NEVER AGAIN

Wizards of Nevermore

Michele Bardsley

A SIGNET ECLIPSE BOOK

SIGNET ECLIPSE
Published by New American Library, a division of
Penguin Group (USA) Inc., 375 Hudson Street,
New York, New York 10014, USA
Penguin Group (Canada), 90 Eglinton Avenue East, Suite 700, Toronto,
Ontario M4P 2Y3, Canada (a division of Pearson Penguin Canada Inc.)
Penguin Books Ltd., 80 Strand, London WC2R 0RL, England
Penguin Ireland, 25 St. Stephen's Green, Dublin 2,
Ireland (a division of Penguin Books Ltd.)
Penguin Group (Australia), 250 Camberwell Road, Camberwell, Victoria 3124,
Australia (a division of Pearson Australia Group Pty. Ltd.)
Penguin Books India Pvt. Ltd., 11 Community Centre, Panchsheel Park,
New Delhi - 110 017, India
Penguin Group (NZ), 67 Apollo Drive, Rosedale, North Shore 0632,
New Zealand (a division of Pearson New Zealand Ltd.)
Penguin Books (South Africa) (Pty.) Ltd., 24 Sturdee Avenue,
Rosebank, Johannesburg 2196, South Africa

Penguin Books Ltd., Registered Offices:
80 Strand, London WC2R 0RL, England

First published by Signet Eclipse, an imprint of New American Library,
a division of Penguin Group (USA) Inc.

First Printing, March 2011
10 9 8 7 6 5 4 3 2 1

For Reid

ACKNOWLEDGMENTS

I would like to thank Claire Zion for asking me, "Do you have another series idea?" and for letting me answer that question with the Wizards of Nevermore.

I'm extremely grateful to Agent Awesome, aka Stephanie Kip Rostan, and the wonderful Monika Verma, who handle the hard parts of the business and let me write (and whine . . . er, a lot).

I adore my editor, Laura Cifelli, and the scarily efficient Jesse Feldman. They are the reason I write better books. In fact, I owe a world of thanks to all of Team NAL. They are dedicated and brilliant. As the song (*Glee* version, of course) says, "My life would suck without you."

I would like to express my eternal gratitude to my Minions and to all my fans everywhere. Because of you, I live my dream every day. I write. You read. We make a good team, you know? And finally I would like to thank my children. You make life interesting, and best of all, you make me laugh. Not always on purpose, but still . . . I love you beyond reason. Even when you're making me freaking crazy. (No, really. Love you lots.)

*And his eyes have all the seeming of a demon's
    that is dreaming,
And the lamplight o'er him streaming throws his
    shadow on the floor;
And my soul from out that shadow that lies float-
    ing on the floor
Shall be lifted—nevermore!*

—From "The Raven," Edgar Allan Poe

Origins of the Magicals
and the Mundanes

Once, all humans could touch magic.

Then the world fell into terror and ruin. Magic became a weapon of cruelty, of war.

The heart of the Goddess broke.

It was She who severed the link between humans and magic. But the world did not become a better place. Humans born without the innate ability to connect to the sacred energies were even more susceptible to the Dark One's influence.

The Goddess decided to return magic through the bloodlines of six champions, pure in heart and in spirit. To keep the balance, She gave each a specific element to use and to protect. So that they would remember their responsibilities to the earth and its creatures, She asked them to choose a symbol.

Jaed, keeper of fire, chose dragon; Olin, keeper of air, picked hawk; Kry, keeper of water, took shark; Leta, keeper of earth, asked for wolf; Drun, keeper of life, wanted sun; and Ekro, keeper of death, chose raven.

The Goddess imbued each symbol with the essence of the living things that represented Her Chosen. These emblems were etched into the very flesh of the champions, that they might remember their purpose—to protect life and keep the balance.

Only their progeny could access the sacred energies,

and they became known as magicals. Those who had no elemental connections became known as mundanes.

As time passed, the purity of the Chosen's lines was weakened, compromised, changed. Powers intermixed, and the line of Drun nearly died out completely. However, every so often, a magical would be born with the ability to control life, and these rare beings became known as thaumaturges.

Two thousand years ago, the Romans created five Houses: House of Dragons, House of Hawks, House of Wolves, House of Sharks, and House of Ravens. They also created the first Grand Court, made up of representatives from the Houses, to govern all magicals. The original building in Rome is still used today. (Not long after the American Revolution, a second Grand Court was established in Washington, D.C.) Children who showed strong connections with a particular element aligned with the appropriate House and were trained by Masters in the magical arts. As a sign of loyalty to both their heritage and their House, all members were tattooed with the symbols chosen by their ancestors—a tradition still strongly adhered to.

Though governed separately, most magicals and mundanes live side by side all over the world. Some choose to live within communities created to serve only their own kind, and others align with a particular House to gain their protections.

Whether magical or mundane, there is one truth that binds all: It is the heart of human struggle to seek balance between good and evil.

Prologue

Ten years ago . . .

Gray Calhoun shut the front door behind him and paused in the foyer, his skin prickling. The entire house was dark and quiet. Typically, their housekeeper greeted him, standing as his wife's sentry to make sure he took off his shoes and put away his Court robes. It was strange not to hear Cook's usual dinner-preparation noises—pots banging and Swedish curse words flying.

The silence—and the sense of emptiness—unsettled him.

"Kerren?" he called out.

"Upstairs," she answered.

He breathed a sigh of relief. This morning, after the shocking revelation about the Rackmores hit the Grand Court's chambers, she'd called him before he'd even gotten their home number dialed. *"Stay there, Gray. Do your job. I'm fine. I have you, remember?"*

"Damn the Grand Court," he'd said, and she'd laughed, then made him promise not to come home early. He wanted to hold his wife, and tell her he didn't care that she was a Rackmore. He loved her—and love meant loyalty. His heart aching, he moved toward the staircase.

"Don't you dare come up here with those shoes on!"

He looked down at the foot hovering over the first polished wood stair, and chuckled. The knots in his stomach unfurled. Feeling lighter in spirit, he returned to the foyer and toed off his shoes.

They'd been married for nearly two years, after a whirlwind six-month courtship. Kerren's parents had welcomed their engagement announcement far more easily than his mother. Leticia Calhoun had thrown every excuse possible at him: *You're too young. You're too new to the Grand Court. You're a Dragon. She's a Raven.* And on and on. Eventually, though, she'd given her blessing.

Despite his mother's worries, he was happily married, and his career was on the fast track. His mediation of several ongoing internal disputes within the House of Dragons led to unheard-of cooperation, and creative resolutions. The success of those negotiations gained him many friends, a very few enemies, and, just last week, the highest accolade offered by any House: Wizard of Honor.

He put his shoes in the foyer closet, and took off his robes, hanging them up. He probably shouldn't have been surprised that his wife had given the staff the day off. When the world felt the reverberations of what some were calling the "great reckoning," all hell had broken loose.

The wealth of every single Rackmore had disappeared.

All day, details had been plucked from speculation and rumors until an enterprising scholar had dug through the Great Library's archives. He'd found a single diary entry from Pickwith Rackmore, Earl of Mersey—a well-known Raven who'd risen in that House's ranks quickly in the sixteenth century. Pride radiated in the words the man wrote about a ritual in which his entire family had called forth a demon lord. They'd made a bargain for wealth—a whole "spin straw into gold" scenario that would last five hundred years. The most sickening part detailed the sacrifice of the earl's youngest daughter and her husband.

They hadn't cared that later generations would reap what they had sown. Death magic and collusion with demons were the two biggest sins a magical could commit. And not only had the Earl of Mersey and his family done both, but they'd also forever intertwined themselves with the House of Ravens.

The fallout would be tremendous.

But those were worries for later. Now he wanted to focus on the needs of his beautiful wife. Kerren was strong-willed and practical. If there was any Rackmore who could weather the storm, it would be her.

Besides, she had him—and he would never abandon her.

Gray took the stairs two at a time. It was dark upstairs, too, but he managed to find his way. Kerren stood in the middle of their richly appointed bedroom, which was cast in shadows, thanks to the single bedside lamp she'd left on.

Kerren was dressed in a diaphanous silver gown that clung to her curves, and offered him a feast. He knew well what lay underneath that simple dress, and he couldn't wait to take it off her. She was so lovely. Her long blond hair hung in silky curls that draped her shoulders. One hand reached out for him, while the other stayed behind her back.

"What are you hiding?" he asked, amused. It was a game they often played. Sometimes, she had a can of whipped cream or a jar of caramel, and other times, she presented him with trinkets she'd found on her shopping excursions.

"It's a surprise," she said coyly.

"Can't wait," he murmured, leaning down to brush his lips across hers. "How's your family?"

"Oh, fine," she said. "They've already made arrangements—but they did say thank you for offering them the spare rooms."

"Our house is big enough for ten people."

She sighed. "You're not going to talk about having babies again, are you?"

"No," said Gray, though he very much wanted to start a family. Kerren said she wanted children, but she always tabled the topic whenever he broached it. Instead of saying anything else, he lowered his head to give her a proper kiss.

"Gray," she murmured, stalling his progress.

He looked up, brows raised. "Hmm?"

"You would do anything for me, wouldn't you?"

"Of course," he said instantly.

She stepped out of his embrace, but kept her hand on his forearm. Her eyes gleamed. "I had hoped to keep you," she said with a regretful smile.

Before he could respond to such a strange declaration, she placed that pale, perfect hand against his chest and whispered, "Kahl."

Pain radiated through him, clogging his throat, throbbing in his eyes, bubbling in his veins. He tried to scream, but no sound could escape through the agony crawling up his windpipe.

His vision grayed at the edges as he stared down at his wife.

"You said you'd do anything for me." The arm she'd had tucked behind her swung up in a wide arc. In her hand, she clasped an obsidian cudgel. The smooth stone smacked him hard in the temple.

Stars exploded behind his eyes.

Then the world went black.

*   *   *

Gray awoke to the stench of sulfur, and the chill of stone beneath his bare skin. His wrists and ankles were manacled to the granite. He felt the dark magic pulsing in the metal, and the thick ugliness of it stifling the room. His right side burned, as though acid had been dribbled from his temple to his shoulder.

He tried to call his magic, but it was useless. The metal dampened his abilities. Besides, not only was there no living thing from which to borrow energy, but also the negative vibrations of this prison suffocated any hint of good.

Bile rose in his throat.

"The heart of a Dragon." Kerren's voice issued from the darkness, seconds ahead of the woman. As she walked toward him, looking coldly beautiful in that damned silver gown, torches flamed to life. He could see now that he was in a small cavern, the craggy walls a mixture of black and red. The rectangular rock on which he was pinned was the centerpiece. "All that my lord wanted was me—and the heart of a Dragon."

"Your lord?" he rasped. Betrayal sat like an anvil on his chest. "What have you done, Kerren?"

"What I must." She stopped near the edge of the altar and let her gaze rove his naked body. "Such a shameful waste." She trailed a hand down his inner thigh, then encircled his hip with a sharp nail.

He hissed in pain.

She grinned, and he saw the madness glittering in those chocolate brown eyes, the hint of crazy proffered by that cruel mouth. Oh, Goddess. Not Kerren. Not his wife. "This is a nightmare," he whispered.

"Not yet," she said. "You know, Gray, you were very sweet to be so worried about me." She patted the wound she'd caused on his hip. "The Rackmores weren't all that interested in their own history—not until today. All our collective paperwork was tossed into our private archives at the Great Library. Piles and piles of moldering ledgers and diaries and personal letters. When I was seventeen, a small indiscretion of mine angered my father so much, he decided to punish me."

"What the hell are you talking about?"

She spread her fingers against his lips. "Shush. I'm telling a story. I'm not without compassion, you see. I thought you should know why you're going to die."

The blood drained from his face. Kerren wanted to kill him? Why?

"No more questions, Gray." Her gaze was that of a stranger, as hard and cold as muddy ice. "If you interrupt me again, I'll stab you through the heart, and you can go to the darkness not knowing a gods-be-damned thing."

He pressed his lips together, mostly because he didn't want to feel the soft reminders of comfort and pleasure the treacherous woman had once given to him. She feathered her fingertips down his cheek and let them rest on his aching shoulder as she leaned against the altar. He knew he should try to think of ways to free himself, or reason with her, but shock had numbed him. His thought processes felt sluggish, and his body clumsy, probably the result of the poisonous magic that surrounded him.

"My punishment was to organize the archives. It took a whole summer. My stupid baby sister went to Paris while I toiled away in that tomb. But I found some very interesting things. For instance, the Earl of Mersey's diary, his personal spellbook, and a little prophecy he'd written before his death. Imagine my surprise when I read all about the demon bargain and found out that in a few short years, I would be penniless.

"Me? Poor? I don't think so. I used the same sum-moning spell, and called forth my own demon lord. He's very handsome and virile—a real devil in bed." She winked at him, and nausea churned in his guts. "In exchange for me keeping my wealth and accumulated pretties, all he wanted—other than me, of course—was the heart of a Dragon. Your heart, to be precise."

"You don't love me." The realization slashed at him, and self-pity was the salt on those wounds. Everything he'd believed about the woman he'd married was wrong. He'd been fooled and cuckolded.

Kerren watched the play of emotions on his face with avid interest, and Gray realized he was giving his socio-pathic wife quite the show. He did his best to blank his features, but she merely laughed. "You can't hide from me. Or from destiny."

Then she produced a wicked dagger and pressed it against his chest. Blood welled where it bit into his skin.

"I liked you. I enjoyed you. I fucked you." She leaned close, her breath ghosting over his mouth. "But no, my darling, I never loved you."

"Please," he said as tears fell. He wasn't sure what he was begging for—mercy or death—but he couldn't stop the rejoinders. "Please, Kerren. *Please.*"

Disgust entered her gaze. She curled back her lips. "I never expected you to simper. You're pathetic." Then she raised the dagger and screamed, "For Kahl!"

Her aim was true, vicious, and supernaturally strong.

The double-bladed dagger slid through muscle, bone, heart, lung, flesh. He heard the tip of the blade scratch the stone; then he managed one hoarse scream before the sharp agony abruptly faded.

In the viscid dark of hell, Gray's soul struggled.

Trapped, whispered a thousand voices, *betrayed.*

You are nothing. No one. You are unloved. Unwelcome. Unheralded.

No, he screamed. *I am Gray Calhoun. I am a Dragon. I will live.*

Become one with us. You are the dark. You will always be the dark.

Pain ripped through him. Though he had no body now, the agony was just as real. He accepted every lightning bolt of anguish, every jagged strike of terror. *I will not bow to you,* he yelled. *You will not break me!*

Then the monster appeared. Its awful smile displayed razor-sharp rows of bloodstained teeth. Gray could discern no other form to go with its terrifying visage—just soulless black eyes, leathery skin, and that terrible grin.

The heart, it demanded, *give me the heart.*

I will not give you anything. Ever. Gray battled through the sludge, exerting his will. *I belong to the Goddess. I call upon the blood of my ancestors, the righteousness of all good Dragons, to help me.*

You are the dark, cried the voices, *you are one of us.*

Light burst through the blackness, and the voices screamed in frustration.

A huge claw reached through golden brightness and grabbed Gray. He was slammed back into his body. The knife was expelled, the horrific wound closed, the chains shattered, and then he was lifted from the altar, and shoved up, up, up through fire, through rock, through earth, until he came to rest on soft, dewy grass.

Gray took a shuddering breath and opened his eyes. Above him, he saw leafy tree branches reaching up as if trying to tickle the full moon. A glance around confirmed he was in some sort of wooded clearing—which could be located in California or France or anywhere in between. He had no idea where he was, only that he was free.

Within himself, he felt the slither of scales, the heat and shape of something foreign.

He had escaped hell.

But he had not come out alone.

Chapter 1

Present day . . .

"Marry me."

The man filling up the doorway in front of Lucinda Rackmore didn't bat an eyelash. His expression didn't change, either. His blue gaze was still parked between sorrow and cynicism.

Gray Calhoun didn't look like a wizard. His hair was too long; the shaggy tips brushed his shoulders and the front strands carelessly framed his face. He might've been considered handsome if his nose didn't crook in the middle and if the planes of his face weren't as sharp as blades. A faded scar on the left side of his face twirled from his temple down his neck, hiding beneath the collar of his T-shirt. The thin white lines formed intricate patterns. She knew he had not healed the disfigurement magically because he was a man who liked reminders.

His tight black T-shirt showed off his muscled form and his faded jeans did the same. His feet were bare, the clean, square nails cut short. Unlike most of his kind, he didn't display blatant symbols of his power. But she knew that somewhere underneath his T-shirt was the tattoo of the House of Dragons, and the mark that designated his rare status.

"Please," she said. *"Gray."*

She couldn't stop the recrimination that echoed inside the plea. A muscle ticked in his jaw and pain flickered in his eyes. He'd heard the censure, wrapped in the poor clothes of beggary, and then passed his own judgment.

"Good day to you." He straightened his six-foot frame. He turned away, as so many had before him, and she knew he would close the door in her face. Though she didn't deserve even his tiniest consideration, she couldn't bear another rejection. *If only I could rest... just for a moment.* She couldn't remember the last time she could take a full breath or what it was like to have a heartbeat unhindered by fear. Her feet throbbed from endless walking. And every day, every moment, she looked over her shoulder, waiting for the inevitable— because she would be found and she would be dragged back to New York.

Bernard Franco was not a forgiving man.

Gray hesitated, clutching the edge of the doorjamb and looking at her coldly.

"You married my sister," she whispered. Desolation tainted her voice.

"I took vows with her because I loved her." His twang was more pronounced. He had once called it "cowboy cadence," the way Texans chewed on their words before letting them out of their mouths. Gray had been born and raised in eastern Texas. He knew something about disgrace, too, though he'd been a victim. She couldn't claim innocence. She'd had nowhere else to go, so here she was, raw from her own wounds, and forlorn enough to ask for Gray's help.

"Let me explain. Please."

His gaze cut past her to the deserted street in front of his house. The yard was overgrown and weed-strewn, the sidewalk leading up to the house cracked and uneven. Not even the wide porch offered a welcome. It was empty of furniture, the planks gray with age and too much rain.

"Even a novice wizard could detect the curse on you," he said. "You're poison, Lucinda."

"It's a . . . a misunderstanding." She whispered the lie, afraid to give full voice to it. What she had done to earn the curse hadn't been a misunderstanding at all.

"What did you do to gain the wrath of your lover?"

So, he knew about Bernard, and his formal tone indicated his opinion about her ex. Or maybe he was trying to keep the distance between them—not that the chasm needed to be any wider. The tiny flame of hope she'd kept alive all the way to his front door petered out and died.

Gray wouldn't help her.

She reached out to touch his arm, but he pulled back. "I'll . . . I'll pay you."

It was the wrong thing to say. Even as she realized how far her own desperation had pushed her, she couldn't snatch back the words, or the sentiment.

Gray's eyebrows slashed downward, and anger sparked in his eyes. "You know better than to lie to me. You don't have money anymore, and you never will." He shook his head. "Getting screwed over by one Rackmore witch was plenty enough for me. Go seek your protection elsewhere."

Anger punched through her weariness. "I don't remember you being such a bastard."

"Ten years ago," he said, "I wasn't." He gave her one last searing look. "You can thank your sister for that."

"I'm not my sister."

For an aching second, she saw pity snake through the fury of his gaze. Then he said, "You're still a Rackmore. Go away, Lucy. Just . . . go the hell away."

She wouldn't make it easy on him. Oh, who was she kidding? Gray's heart had turned to a husk years ago, and *that* was certainly his fault. Lucinda stared defiantly into his eyes until the door closed. Its soft click echoed Gray's apathy. Her throat knotted and her eyes went hot, but . . . *Fuck that.* The weather seemed to empathize with her, and the ominous gray clouds crowding the sky began to weep.

She picked up the duffel bag filled with all her worldly possessions and dragged her sorry ass to the edge of the portico. Gray's house was an old Victorian, now a faded, peeling pink. The house looked as neglected and mournful as its owner.

Gray had truly been her last hope. A long shot that hadn't paid off. The moment Bernard issued his edict, all her friends and acquaintances had turned their backs on her. No one wanted to help her, and she didn't blame them. Bernard was a difficult man. And by "difficult," she meant he was a soulless cretin.

That was what she got for being the mistress of a wizard from the House of Ravens. *No, that's what you got for interfering with his sick pleasures.*

Sometimes, in her darkest moments, she thought dying would've been easier.

No beings born with the ability to wield magic could have their powers stripped. But powers could be bound. Powers could be warped. Bernard's curse had done such a thing to her thaumaturgy. He hadn't done anything to her aquamancy, but that particular power wasn't much of a threat to him.

Only the wizard who issued the curse, or the tribunal of his House, could remove it. No way could she approach the House of Ravens for a pardon. They had more reasons than she could count to hate the Rackmores—and just because one of their politicos had bedded her, that wouldn't soften their black hearts. The irony was that the Rackmores used to rule the House of Ravens.

Bernard had been busy making sure no wizard from any House would look at her, much less share the same sidewalk with her. Worse, the minute she was spotted anywhere, her location was reported to Bernard.

He almost caught up to her twice. That was when she went off the grid. No using IDs, no staying in motels or renting cars, no hitchhiking on main roads, and using magic only when necessary. It had been three months since she'd escaped, but he wasn't a man who let go of his possessions. Not ever.

She'd embarrassed him. Hurt him. And then she'd stolen from him.

Gray had been right: She was poison and would be until Bernard could be forced to remove the spell, but more than that, she wanted to be free of him. She wouldn't go back to the penthouse, to him, ever.

Marrying Gray would not nullify the curse, but it would ensure her protection. Not even Bernard would risk the wrath of a Wizard of Honor—the highest level bestowed on any magic wielder—especially one from the House of Dragons. Even though Gray hadn't been active in years, he was still very well respected. Gray may have given up his place in the House, but the talent, power, and skill that had originally earned him the honorific were still his to command.

Besides, some things you couldn't give back.

Tucking her chin down and pulling up the hood of her green cloak, Lucinda hurried down the rickety stairs and splashed through the puddles dotting the cracked walkway. In the first week of March, winter still held dominion in Texas. The rain splattered coldly on her face and dribbled mercilessly into her shoes. She trudged away from the Victorian and headed toward the street, which she could follow to downtown. She had enough cash left for a simple meal. Maybe resting for a bit and eating something would clear her mind enough to figure out what to do next.

Anguish filled her as she trudged down the sidewalk. Holy hell, she'd gotten herself into trouble. Nobody who wanted to live got on the wrong side of Bernard Franco. At first, Lucinda had genuinely believed that he'd cared about her. For a while, he'd indulged her fantasy of a real relationship. She hadn't known she was one among many mistresses—his little harem of horrors. Lucinda realized too late he was incapable of love, just like he was incapable of mercy.

How did I not know?

Even at the end, when she'd figured out what he'd done to her, she had no one to blame but herself. She was in Nevermore begging at the door of Gray Calhoun because of the choices she'd made.

Everything had a price. And now, she was paying what was owed.

Did she really deserve anything less?

Mexico was the only viable option now. Bernard had enemies there, so he would be less likely to follow her into the country. She could stick close to the beaches and use her aquamancy to earn a living. Very few from the House of Sharks lived landlocked, choosing to live in seaside towns or on islands or on boats. Her water gift wasn't strong enough for her to seek refuge from the House—and Sharks tended to be cold, far too practical, not to mention predatory. People with her level of skills found themselves either in the entertainment business or as glorified dishwashers.

At this point, she was so broke that she was more than willing to wash dishes for a few bucks. It was better to barter for the things she needed than to try to earn coin to pay for them. She could trade her skills for food and shelter in Mexico. Magic wasn't as regulated, and it would be easier to hide there, too.

Up ahead, Lucinda saw the square brick buildings that lined Main Street. Unlike most small towns, Nevermore hadn't embraced modern progress. There weren't any strip malls or fast-food joints like those that plagued other places. Most small towns attempted to preserve some of their heritage, mostly for the sake of tourism, while inviting in as much big city as they could handle.

Nevermore probably looked the same now as it had in 1845.

She hadn't seen a car or a person since she'd left Gray's home. It was lonely out here.

The gentle rain changed its intensity and rhythm. It slashed down, cold and angry. Adjusting the strap, Lucinda heaved the duffel bag over her shoulder and quickened her pace. By the time she reached the Piney Woods Café, which sat on a corner intersected by Brujo Boulevard and Main Street, she was soaked to the skin. Above the row of fogged plate glass windows was a peeling hand-painted sign. A shower of gold sparks spit out around a scraggly bunch of pines shaped to form the name of the restaurant. She assumed the sparks were supposed to represent magic, but instead it looked like the trees were going up in flames. Beneath this travesty of art was the claim that the diner had been serving Nevermore for more than a hundred and fifty years.

She stood outside, shivering, unable to seek the warmth and shelter she needed. She was so tired of being judged and rejected. Not one person she'd asked had helped her. Going to her sister had been out of the question. Kerren had always been a bitch, but the night she sacrificed Gray, she became something worse: a half demon. She apparently hadn't read the fine print on her marriage to Kahl. Three days every month, Kerren returned to her human form and the earthly plane, usually to wreak havoc on her husband's behalf—and hit whatever shopping mecca was nearby.

Lucinda swung open the door, cringing as a bell clanged above her head. Was it too much to ask to walk into a place without gaining every occupant's immediate notice? Not that she could've hidden the fact she was wet, a witch, or a stranger.

She remembered how Gray had often spoken about the coziness of small-town living, but he'd also said most everyone knew your business—sometimes before you did.

That did not appeal to her.

Back then, Gray always had a twinkle in his eye and a kind word for everyone. She'd been too caught up in her own teenage drama to pay him much mind. He'd been her older sister's boyfriend, and therefore someone to be dismissed. His and Kerren's wedding had taken place at a small venue with family and close friends: A battle Gray had won, since her sister had very much wanted a huge, glamorous affair. She remembered very little about the nuptials—only that they had interrupted her own, more important plans for a Saturday afternoon.

She shuddered to think about the girl she'd been. And the woman she'd become hadn't been much better.

Maybe she, more than any other, deserved the Rackmore curse.

Now that Lucinda stood inside the establishment, she wasn't sure what to do next. The utter silence frayed her nerves. Water from her soaked cloak dripped onto the cracked linoleum, and she watched the drops splatter. Courage fled, but she managed to peek from underneath her hood.

Everyone was staring at her.

"Sorry. We're closed." The speaker was a chubby woman sitting behind the counter, a magazine in one hand and a cigarette in the other. She wore a pink jogging suit and a pair of scuffed white Keds. Her hair was a tight cap of dull gray curls, her eyes icy blue, and her mouth a thin line of censure.

Lucinda's gaze flicked to the full café, and back to the woman.

"I'll wait for a table," she said.

"No need," said the woman. "We ain't serving."

Lucinda could smell the typical comfort fare—crispy fried chicken, meat loaf with tomato sauce, and even the peppered gravy that topped homemade mashed potatoes. And she definitely heard the clattering sounds of people in the kitchen whipping up all that wonderful food. Her mouth started to water, and her stomach growled.

"Go on, now," said the woman, nodding toward the door. "Git."

"I don't understand," said Lucinda stubbornly. Only she did understand. They knew she was a Rackmore, and they wanted nothing to do with her. News in small towns really did travel fast.

"This here is private property. I reserve the right to refuse service to anyone," said the woman. Her eyes flashed with disgust. "We don't got nothing here for you." She smiled grimly. "Maybe you should head on over to Ember's. Bet that crazy bitch would welcome you with open arms."

"Mama!" A young woman bustled forward, smiling. The rude lady rolled her eyes and took a drag off the cigarette. The girl was rail thin—opposite in form and manner to her mother. She wore a yellow waitress outfit covered by a frilly white apron. Order pads and pens stuck out of the pockets on the front. Her brown hair was tugged into a ponytail and her blue eyes were much kinder. She sent Lucy an apologetic look. "Welcome to Nevermore," she said. Then she flinched, obviously not wanting to sound too friendly. "Are you staying in town?"

"No," said Lucinda.

She nodded, nibbling on her bottom lip. Her glance flicked to her mother, and then back to Lucinda. "I'm so sorry. Really."

"Don't apologize," chastised her mother. "She ain't got no cause to be here."

"Ember's tea shop is just across the street," said the girl. "Her place is neutral ground."

Her gaze was filled with urgency, and Lucinda responded to it even though she had no idea why the girl would be so concerned about her welfare.

"Thank you," she said.

"Hurry yourself on over there," chirped the waitress, making shooing motions with her hands. She slanted a gaze toward the back of the restaurant, and then looked at Lucinda. "Get some of Ember's chamomile tea. It's real soothing."

Her smile seemed more brittle than bright, and if Lucinda weren't drowning in her own emotional morass, she might wonder what problems the girl had. It was obvious she wasn't happy. Then again, dealing every day with that mother of hers would no doubt wear down any soul.

"Good day to you," she said to the waitress, echoing the dismissal Gray had given her earlier. She pulled up the hood, dragged the duffel over her shoulder, and went back out into the storm.

Even though the rain pelted her relentlessly, she felt as though something heavy had been lifted off her shoulders. The Piney Woods Café had been oppressive, the atmosphere weighted down by the negative emotions of its owner. Though it was worse in the café, the energy imbalance affected the whole town. She'd felt the shift the moment she'd arrived. It was almost as if Nevermore were sliding up and down a teeter-totter. Still, it was a lovely place. Despite the magical quavering, there was an underlying sense of peace—masked, yes, but there. It seemed to be waiting. For what, she didn't know. Lucinda trudged down the sidewalk. She'd hitched most of the way here, but with the sky wailing like a toddler amidst a temper tantrum, she wouldn't get a ride to Dallas, much less one all the way to the Mexican border.

Her body shook, from cold, exhaustion, and lack of food. She gripped the strap of the duffel. *C'mon, Luce. You'll be all right.* Sighing deeply, she stopped on the corner, and studied the bricked street. Two lines of black bricks laid in the opposite direction of the red ones delineated the crosswalk. There wasn't a stoplight, or even a stop sign. She wondered how traffic was managed. Then again, how much traffic could a town with a population of 503 actually have?

Feeling trepidation, Lucinda looked around. Her neck tingled, and she had the distinct impression someone was watching her. Probably a few people from the café had their noses pressed against the window waiting for her to get struck by lightning.

No one was on the street, and though several cars were parked along the curb, none were actually on the move. Nevermore was such a quiet place. What was it that Gray had once told her? Oh, yes. That as soon as the streetlights came on, Nevermore rolled up its sidewalks. After the excitement of living in Europe and New York City, she wouldn't have thought she'd ever consider living in such a tiny town. No gourmet restaurants, or theater, or coffee shops, or Neiman Marcus anywhere in sight ... mere months ago she would've been appalled. But today, with nothing except a few clothes and even fewer bucks to her name, and no one to give a damn, Nevermore seemed more like sanctuary. It was almost as if she could belong here.

Don't be silly, Luce.

Even if Gray allowed it—and he wouldn't—she could probably expect the same treatment she'd gotten at the café. At least in Mexico, no one would care who she was. A lot of outcasts ended up there because, like her, they had nowhere else to go.

Goddess, she was tired.

She stood on the curb, trying to decide if she should head toward the highway, or check out the tea shop—at least until the storm abated. Through the sheets of gray rain, she spied the place across the narrow two-lane street. The corner brick building was two stories, flat on the top, and painted purple. It looked as square and squat as a piece of birthday cake. The gold lettering on the single, large tinted window read:

Ember's Tea and Pastries
All Are Welcome Here

"I hope you mean that," muttered Lucinda. A hot cup of chamomile with a lemon scone sounded like heaven. She looked both ways, then stepped off the curb and started across the street.

When she got to the middle of the crosswalk, the roar of an engine startled her so badly, she stopped and swung toward the noise. Barreling down the street was a black Mustang with red-and-yellow flames painted on its hood.

It was headed straight for her.

Lucinda immediately tapped into her aquamancy, directing her magic toward the rain. She aimed the swirling blue power toward the raindrops sluicing between her and the car.

"Ice!" she screamed.

Instantly, the drops turned as sharp as daggers. She directed the shards toward the tires. Hundreds of the sharp icy drops dove into the treads.

The car was about twenty feet away when all four tires exploded.

Lucinda dropped her arms and ran across the street, her duffel bouncing on her backside, her heart pounding. Magic trailed in her wake because she hadn't properly released it. She slipped on the wet sidewalk and skidded toward the building. She grabbed the corner to right herself and then turned around, pressing her back against the purple brick. She called the magic back to her, releasing the glowing blue ropes of power, and offering a quick prayer of thanks to the living things from which she'd borrowed energy.

The spinning car screeched to a halt in middle of the intersection.

The front end pointed directly at her as though it were a compass and she were north. The windows were tinted so darkly, she couldn't see who was in the car, or how many might be inside. Its engine revved ominously. The driver was letting her know he'd fully intended to mow her down, and given another opportunity, he would do so again.

Yet, he wasn't so brave that he was getting out of his car to challenge her directly.

"Screw you," she muttered. She flipped off the Mustang, and whoever the hell was in it, then scuttled toward the door to the tea shop and bolted inside. She wasn't feeling so brave today, either.

"Well, now. Here you are." The odd statement tinged

with a Jamaican accent was issued by a cocoa-skinned woman standing a mere foot away.

Lucinda warily wondered if the lady had witnessed what had happened outside, and then she wondered if she should explain—or maybe even report the incident. After a moment of consideration, she decided it'd be better to pretend like nothing had happened.

The woman smiled widely, showing off a set of sparkling pearly whites. She wore a pair of purple-tinted glasses. Actually, one side was purple tinted, and the other was blacked out completely. She was at least six feet tall and wore a purple dress that clung to her curvaceous form, and a pair of black high-heeled boots with purple roses stitched on the toes. Her long hair was a mass of tiny braids in various shades of purple, and those not purple were jet-black.

"I'm sensing a theme," said Lucinda as she stared at the woman. Then she grimaced. "Sorry. That was rude."

"Was it, now?" asked the woman. "Purple's me color. 'Tis my magic, my ju*ju*, you see? Ain't no shame in embracing who I am."

"I envy that."

"Well," said the woman as she sized up Lucinda. "Got to know who you are first before *you* can embrace *you*." She nodded. "I'm Ember. Come in and rest."

The simple but heartfelt invitation blindsided her. "Th-thank you."

"Oh, now. We need some TLC right here." Ember took the duffel right out of Lucinda's hand. "C'mon, chil'. I'll get you fixed right on up."

"I . . ." Lucinda froze. Her savior turned and marched toward the back, leaving her no choice but to follow. Yet, she hesitated. The tea shop was dimly lit, and there were swirls of fabric everywhere, but it offered coziness . . . no, more like tranquillity. The small foyer where she stood was a couple feet away from a long counter lined with black leather seats. It looked like a bar, but the bottles lining the glass shelves on the wall behind it had nothing to do with alcohol. It smelled earthy in here, no doubt due to the incense burning at regular intervals.

Then she noticed she had the scrutiny of someone sitting at the bar. He was a big man, not an ounce of fat on him, either. He glared at her from underneath a worn black cowboy hat. His uniform was tan outlined in black, a gold five-point star glittering from the upper right side of his chest. He wore a big black belt with typical law enforcement tools: a gun, handcuffs, a baton, and a pouch, no doubt filled with justice gems or other approved magical items.

She swallowed the knot in her throat.

"New in town?" he said in a gravelly voice. "You check in with our visitors' center yet?"

"Visitors' center" was the nice way of saying "magic checkpoint." Big cities usually had embassies from all the Houses. However, many smaller towns like Nevermore allied themselves with a certain House, in order to receive funding and protection. Any town under the auspices of magicals had to live under the laws enacted by the appointed Guardian.

Nevermore was a Dragon town, and the Calhouns had been its Guardians since day one. Gray didn't care what happened to her; she seriously doubted he would intervene if the sheriff decided she needed quarantine.

"I'm not staying," she said. "Just passing through." She shrugged. "Visiting an old friend, actually. Gray Calhoun."

His eyes were a bright shade of green, much lighter than her own, and filled with suspicion. He narrowed his gaze. "You know Gray?"

She'd thought throwing Gray's name out there might

buy her a pass from the sheriff's scrutiny, but she'd been wrong. She'd garnered even more of his attention.

Her tongue felt glued to her mouth. Right. Like she would admit to anyone that she'd come to Texas to beg the protection of her ex-brother-in-law—you know, the man her sister had all but killed more than a decade ago. And she sure as hell wouldn't admit that she was a Rackmore. It seemed like everyone she'd run into since the great reckoning had a Rackmore to thank for some kind of misery.

"Shut it, Mooreland. You're scarin' me chickie to death," said Ember as she returned. She wasn't holding the duffel. Lucinda wanted to trust the woman, but her stomach squeezed at the idea that her worldly possessions were no longer within her view. She didn't have much, and she didn't want to lose what few things she had left.

Mooreland looked unrepentant. "Just don't want any trouble."

"Then quit makin' some," chastised Ember. "My place is neutral ground. You got no jurisdiction here. Drink your tea and meditate on improvin' your people skills."

Mooreland's gaze flicked down at the steaming mug in front of him. He looked at Lucinda as if to say, "I'm watching you, sunshine," then promptly ignored her. She was surprised he hadn't responded to Ember's baiting. Then again, she could throw him out without consequence. Only the holder of the deed determined what happened on neutral ground.

"C'mon." Ember took Lucinda's hand and tugged her through a series of small tables, past a stage with flowing purple and silver curtains, and tucked her into the back booth, which kept her hidden from prying eyes. "Let's get that cloak off you. I'll throw it in the dryer."

"You have a dryer?"

"My apartment's upstairs," she said. "Me and my husband, Rilton, bought this building a few months ago."

"You're new here?" she asked. "And people were nice to you?"

"I don't move to dis town 'cause I want to meet nice people. I come 'cause dis where I'm supposed to be. We all got destinies, chil', and mine is here." Ember's accent had thickened considerably.

"It's truly neutral ground?" Gratefully Lucinda slid into the booth, right next to her duffel. She wanted to cuddle up to it and sleep, but it was wet and lumpy and filthy, and she wasn't exhausted enough to not notice.

"All who enter here are safe." Ember draped the wet cloak over her arm. "Now. I'll bring you something, something just right."

"Wait." Lucinda unzipped a pocket on her duffel and dug into it. Her fingers poked through a hole that hadn't been there earlier. The four dollars and eleven cents she had left was gone.

She should be used to it by now, but she still found herself devastated by the loss. "I don't have any money."

"Seems like you don't got a lot of things," said Ember. "Don't you worry about payin' me."

"No menus?" asked Lucinda, and then wondered why she'd posed the question.

Ember laughed. "Why do people need menus in here? Dey don't know what's good for dem."

"But you do?"

"Of course, chil'." She smiled. "Sit dere and relax. I bring you just da ting."

"Ember." Lucinda swallowed the knot in her throat. "I'll never have money. Not ever. My name's Lucinda Rackmore." She waited for the inevitable expression of distaste, waited for Ember to invite her to leave, waited for the rejection that always came.

"Hello dere, Lucinda Rackmore. Welcome, welcome." Ember reached down and patted her on the shoulder, then turned and sauntered through the door a couple feet away. It swung open and allowed out the sounds of food preparation as well as the sweet smells of baked goods.

Ember's kindness poked holes through Lucinda's fragile control. Everyone she'd known had turned away from her, and this stranger had offered her both comfort and help—even after she'd revealed she was a Rackmore witch.

It was too much.

Lucinda laid her head down onto the table and wept.

Chapter 2

"That's no way to talk to a lady, son," called out a cranky old voice from the kitchen. The Texas accent twanged all the way through his words. "I expect better from my kin."

"Yeah, dude," chimed in another voice, this one younger and all 1980s California. "Total asshole move. You suck."

Gray Calhoun rolled his eyes. He didn't need advice from his grandfather, Grit, much less admonishment from Dutch the Surfer.

For the last five minutes, Gray had been leaning against the front door, trying to breathe. Narrow windows lined the heavy wood door, and he'd watched from one while Lucy trudged off the porch and down the street, the rain beating at her as she headed toward downtown. He almost expected her to turn back, to try again. It was obvious she had no pride left. He'd never seen anyone, much less the once haughty, spoiled Lucinda, so achingly desperate.

Even though he owed her nothing, he still felt guilty.

He shouldn't have slammed the door in her face. At least he could've given her some lunch and allowed her to rest before sending her away. Hell, he could've even given her a ride to the bus station and gotten her a ticket to Dallas or Houston or wherever.

He really was an asshole.

His temple throbbed, and he reached up to trace the top of the scar. Lucy hadn't given him the mark, or the bad memories, or the nightmares. She hadn't condoned her sister's actions or tried to do the same to anyone else to save herself. Not that he thought whoring for bastards like Bernard Franco made her any better. Still, she'd traded herself instead of someone she claimed to love. He couldn't forget, either, that she'd been just a kid when the Rackmore curse initiated. She'd had to rely on her mother and then on her mother's lover for survival. She'd never had to take care of herself. She knew only how to be taken care of . . . so how could she resist the slimy charms of a wealthy and powerful wizard like Franco?

Kerren, on the other hand, had been an adult—married to someone powerful, to someone who'd loved her. To *him*, damn it. He would've moved heaven and earth to help her, but she didn't ask. She'd already put plans into motion to save all that she valued—and he had not been among those.

He'd completely misunderstood his wife's true nature. All those quirks he thought so adorable were just manifestations of selfishness. Oh, she'd been good at pouting. Very good at using sex to soften him, or to thwart him. He'd been enamored by her beauty and her luscious body, but she was also a keenly intelligent woman, quick-witted and forward-thinking. He'd believed that he had found his match. Not even the night she'd killed him brought him such pain as the knowledge that she had not loved him. She had chosen him, and manipulated her way into his life, so that she would have the heart of a Dragon to give her demon lover.

Bitterness rose, tasting metallic and vile. Ten years.

He should be over what happened. It wasn't that he had any feelings left for Kerren. She could go to hell, or rather, she could stay there. What she had wrought by the ritual had exacted a price neither had expected. He still had nightmares, though they were few and far between.

Damn it.

He rubbed a hand over his face.

Having his past walk up to him and beg for help was the last thing he'd expected. And he'd had enough of surprises, especially surprises from the Rackmores. While he spent years trying to figure out what had happened to him, and how to control whatever had come out with him, the magicals dealt with the Rackmore fallout. The Houses revoked Rackmore memberships—and refused new members with Rackmore bloodlines. Lawsuits were filed. New laws were proposed, rejected, proposed again. Many Rackmores left the Houses of their own accord, and others held on to their positions tooth and nail while fighting for their rights.

Hundreds committed suicide.

Lucinda's father had been among those casualties. Her mother, Wilmette, had soldiered on, taking on a wealthy lover to ensure the security of her youngest daughter. She had publicly disowned Kerren, going so far as to complete magical ritual and mundane paperwork to remove the woman from the Rackmore rolls.

It took two years for the Grand Court to issue its edict. Rackmores had colluded with demons and performed death magic; therefore, they no longer had the rights and privileges of any Houses. It didn't matter that current Rackmores hadn't made the deals and that they were suffering enough already—the rules for magicals were different, and oftentimes far more harsh, from those for mundanes. Magicals had a bigger responsibility to the world, and therefore paid a higher penalty when guilty of abusing power.

The House of Ravens suffered the most membership loss, since so many of their witches and wizards were Rackmores. Those who were left felt betrayed and resentful. After two thousand years of being one of the strongest Houses in the world, they became the smallest and the weakest. It was unpardonable. The Ravens soon became the Rackmores' greatest enemies.

Despite the inconvenience of his escape, Kerren had left him alone. Why would she bother him? She'd gotten the blood price she needed to save herself. He'd spent a lot of time trying to heal from what she'd done to him, not only physically, but emotionally and mentally. He knew everyone believed he'd been so overwrought by his wife's betrayal, so weakened by her attempt to kill him, that he was no longer capable of fulfilling his duties in the House of Dragons.

It was part of the truth. The other part was something he had never admitted. He'd never spoken to anyone, not even his own mother, about his death and resurrection. Those secrets were his burden alone. What did it matter? He had a life of his own making, one that satisfied him, even if he sometimes felt as though he was in hiding, or, worse, running away.

Lucinda Rackmore.

Why had she even bothered to seek his protection? And to ask *him* to marry *her*? Was she insane? He barked out a harsh laugh. He'd been doing fine. Just fine. Now his past was mucking about in his present and he didn't like it.

"You gonna finish this spell?" called his grandfather, still as cranky as ever. "I ain't got time to sit here all day at your beck and call."

"Yeah, dude. If you're done being mean to the babes, we could totally use your help."

"All right, already!" called out Gray. It wasn't like Grit or Dutch could go anywhere—they were soul-imprinted books. He'd inherited his grandfather, who'd befriended Dutch while doing the requisite year in the Great Library. When the time came for Gray to claim the old man, Grit hadn't wanted to leave his friend. So now Gray was stuck with two smart-asses. "Don't get your pages in a ruffle."

"We heard that, dude!"

Gray rolled his eyes as he pushed away from the door, and strode toward the kitchen. His mind churned with the images of Lucinda trudging through the rain toward downtown Nevermore. Midway through the living room he stopped. *Shit.*

He told himself she was strong. She'd made it this far, and she could find her way out of town on her own. He wasn't responsible for her. She wasn't a kid anymore. But he had an excellent imagination, and playing out was scenario after scenario of all that could go wrong for a Rackmore witch in Nevermore.

"I'm going to town," he yelled as he pivoted. He needed to change clothes and put on shoes, not to mention rustle up a suitable coat.

"Dude!" called Dutch. "Bring us back some doughnuts."

"None of them sissy jelly doughnuts, neither," added Grit. "But them cake ones are all right."

Gray ignored their requests and hurried up the stairs to his bedroom. In their current forms, neither Grit nor Dutch could eat. But they liked the smell of food a lot, especially desserts.

He stripped off his clothes and redressed in a pair of faded Levi's and a gray cable-knit sweater. Miraculously, he found a pair of clean socks, and after a search through the mess littering his closet floor, he was able to extract his black cowboy boots.

The coat was the issue.

He'd misplaced his usual "I'm the Dragon Guardian" garment. It was an informal hooded black cape with a gold dragon stitched on the left front side. He hadn't seen it in a while, not since he'd ventured to town. . . . He frowned. He hadn't been in Nevermore since the winter-solstice celebration. Crap. Had it really been that long?

The problem with the way that he lived was that he tended to drop whatever he was taking off where he was standing at the moment. Every so often, he spent a solid week digging himself out of his mess, but the debris-free look never lasted long. Hell, he couldn't remember the last time he'd done a thorough cleaning, which was probably why he couldn't find a damned thing.

As the Guardian of Nevermore, he had to meet certain . . . er, dramatic expectations of the townsfolk. Nevermore had always been a Dragon town, and not only had his family helped to found it along with a few hundred humans, but they'd also been the appointed protectors.

Unfortunately, the Calhoun line had dwindled down to . . . him. When he returned to Nevermore five years ago, only his grandfather was left, and the old man was in no shape to perform the minimum duties, much less the actual protection spells. Gray's mother had long since left to pursue her own political goals in the House of Dragons, and had groomed her son to do the same. She hadn't returned to Nevermore—not since the day she had helped her son move back into her father's house.

Back when he'd had political ambitions, he had no problem following in his mother's footsteps. Like her, he wanted to make a difference. And, too, he'd loved playing the games, all that maneuvering and positioning. He didn't always win, but he always learned something new, something he could put into his own little bag of tricks. He'd been good at his job, and he'd loved the energy, the ambition. It was hard to believe that at one time in his life he had felt like he could conquer the world.

His father had died when he'd been barely old enough to walk, and Leticia Calhoun had never married again, despite the numerous propositions she received. As politically motivated as his mother was, she would not marry to strengthen an alliance. *Once you've been in love,* she'd told him in a rare moment of melancholy, *you can never settle for less.*

He had loved Kerren, or at least thought he had. His mother had never been thrilled with the idea of him walking a Rackmore witch down the aisle. The Dragons and the Ravens didn't exactly coexist peacefully. When he looked back now, he wondered if in some small way he'd known they didn't have the kind of soul-deep, can't-breathe, would-do-anything kind of love his mother had shared with his father.

"Except it's all a bullshit fairy tale," he muttered as he unzipped the black bag hanging among his sweaters and T-shirts. His mother longed for the man she could never have, and had painted love as bright and alluring as a fairy's wings.

Argh! If only he could find the cape, he wouldn't have to find substitute attire. He pulled out the red robe first, and grimaced. He hadn't worn it since his last day on the House floor, the morning he gave his formal resignation to the Court. He jammed it back inside and grabbed the hanger next to it.

Gods-be-damned!

Why had he even kept the white robe in which he'd been married? He tossed it to the floor, disgusted. The magic of the symbols sewn into the fabric no longer had meaning or power. He shouldn't have kept the stupid robe. It wasn't like he didn't have enough reminders about his failed marriage and his treacherous ex-wife.

Irritation turned to anger. He shouldn't even be going into town. For what? To save Lucy? He didn't exactly have pleasant memories of her. It wasn't that she was a bad kid, just a self-absorbed one. She couldn't be bothered with anyone or anything that didn't have to do with her, an attitude that had a lot to do with being a typical teenager, and even more to do with being spoiled by wealthy, indulgent parents. Not to mention she was a thaumaturge—once courted by all the Houses, even the Dragons. His own mother had put aside Lucy's Raven heritage to woo her. "Thaumaturge" meant "miracle worker" in Greek. Someone with Lucy's ability could manipulate life itself—heal grievous wounds, fix broken bones, take away diseases. He'd heard that skilled thaumaturges could breathe the very life back into a body.

But being a Rackmore had tainted her—and once the Grand Court issued its edict, no House could accept her as a member, even if they had wanted to risk it.

As Gray extracted a third mystery coat, he wondered if he should just leave her alone. She was destitute, but he couldn't save her from that. She'd always be without money, thanks to the actions of her greedy ancestors. No. What got to him now was remembering the forlorn look in her green eyes, the sharpened features and frail form that suggested starvation, the slump of shoulders bearing too heavy a burden, and the hopelessness that covered her far better than that worn green robe.

He'd killed her hope completely. He'd seen the way the light had died out of her eyes when she realized he wouldn't help her. How many people had already slammed their doors in her pretty face?

Fucking Bernard Franco. He'd always been a prick, even before he "resigned" from his position in the House of Ravens. After the last and worst scandal, rumor had it he was given an ultimatum by the House's Inner Court to leave of his own accord. Worse still, some said that he'd been paid off to keep the House's darker secrets. Lucy had been in his bed, accepting his gifts, enduring his humiliation, playing the simpering paramour.

It sickened him.

He gripped the black leather duster in his hands. Old magic pulsed in its seams; memories of days gone by—and people, too—whispered from the leather. He realized it was his grandfather's, and before that, it had belonged to other Calhoun men. A red dragon shimmered across the back, a powerful symbol of his House and family. He'd never worn it, but the old coot had made it clear he wanted Gray to wear these threads.

He'd never donned the coat because then . . . he'd have to admit he was fully committed to the auspices of guardianship. That *this* was his life, and always would be. Even after five years of living here, he didn't feel as if he belonged in the very town he grew up in, and though he did all that was required of his office, he wasn't a social kind of guy. He didn't want to get close to anyone, even old friends.

He didn't care what that meant, either.

Gray put on the duster, and left the house before he changed his mind. Usually, he'd walk to town, but since he wasn't sure where Lucy had gone or where he might find her, not to mention he was going out into the unrelenting storm, he decided to take his grandfather's old Ford truck. It was a rusted bucket of bolts, but it ran well, and it was good enough to take Lucy to the bus station. All he had to do was buy the girl a ticket to wherever she wanted to go. Then he could quit feeling like a jerk, and she could keep running away from Franco.

He didn't figure she'd actually stop in town. She was a practiced enough witch to feel the negative energy undulations. She'd probably been in town ten seconds before everyone knew about her arrival and had passed their judgments. They didn't even need to know that there was a history between Lucy and their Guardian. Being a Rackmore was reason enough for most folks to distrust her.

His house perched on a large hill that overlooked downtown. The street in front of the old Victorian ended abruptly, but Main Street passed to the left of his home. He pulled onto it, taking a right. If he'd gone left, the paved road eventually gave way to gravel. There were three family farms out that way, and the road petered out at the entrance to the Gomez farm.

When Gray got to Brujo Boulevard, he turned right and just past the school, he took a left on Cedar Road. It was the only street that led to the highway; there was no other way in or out of town, at least by car.

The storm had worsened, and the windshield wipers sucked. Rain fell in thick, chilled sheets of silver, and even though he didn't want to be, he was worried about Lucy surviving in this crap. Guilt assailed him once again, but he shoved it away. *She's not my fucking problem.*

Only she was.

Gray slowed the truck and peered through the torrents. Damn. She'd fallen into a ditch, gotten a ride, or squirreled away someplace. He pulled onto the shoulder, and stared out the windshield. He didn't want to use a summoning spell. He had no idea where she was, and if she'd made it out of town, he sure as hell didn't want to draw her back. And a tracking spell wouldn't work if he didn't have a possession of hers. He could use something as small as a hair, but he didn't even have that.

Maybe she ran into the sheriff. It was possible his

old friend would stick her in magical quarantine. Taylor Mooreland's father had run off with a Rackmore witch—at least that was what Edward had admitted to in his note. He'd been too cowardly to face the woman he'd betrayed and then he'd left his wife, Sarah, to raise their seven young children alone. Taylor had been the oldest at fifteen and had taken over as "man of the house." Gray's lips twisted into a frown. Taylor probably wouldn't stick Lucy into the equivalent of wizard jail just because she shared a lineage with the woman responsible for breaking up his family.

Then again . . .

No one was on the road. Only a fool would be out in this weather—and he was definitely feeling foolish. Annoyed with his need to rescue the damsel in distress, he turned the truck around and headed back into town.

He parked in front of the Piney Woods Café. If Lucy had dared to go inside, she wouldn't have received a warm welcome. Cathleen Munch was a bitter woman, and it was definitely a case of the apple not falling far from the tree. She and her mother, Cora, had lived in a run-down trailer by the lake. Apparently, Cathleen's father had drowned in the lake, though that happened before his time. Losing her husband turned Cora mean. She raised her daughter to hate everyone and everything as much as she did.

The café was the only place in town to catch a bite, so even people who didn't like Cathleen or the imbalance of energy around the place would stop by—mostly to order their food to go. But Cathleen didn't care about making friends. She liked money.

Another reason she would've tossed penniless Lucy out on her ass.

He sucked in some deep breaths and reinforced his

magic shields. He didn't want anything he picked up in the café sticking to him. The shield acted like Teflon to bad vibes. And Cathleen had plenty to go around.

Gray hurried through the rain and ducked inside. He stopped in the foyer, shaking off the drops that clung to his duster, and nodded to Cathleen. She sat, as usual, behind the register smoking a cigarette and perusing a gossip rag.

"Get something for you, Guardian?" she asked. Her voice echoed with a sneer, but she tempered it with a thin smile.

He knew better than not to order. Nothing made Cathleen surlier than someone trying to breathe her oxygen for free. Luckily, the food was actually good. "Piece of coconut cream pie," he said. "You got any doughnuts?"

"Late in the day ~~for~~ those," she said, lips puckering. "But I think there're some jelly ones left."

Gray grinned. "I'll take 'em." The grin was for what would result when he plopped noncake doughnuts in front of Grit and Dutch, and boy, was he looking forward to that, but Cathleen straightened on her stool and fluffed her hair.

He toned down his smile, and looked away, catching a glimpse of Marcy dashing through the door marked RESTROOMS. Her distress seeped through his shields.

"That girl," snapped Cathleen, "deserves everything she gets. You know, she tried to help that Rackmore bitch?"

Gray resisted the urge to aim a fireball at Cathleen's head. Instead, he kept his smile, and turned. "Rackmore?"

"Yeah. Came in earlier all wanting me to feed her. I made Marcy mop the foyer. Didn't want no Rackmore germs infecting my place." She sniffed. "You gonna do something about her? Went over to Ember's. Walked herself right into that hoodoo bitch's shop."

It seemed that all women, other than herself, qualified as bitches in Cathleen's estimation. He hadn't met Ember, much less been in her tea shop. He'd asked the sheriff to welcome the new residents in his stead.

His gut twisted again. Had he really the nerve to think he'd been doing his job? Guilt crawled over him like red ants, stinging him endlessly. He didn't like feeling this way. He didn't like feeling *any* way.

"How's that pie and those doughnuts coming?" he asked.

Cathleen realized that her only help had stepped out, so she would have to wait on him. She wasn't happy about it, but since Gray had jurisdiction above all others in town, she reluctantly slid off her stool to go fill his order.

He decided to track down Marcy. It bothered him that she seemed upset, and bothered him even more that her stepmother seemed to think she deserved to suffer. The door marked RESTROOMS opened into a dark, narrow hallway with paneled walls and dusty pictures of the café as it had looked when it first opened in 1845. It was one of the first businesses built by the mundanes, and Gray remembered the previous owner, Cathleen's father-in-law, Wilber Munch, with a lot of fondness. His son, Leland, had been a nice guy, a little too malleable when it came to the whims of women.

On either side of the hallway were the doors to the men's and women's restrooms. And all the way at the back was a black metal door with a big red EXIT sign above it. He assumed it was an emergency door, broken no doubt, because Cathleen was too cheap to fix up the place.

He pushed through it. The rank smells of garbage hit

him so hard he gagged. Goddess almighty! The last time
he checked, the town had trash service. As he stumbled
outside and looked around for Marcy, he noted how
refuse overfilled both Dumpsters tucked into the tiny
alley.

Gray moved away from the stench-filled morass
and toward the end of the alley. He spied Marcy easily
enough, since she was wearing a bright yellow dress. She
huddled in the corner, under a portico that offered little
shelter from the sluicing rain, her hands covering her
face. "Marcy?"

Startled, she looked up, hiccuping sobs. He saw the
shiner on her left eye. It was fresh, as was her split lip,
which was still bleeding. Anger burst through the rem-
nants of his apathy. Had he stopped so thoroughly giving a shit about anyone else that he let the whole town
go to hell?

"What happened?"

"N-nothing. I . . . uh, ran into a door."

"Either you tell me what happened," he said softly,
"or I'll do a truth spell on the entire café to find out who
hurt you. I'll learn everybody's secrets, including yours."

"Guardian. Please." She shook her head. "I c-can't."

"You can trust me, Marcy."

She stared at him, eyes wide, and opened her mouth.
Then she shuddered and shook her head. Gray was as-
tounded that she was more afraid of who hurt her than
she was of him. He realized that, somewhere along the
way, the town had lost faith in him. He couldn't actually
remember the last time someone had come willingly to
him with a problem or concern. He had assumed that all
was well because no one bothered him.

It seemed that no one bothered him because they'd
realized he didn't care. A point he'd driven home by
performing perfunctory magic, showing up only on fes-

tival days, and doing his yearly pilgrimage to the House in Dallas to reaffirm the town's loyalty to the Dragons. He never came to Nevermore otherwise, never mingled with the residents, never tried to be more than the Dragon Guardian who lived in his big house on the hill.

I'm not just an asshole. I'm the biggest asshole on the planet.

If Lucy hadn't shown up and stabbed his conscience, he wouldn't be out here. He wouldn't even know about Marcy's trouble or that the café was in near ruins. He wasn't sure if he should be grateful to the little witch or be even more pissed at her. He studied Marcy's young, pale face, and decided Lucy deserved thanks. And, he supposed, his help.

But he wasn't going to marry her.

"Tell me who hurt you, Marcy." He didn't want to touch her, didn't want to make her fear that he would hurt her, too. Instead, he looked deeply into her eyes, and held her gaze. Tears rolled down her cheeks and her mouth quivered.

"What will you do to him if I tell you?"

Kill him. Maim him. Kick his balls into his throat. "You know the rules, Marcy. The Guardian decides punishment for transgressions within the town's borders."

"Y-you'll have to h-hear both sides of the s-story?"

He nodded. That, too, was part of the process.

"I love him," she whispered. She looked at Gray, her expression haunted. "How is it possible to love someone who can do such awful things?"

His heart clenched—the same heart Kerren had skewered with her betrayal and then her dagger. "Sometimes we're blinded by our emotions. But we always have choices."

"Yes," she whispered. "That's true."

"Then tell me his name, and I'll protect you."

"Protect yourself!" She shoved him away, and ran. Gray stumbled backward into a soggy stack of wet cardboard boxes and fell on his ass. Cursing, he rolled to his side and staggered to his feet—just in time to watch Marcy stop at the corner of the café, turn, and yell, "Save the witch, too. She's in trouble. We all are!"

Then she disappeared.

Gray took off after her, but when he reached the street, she was gone. The rain washed everything away, any trace she might've left to create a tracking spell, though he could probably find something of hers in the café. Or he could just go to the house she shared with Cathleen and catch her there. He clutched the corner of the building, his side aching, and thought about what to do next. He doubted Marcy wanted to be found, but too damned bad. And what was with all the warnings about saving Lucy and everyone being in trouble?

He hated to feel indecisive, especially when being pummeled by cold rain and the stench of the café's refuse. Well, he might not be able to do anything about either Marcy or Lucy right this second, but he sure as hell could remind the citizens he was the Guardian of Nevermore.

Gray reentered the café through the emergency door and went into the men's room to dry off. If he was anywhere else, he'd draw energy to create a drying spell, but with all the negative vibes here, he didn't dare try. He might end up being engulfed in flames—because like attracted like, and evil created evil. Magic was about keeping balance, and most spells borrowed energy from whatever living things were around. Once the task was completed, wizards and witches had to release the energy again, and send it back.

Keeping the balance was important.

He'd let the café get out of sync. He'd let the whole

town get out of sync. Come to think of it, he wasn't exactly in balance himself, so it wasn't a surprise he hadn't noticed the world around him crumbling away, shifting dangerously. Nevermore was vulnerable, and it was his fault. With the town out of magical alignment, portals could open—those that allowed in gremlins, which were annoying but mostly harmless, or those that invited in demons, which were also annoying, but a lot more dangerous. All of demonkind was magically bound to hell, and even if they managed to scrabble onto the earthly plane, either by portal shifts or by summoning spells, they could never stay for long. Still, it took no time at all for a demon to wreak havoc or, worse, make bargains with mundanes or magicals, and fuck up the sacred energies. Honestly, he was surprised a portal hadn't popped open right in the middle of the café.

He'd put everyone in jeopardy, but he could fix it. Nothing bad had happened yet. Marcy's warning still worried him, but he'd know if a portal had opened, or if demons were hanging around. That kind of magic couldn't be hidden, especially not from him. He chased away the doubts filling his mind, the ones that said he was rusty, that he was blind, that he was too far gone, that it was too late.

It's never too late.

Grit had lived by that phrase. And Gray had believed it, too—until Kerren showed him that sometimes, it damned sure was too late.

The duster had kept most of the rain off him, but his jeans were soaked from his fall, and his hair was a mess. He combed back the wet strands as best he could, and called it done. He didn't spend too long staring at himself in the mirror. He couldn't quite meet his own gaze, not yet ready to face his shame.

He exited the bathroom and returned to the front counter. Cathleen waited at the register, her impatience evident in her narrowed gaze and twitching fingers. Gray looked down at the small Styrofoam box and the greasy paper bag. He had no stomach for either the pie or the doughnuts.

Cathleen tapped the keys on the old-fashioned register. Magic tended to suffocate sophisticated gadgets, so most folks didn't bother with technological upgrades, at least not in towns protected by magicals. Gray pulled out his wallet and thumbed through the cash.

"Five eleven," said Cathleen. "I had Josie dip the doughnuts real quick, so they're fresh."

Gray handed over the bills, and grimaced. That explained the grease on the bag. The doughnuts had probably been sitting around in the back for Goddess knew how long, and that was why she'd thrown them in the fryer.

Cathleen carefully counted back his change, her expression morose, and then slammed the metal drawer shut. She still had enough respect for his position that she didn't waddle over to her stool and pick up her magazine immediately.

"When's the last time your garbage got picked up?" asked Gray.

She blinked at him, as if she couldn't quite process the question. Her lips drooped into a limp frown. "What?"

"Your Dumpsters are overflowing. It's against city code to litter."

"I ain't littering."

"Have you been in the alley lately?" asked Gray pleasantly. "Nevermore has garbage service twice a week. It doesn't look like the café's trash has been picked up in a long while."

Cathleen licked her lips nervously. Her gaze filled with uncertainty. "I can't help it if my employees ain't doing their jobs proper."

"Actually," said Gray in the same pleasant tone, "you can. Because you're the proprietor—that makes you responsible for the well-being of this property, your employees, and your customers."

"She canceled the garbage service."

A young man extracted himself from a counter stool and sauntered toward Gray. The boy was tall and thin, dressed in a red coverall. On the upper right side was a small gold dragon with "Nevermore Sanitation" stitched above it, and below it, the name "Trent." His hair was short and spiky, the tips colored neon red. A flame tattoo crawled up his neck. Gray could see multiple holes in his ears, and realized the boy probably wore piercings when he wasn't on the job.

Trent stopped next to Gray, and leaned on the counter, his insolent brown gaze on Cathleen. "She called a couple months ago complaining about the service fees. She told the boss she wasn't gonna pay for pickup anymore, so he told us to skip her on our route."

"Why wasn't this brought to my attention?" asked Gray.

Trent's gaze flicked to his. "Why would it?" The question held puzzlement, not resentment. He tossed a ten-spot onto the counter and saluted Cathleen.

"You're not welcome here no more!" she screeched. "I won't serve you again, you half-breed bastard!"

Trent grinned and wiggled his fingers at her. "I prefer Ember's anyway. It smells too much like old bitch in here." He left, the door slamming shut behind him, the bell over the doorway jingling loudly in the ensuing silence.

The kid had balls. Gray liked him. He turned toward Cathleen, relishing her look of outrage.

"Cathleen Munch, I find you in contempt of the city ordinance 3.125, proper disposal of refuse." Gray was kinda surprised he remembered the actual ordinance. Maybe he wasn't so out of practice, after all. "I order you to remove the garbage from the alley, and hereby give you verbal notice of inspection. As specified by our laws, you have forty-eight hours to prepare for the arrival of myself and my appointed inspectors. Until then, I'm closing the café."

Cathleen's eyes went wide, her mouth flopping open. Then she started to sputter, her arms waving. "You can't! You'll ruin me! I demand a lawyer!"

"If you do not wish to abide by Dragon law," said Gray evenly, "then do not live in a Dragon town." He turned to the patrons still sitting at their seats and staring at him. "The café is closed. *Leave.*" Everyone knew a Guardian command when they heard it. They scrambled from their seats, nearly trampling one another to get out of the café.

"Wait!" screamed Cathleen. "Y'all still gotta pay! *Wait!*"

No one paid attention to the screeching purple-faced woman. Her fury hit Gray's shields like hot grease, sizzling and popping. Gray was too strong a wizard and Cathleen too much a mundane for her emotions to affect him magically, but he was still amazed by the strength of her hatred. It almost had its own heartbeat.

Soon, everyone was gone, except the overworked short-order cook. Josie Gomez ambled out of the kitchen holding her big red purse under her arm. Gray had gone to school with her. She'd been a sophomore when he was a senior, worked hard not only in her classes but on her family farm. She was one of three girls, with two much younger sisters, and she was also one of the few kids who never talked about getting out of Nevermore. She liked her family, the town, and her life, in general. She was short and curvy, her caramel skin radiant, even though she'd just spent hours in a hot kitchen. Her black hair was twisted into a long braid.

"Gray," she said. "It's good to see you."

"Don't you talk to him," screeched Cathleen. "He's shut down my business. And I ain't paying you, neither. You don't work, you don't get paid. I don't care how sick your daddy is."

Fire erupted from Gray's fingertips. Josie's eyebrows went up. "I understand the feeling," she said. "But she's not worth it."

It was an effort to put out the flames. His anger was almost tangible.

Josie turned to Cathleen. "I've put up with a year's worth of bullshit from you. You're a bitter, mean woman with a shriveled soul. You're going to die alone, Cathleen. And no one will ever mourn you."

Cathleen sucked in a shocked breath, her chubby little body quivering with fury. "How dare you!"

"How dare *you*!" said Josie. "I quit."

Cathleen huffed in outrage and crossed her arms, apparently thinking about what kind of meanness she could do next. Or maybe she was grappling with the idea of losing the only cook willing to work for her sorry ass.

Gray touched Josie's shoulder. "Angel's sick?"

"Cancer. He's getting treatments. We have hope." She gave him a quick hug. "Drop by if you can. He'd love to see you."

Gray felt another pang of guilt. He sucked as Guardian. Big-time. He nodded to Josie, and then watched her leave. Fury boiling, he turned toward Cathleen. She was still reeling from Josie's exit speech, but he didn't give a ripe shit.

"I'll return in forty-eight hours to complete the inspection," he said. "If even the teeniest tiniest thing is out of place, if you're within a hair's violation of any city code or Dragon law, I'll close the café permanently."

"You wouldn't," she sneered. "This is the only place in town to eat. It's been here since the beginning. People'll get mad if you do something stupid, Guardian."

Gray leaned over the counter and captured her gaze. "I will close the café," he repeated, "and then I will ban you."

Something like fear slithered across her expression, but Gray got the odd feeling it wasn't because of him.

"Fine," she spit out.

He left the items he'd purchased on the counter. Thinking about eating anything made in this joint turned his stomach. As he turned to go, Cathleen hissed, "Now that you're done botherin' decent folks, you gonna do something about that Rackmore bitch?"

"I am the Guardian," he said in low, steely voice. "I suggest you remember that I am capable of much more than merely closing your place of business and bespelling you into leaving."

This time when fear flashed in her eyes, Gray knew it was because of him. She stepped back from the counter, her expression uncertain. It was as if she'd realized the puppy she'd been teasing was really a hellhound. He had no doubt she was remembering that he was not only a Dragon but also a wizard who'd literally been to the domain of the Dark One—and returned to tell the tale.

"You wouldn't disappear me," she said, her voice thin with terror.

His lips split into a feral grin. "The hell I wouldn't."

He turned to go, and then he paused and looked over his shoulder. "Just so you know, I'm extending Lucinda Rackmore magical privileges and residency in Nevermore. The next time you see her, I suggest you be polite."

Chapter 3

"We're fucked." The panicked voice echoed through the dimly lit basement as the big man clambered down the stairs, scuffling toward the table filled with magical objects. "We gotta bolt."

"No, Lennie." The black-robed figure reached out and stilled the movements of his friend, who was gathering up the items and stuffing them into his pockets. "We'll move up the timeline."

"Two days!" screeched his companion. "Are you shit-stupid? The portal—"

"Is already starting to open."

"It is?" He paused. "We'll be rich then. Right?"

"You'll be showered with gold," he lied. Oh, there would be wealth galore, but not the kind that could be spent. Magic. He needed it. Craved it. *Deserved* it. And demon magic was the most powerful. All he had to do was call forth a demon lord and barter for it. Soon, Gray Calhoun would be in hell where he belonged . . . and the Guardian's magic would belong to him.

It had taken him five long years to gather the items so carelessly stuffed into his friend's pockets. His power had been too diluted with mundane blood to use without some sort of amplification. Once he had the magic, he wouldn't be so gods-be-damned weak. Then he could close the circle. What had been started in his childhood could be finished. When he was strong, stronger than any of *them*, they would all know the truth, and they would bow before him—no, scrape and beg. He would make a far better Guardian than whiny, pathetic Gray Calhoun.

"I'm worried."

His big, dumb, naive friend was such a nuisance.

"No need. Everything's under control."

"Miss Ember said—"

His sigh cut off the statement. "I told you not to listen to Ember's ramblings." He patted Lennie on the shoulder. "Is that why you tried to run the witch over?"

"Thought I could take care of her, you know? We don't need a Rackmore here messing things up."

We don't need you messing them up, either, he thought. Bringing his old buddy on board had been a mistake born from sentimentality. Had he not learned his lessons about hardening his heart? His friend had been useful, but he feared he would soon be nothing more than hindrance.

"Put the objects back. I have another errand for you."

Reluctantly, the man put back all the items he'd taken, straightening them out in neat rows. "I thought we had everything we needed."

"We did." He looked down at the table, at the power that glowed among the magic-made artifacts. He needed only one more—the key to making them all work. The one that had been taken from him. "You must promise not to hurt the witch. I need her."

"For what?"

His gaze flicked over his friend's suspicious expression. So many ignorant people believed the Rackmore curse was like the plague—if you touched a witch, you might lose your money, too. They didn't understand the intricacies of the demon magic, the beauty and precision of the spellwork required to divest thousands of Rackmores of their wealth and keep them from it forever. He appreciated the artistry of the curse, the cruel orchestration required to create such a delicate, unbreakable web of misfortune. He was fascinated by it, admired it, and wanted, above all, to learn how to master it.

"I promise you," he said, "that the witch will not live. But before she dies, she will serve our purposes well."

"If you say so. Well, what crazy-assed thing do you want me to do now?"

He smiled, drew big, dumb Lennie away from the table, away from the magic they'd stolen, and told him what to do next.

"Well, now. Here you are," said a female's Jamaican-tinged voice. A tall, voluptuous black woman stood in the foyer. She was draped in shades of purple and black, her beringed hands clasped in front of her.

"I'm sorry," Gray said. "Were you expecting me?"

Her deep-throated laughter threw him off guard. Unsettled, he watched as she slapped her thigh and hooted. "Expecting you. Oh, da Goddess, She has a sense of humor, dat one. *Expectin'* you."

"I'm afraid I don't see the humor," said Gray.

"No," she offered, her merriment tapering off, "you wouldn't. When's the last time you found anything to smile about, Guardian?"

It seemed no one in this town, not even the new residents, respected his position. He'd admit he hadn't exactly been the best Guardian, but he was determined to do better. The town and its citizens deserved no less. Still. His ego was taking a bruising today—and he had no one to blame but himself.

"Oh, now. Don't you worry," she said, stepping forward to grasp the crook of his elbow. "Everything works out for a reason. Just not always the reason you like. Or want. But sometimes, you can't see what's best for you." She tapped her left temple, which drew his attention to the blackened side of her strange eyewear. He sensed the magic of the lenses, but he also realized that she had shields up, too. He reached out, trying to figure out what was so odd about her power, but she made a *tsk*-ing sound and waved a finger in a you're-being-naughty gesture.

"Now, now. You stop dat. I promise I only bring good juju to Nevermore."

"You'll forgive me if I'm a bit skeptical."

She chuckled. "Not so skeptical dat you didn't come to meet me and my Rilton face-to-face. Not so worried then, were you?"

He noticed her accent strengthened every so often, sorta like a radio station that kept fading in and out. He didn't like that she was right about him skipping her intake interview. He'd let Taylor handle processing the new magicals. But Taylor was a thorough bastard, even more skeptical than Gray, and hated change, especially when it included adding new people to the town's roster. If Ember and her husband passed his inspection, then they must've impressed the hell out of the sheriff.

"So. You lettin' her stay." Ember's statement startled him into realizing she'd been leading him toward the back of the tea shop. She hadn't phrased a question, and he had no problem figuring out "her" meant "Lucy."

"She's here?"

Ember stopped in front of an empty booth and looked down at it. Gray offered a cursory examination, but noted only that the table was wet and there were lingering smells of rain and earth. He opened his senses wider, and emotions filtered through his shields: desperation, relief, panic.

Lucy.

"Where did she go?"

"Don't know." She shook her head. "Sometimes, when people are damaged, dey view tings from upside down."

Gray's brows went up. "What does that mean?"

She sighed, as if he'd disappointed her. Irritation flashed through him. He wasn't a damned novice, and he hated that she made him feel like one. Battling his own impatience, he kept his gaze on her and waited.

"You ever play the opposite game?" she asked.

"Sure," said Gray, "when I was a kid."

She nodded. "Right. So everything you say and do during the game is the opposite of what you mean. But for Lucy, it's no game. She freed herself from a bad situation. Bad people. She learned to believe she has no worth. So, when someone is kind to her . . ." She trailed off and looked at him.

Gray felt like Ember had punched him in the stomach. Lucy had expected him to be a jerk, even though some small part of her had hoped he would be different from everyone else who'd rejected and shamed her.

"You were nice to her," he said softly, "and she couldn't handle it."

"Opposite game," Ember murmured. "She need some time to figure out how to right her world." She looked at him, one dark eye visible through the single purple lens of her weird glasses. "Maybe she not the only one."

"Maybe," agreed Gray.

"Well, then!" Ember broke into a broad smile and patted his arm. "You stayin' for some tea, Guardian? I got just dey ting for you."

"I'll come back," he promised. "Right now, I have an errand to run."

" 'Course you do. That's her booth. Maybe she leave

something behind." Ember slipped her hand out the crook of his arm, gave him one last pat, and turned away. He watched her go through a swinging door marked KITCHEN ENTRANCE, and then she was gone.

Gray examined the booth. He knelt on the right side, where Lucy's presence felt strongest, and bent low to see if she'd left anything he could use to create a tracking spell. Despite his detailed investigation, he found nothing, not even a thread from her robe or lint from her duffel.

"Shit." He backed out of the booth and looked down at the table. It was still wet from . . . *oh*. Lucy had left something behind all right.

Her tears.

"Stupid," said Lucinda as the rain pelted her. The wind was getting in on the beat-the-witch action, too, slicing at her like machetes. As she trudged down the gravel shoulder of the road, her threadbare tennis shoes soaked, her robe failing to keep off the sluicing water, her body chilled and shivering, she berated herself again.

Stupid. So freaking stupid.

She shouldn't have left the warmth and safety of neutral ground—especially with people like that old bat from the café and that moron in the hot rod gunning for her. Her time with Bernard taught her to trust her instincts . . . at least when it came to sensing an attack. Instincts honed as she'd wandered around for the last three months, tracking down anyone who might help her. Goddess! When she thought about all those times she let Bernard— *No*.

Maybe she'd been a fool. But she couldn't blame anyone but herself for putting up with Bernard. And for what? Security? Yeah, that had worked out well. Pretty clothes, luxurious surroundings, exotic trips . . . she'd handed over her dignity and self-esteem for baubles. There was only slight satisfaction in realizing she'd literally been under a spell, too. Compulsory magic worked best with the already willing.

The Rackmore whore.

Nice how that rhymed. Made it just roll off the tongue.

Lucinda redirected her thoughts. The past was the past. Over, over, *over*.

She pulled the robe tighter around her, but the clasp had broken, so it was a useless gesture. She'd enjoyed its dry warmth, at least for the first thirty seconds of her walk. In no time at all, the rain had pummeled her clothing into wet submission.

The nanosecond Ember handed over the fresh-from-the-dryer robe and excused herself to the kitchen, Lucinda bolted. She felt bad that she hadn't stayed long enough to have tea, but Ember's kindness felt strange—like finding a plate of chocolate-chip cookies after falling into a pit of vipers.

Besides, she didn't want to bring any misfortune to the tea shop.

It was hard not to think of herself as a plague, even though she knew her curse couldn't infect others. One of the simplest laws of magic was that like attracted like. It was why witches and wizards were taught since birth about keeping the balance. Granted, cursed people had little choice in what they attracted, but there were still ways to offset it. And not every magical was interested in keeping the balance at all.

She snorted. Bernard had lost his official position in the House of Ravens, but he still had a hand in it. She'd never been sure exactly what he was doing for his former cohorts, but no doubt it had something to do with overthrowing a small country or controlling drugs or killing kittens.

Beep! Beep!

Startled by the honking car roaring up behind her (so much for those well-honed attack instincts), Lucinda spun around, heart hammering. The worn soles of her tennis shoes slipped in the mud, and she caught a look at the braking lights of a yellow VW Bug as she tried to find some purchase. Her arms pinwheeled as she grappled for balance, but she couldn't compensate for the weight of the bag slung over her shoulder.

For a couple of seconds, she had the sickening sensation of weightlessness as she toppled backward into the ditch. She landed on her side on top of the duffel. The swirling water was deep enough to douse her completely, but not enough, unfortunately, to drown her.

Because death would be an upgrade to her luck right now.

Pain radiated up her hip, and the arm squished between her body and the duffel felt numb. Water swirled up her jeans and under her shirt, and grabbed at the end of her robe. Maybe if she lay here long enough, the earth would open up and swallow her.

Was that too much to ask?

Apparently so.

Aching and tired, Lucinda sat up, dragging her duffel with her. It had been heavy before, but thanks to its thorough dunking, it now felt like someone had tucked an anvil inside it.

"Oh, my gosh!"

In all the wind and rain, the words sounded like a whisper. Lucinda looked up and saw the waitress from the café kneeling at the edge of the ditch and offering her hand.

"What happened to you?" asked Lucinda as she zeroed in on the girl's black eye and split lip.

"Me?" The girl's eyes widened. "What about you?"

"It's just water," said Lucinda. She stood up, irritated. She looked at the muddy liquid swirling around her ankles, gathered her magic, and yelled, "Part!"

The water moved aside to reveal the soggy, rock-strewn bottom of the ditch. She shoved the duffel up the slope, and the waitress grabbed the handles, hauling it up onto the shoulder.

As soon as Lucinda got to the top, she released the magic, silently thanking nature for the little borrow of energy.

"I'm Lucinda." She held out her not too muddy hand to the waitress, trying not to take offense while the girl considered whether to offer hers in return.

Finally, she squared her shoulders and shook Lucinda's hand. "I'm Marcy. Marcy Munch." She flinched. "I know. Munch is a dumb last name. High school was a real bitch."

"So's life," said Lucinda. "Who hit you?"

Marcy's gaze slid away. "You need a ride? I'm leaving for good. I got enough money to get to the border."

"You're going to Mexico?" Lucinda couldn't wipe the suspicion from her voice. Her experience had become this: If something good happened, it was just a setup for the really bad thing headed her way. She didn't like the coincidence of needing a ride and Marcy's sudden departure from town—to the same desired destination.

"Let's get in the car, okay?" asked Marcy. "This weather is crazy."

Lucinda watched as the waitress turned and made her way toward the Volkswagen. Her choice was to slog through the rain until someone else took pity on her, or to get into a warm, dry car right now.

She followed the girl around to the front of the tiny car. Marcy opened the hood and Lucinda threw her duffel into the empty space. Then they got into the car and secured their seat belts. The heat was cranked up—thank the Goddess—because they both were soaked and shivering.

"You didn't pack anything?" asked Lucinda as Marcy put the Bug into gear and coasted onto the road. She noted the grease spatters on the girl's white apron with its still-bulging pockets and breathed in the food smells not even the rain had been able to wash away. "You didn't change clothes."

"No time," said Marcy. "It's good we're leaving. Nevermore's . . ." She paused, apparently unable to come up with an appropriate adjective, and shrugged.

"What about your mom?"

"Cathleen," Marcy hissed, "is not my mother—even though she insists I call her 'mama.' She likes to remind me that she raised me, but she didn't. She married Daddy when I was ten. He went and died four years later and left her the café. Her! She's not even a real Munch!" She blew out a breath and pushed back her wet hair. "My family has owned the café since the town was founded. It's horrible! I'd change everything. If Daddy had just trusted me . . . but I guess he didn't think he'd die. Who does, right?"

"How do you know he didn't trust you?" asked Lucinda.

Marcy slanted her a look of disbelief. "Because I don't own the café. Maybe if I'd been older, he would've changed his will."

Lucinda wondered if the café was supposed to belong to Marcy and her stepmother finagled control of it. What business was it of hers, anyway? She wasn't a resident of Nevermore. And two hours in a place didn't make her an expert on it, or the people who lived there. Still. She couldn't dismiss that someone had used Marcy's face as a punching bag.

"Who hit you?" Lucinda asked again.

"Doesn't matter." Marcy's expression turned mulish. "It won't happen again, anyway. I'm leaving. Mexico will be different. It's safe there."

"Depends on your definition of safe," offered Lucinda.

"Why are *you* going there?" asked Marcy, her tone defensive.

"To escape my ex-lover."

"Oh." She chewed her lower lip. "He's a magical, too?"

"House of Ravens. A real asshole."

"Wow."

"Yeah." Lucinda turned to look out the passenger's-side window. "When I get in trouble, I go big. All the way."

Both women said nothing else, lost in their own thoughts. The buzzing noise of the car engine and the rain plinking against the windows filled up the silence. It seemed like the road stretched into infinity, an effect only reinforced by the overcast sky—and it was already dusk. Since there were no lights on this road, only the yellow glare of the VW's headlights broke through the encroaching black.

Lucinda felt unnerved. The storm coupled with the increasing darkness, not to mention the lonely road and her distressed companion, made Lucinda feel like she was trapped in a horror movie. In a scene right before the monster lunged, or the car crashed, or the—

Shut it! Nothing bad will happen, she thought sternly.

"Highway's just a few more miles," said Marcy. She flashed an uneasy smile. "It can get really creepy around here, especially at night."

Lucinda felt the car lurch as it accelerated. She grimaced. "Maybe going faster is a bad idea."

"We gotta make the highway before the sun sets."

"Why?"

"Bad things happen. That's the truth of it, everywhere. Bad things always hide in the dark." She sucked in a breath. "Anyway. Even though this is all farmland, we're still technically in Nevermore." Marcy had a white-knuckled grip on the steering wheel. "The boundary ends at the highway. Once we're on it, we'll be safe."

Lucinda turned in her seat and stared at Marcy. The green lights from the dashboard highlighted the girl's pale face and worried expression. Foreboding crept up Lucinda's spine like a wave of tiny spiders. "Safe from what?"

"Shit!" Marcy slammed on the brakes. The car skidded on the slick road, fishtailing.

Lucinda was thrown forward, the seat belt locking so hard it knocked the breath from her, and then she was thrust back, her skull bouncing off the headrest. Little white stars danced before her eyes, and her chest throbbed with pain.

The car stopped at an angle on the wrong side of the road, the headlights revealing a barbed wire fence.

Marcy had whacked her head on the steering wheel, as evidenced by the wound across her forehead. She was still conscious, though, and her terror so sharp, Lucinda felt cut by it.

"Did you see him? Right there? Goddess help us!" Marcy jammed in the clutch and shifted into first gear, but the car wouldn't start. The key simply clicked. "Shit! No, no, no!"

"Calm down." Lucinda unhooked her seat belt. "What happened? Who did you see?" She grabbed a fast-food napkin from the center console and tried to dab away the blood trickling down Marcy's temple.

"Stop it!" screamed Marcy. She knocked away Lucinda's hand. "The highway's less than a mile. Can you magic the engine?"

Lucinda shook her head. Her reserves were too low to attempt it. Machinery didn't appreciate magic, and required the kind of finesse she wasn't capable of on her best day.

"We'll have to run." Marcy took off her seat belt and grabbed the handle of the door.

"Wait a minute." Lucinda grabbed Marcy's arm and stalled her. "Tell me what's going on. Who's after us?"

"Please, Lucinda. *Please.* Just run. I'll explain everything when we're safe."

Lucinda looked out the window, into the darkness, and couldn't discern anyone or anything out there. Her shields were up, but she'd still be able to detect any magicals.

But not mundanes.

What had Marcy seen that had freaked her out? Who had scared her so badly she'd nearly run off the road?

"Let's go," said Lucinda. "I'll follow you."

"Run as fast as you can," said Marcy, offering a trembling smile. "Don't stop. Don't look back. Follow the road straight to the highway."

"Okay."

They exited the car, and Marcy took off like a shot. Lucinda followed, keeping her gaze on the flashes of yellow dress within the darkness. She was tired, so tired, and her legs protested. Her lungs hurt, too, no doubt still recovering from the way she'd been slammed around the car. The gods-be-damned rain wasn't helping matters much, either. Water splashed her eyes, got into her mouth, smacked against her bruised body.

Her legs hurt, her lungs burned, her vision faltered.

"Almost there!" yelled Marcy. The words seemed far

away, and the flashes of yellow were getting fewer and fewer.

Lucy was slowing down too much.

The will was there, but not the physical capability. She didn't even have enough in her to call up magic to push away the rain. Her aquamancy was a minor power, anyway. Even at full capacity, she couldn't control the freaking weather.

Lucinda was at a jog now, her legs threatening to give out any second. *Just keep going, Luce. Get to safety, then rest.*

That seemed to be her life motto these days.

Marcy's scream split through the night, the rain, the very heart of Lucinda.

The extra boost of fear-laced adrenaline gave her the push she needed to pick up the pace. "Marcy!"

The girl's screams raked her like poisoned claws. Oh, Goddess! What was happening? Where was she? "I'm coming!" she yelled. "Marcy!"

Up ahead, Lucinda could see the lights of the highway, and yards away the exit ramp. Safety was close. She just had to get Marcy, and they would make it.

Then she saw the girl.

And the man crouching over her.

Marcy knelt on the ground, her hands above her face, her screams raspy and tear-filled. "No. Please!" she blubbered. "I'm sorry! I'm so sorry!"

The huge man wore a black robe that shielded his face, but not his massive hands. He had the sulfur stink of dark magic, but there was something odd about it, like he was wearing it, not issuing it.

One meaty fist delivered a blow to Marcy's stomach, and she fell over, skidding down the gravel.

"Stop!" Lucinda cried out. "Stop it!"

The robed figure didn't even look back at her. Either he didn't hear her or he didn't consider her much of a threat. Marcy was trying to crawl away, but the brute grabbed her legs, and turned her, reaching for the front of her dress.

Lucinda skidded to a stop, and tried to gather some water magic, which wasn't working because her vision was graying, and her body ached so badly, she couldn't think straight. "Stop hurting her!"

The wind tossed away her words. Lucinda decided she couldn't wait to see if her aquamancy would work. She ran and jumped on the man's back, hitting him with her fists. "Leave her alone!"

She might as well have been an ant trying to stop a giant.

He delivered a nasty blow to Marcy's battered face. A sickening crunch echoed, and her head snapped back. The girl went suddenly, terribly still.

"Noooo!" She pummeled the attacker, but he merely dropped Marcy, then reached behind, grasped Lucinda by the robe, and tossed her onto the road.

Terror and grief and anger twisted inside her. Worse, though, was the relief. *He's going to kill me,* she thought, *and it'll all be over. Finally.*

To her shock, he turned away, leaning over Marcy, his hands reaching toward the girl's clothing. Lucinda's mind flipped back to another man, another woman, another tragedy. She no longer saw the attacker hovering over Marcy, but Bernard. He, too, had been leaning over a girl, a beautiful innocent who'd been sacrificed to Bernard's lusts. His hands were bloody; sweat dripped from his brow, his eyes filled with cold contempt. *"You think you saved her?"*

Lucinda snapped back to the present. She gathered as much power as she could, directed it toward the rain, then focused on the bastard who thought he was going to put his dirty hands on that brave girl. She whispered, "Boil."

Every drop that landed on him was so hot, his skin hissed. The robe couldn't protect him from the sheets of hot water. It soaked through, ravaging his skin. He cried out, and stumbled away.

She kept the spell on him, forcing him across the road.

He roared in pain, and satisfaction curled through her. It was wrong to take pleasure in another's torment, but she couldn't feel sorry. Not for him.

Lucinda felt a shift in the atmosphere, a tingle of magic, and then the whoosh of a portal opening. She didn't bother to watch him leave. Instead, she released the magic, and crawled to Marcy.

The rain sluiced away the blood from the girl's face. In fact, it seemed as though the storm was moving on, the fierceness of the rain giving way to a soft patter.

She swept the strands of hair away from Marcy's face. Her eyelids flickered, and then opened.

"Oh, my God!" Lucinda's heart gave a jolt. Her new friend was alive. Hope flared. "I'll get you some help. Just don't . . ." She swallowed the knot in her throat. "It'll be okay."

Marcy coughed, and blood dribbled from her mouth. "Pockets."

For a moment, Lucinda couldn't comprehend what she meant, and then realized she was talking about the apron on the dress. She dug through the pockets, pulling out pads, pencils, napkins, and a red silk pouch.

"Take. Hide. Important."

"You weren't just leaving town, were you?"

"Trying to . . . protect . . . Nevermore." Her eyes were dilating, her ragged breathing slowing. "You. Go."

"Marcy." Lucinda couldn't let her die. She was too

young to be so scared, so abused, so at the mercy of the world. "You deserve better."

The girl's gaze went wide, her breath leaving in one final, soft hush. Her body went limp, and Lucinda thought, *No, not again.* She tucked the red bag into the front pocket of her jeans; then she knelt before Marcy, closed her eyes, and began to weave the golden magic of her thaumaturgy.

The old Ford hurtled down the dark road as Gray followed the sparkling green line created by his tracking spell. The rain had stopped, which made following the magic a helluva lot easier. It would lead him straight to Lucy. This time, he'd make sure she got something to eat, that she had a chance to rest, and then . . . then he'd offer her sanctuary. He couldn't give her his personal protection, not that of a husband, but at least she'd have some safety so long as she stayed within the borders of Nevermore.

What the hell!?

He stomped his brakes. He threw the truck into reverse and backed up. He jumped out and examined Marcy's abandoned car, which was parked diagonally on the wrong side of the road. The headlights were on, both doors were open, and the tracking spell glittered in the passenger seat. Lucy had been in the VW, too.

Why was Marcy's car here? Where had the women gone?

He returned to the truck, a knot of foreboding in his stomach. The green line stretched into the dark, heading toward the highway. Whatever had happened, the ladies had obviously believed they were safer on foot. Or maybe they'd hit something or the storm had made the car stall.

But why would they go toward the highway instead of back to town?

In the distance, he saw a circular blast of shimmering gold. The magic emanating from it was so strong, it made his shields buckle. The tracking spell ended at that huge orb of light. He gripped the steering wheel, the accelerator pushed down all the way, and within moments, he was there.

He stopped the truck on the shoulder, throwing it into park, and jumped out without turning off the engine.

"Lucy!" He was forced to stop a couple feet away. He tried to take in everything all at once. Marcy was crumpled on the ground, her eyes wide and unseeing, her skin tinged gray.

He felt the blood drain out of his face.

Marcy was dead.

Lucy knelt beside her, radiating that gold light. Her hands were moving like a weaver's, and she was muttering incoherently.

Her eyes were completely white, and focused on the body of Marcy.

Shock reverberated through him and locked him into place.

Gray had never seen a thaumaturge in action. But . . . something wasn't right. Lucy was so pale that he could see the delicate spiderweb of blue veins under her skin. Sweat poured off her. Every so often, her body would jerk, as if getting an electric shock. Her hands were bloody, too, but he didn't know if that was from touching Marcy's battered form, or from an injury of her own.

The magic wasn't working. Whatever she was trying to do for Marcy, it was too late.

"Lucy." He stepped closer. "You have to stop. She's gone."

"No!" Her white gaze turned toward him. He was horrified to see the blood seeping from the corners of her eyes and trickling from her ears. Her voice had a metallic ring. "I can save her. I have to save her."

"What are you doing to yourself?" He crouched next to her and reached out to touch her. Her flesh was so hot, it burned his fingertips. He yanked his hand back.

She refocused on Marcy, and the light around her flared. She cried out, but she put her hands above the girl's limp form. "Live," she begged. "Live!"

Blisters started to form on her reddened skin. Her body jerked as if continuously being electrocuted, but she stayed upright. She wept tears of blood, and her nose began to bleed, too.

"Stop it, Lucinda!" He grabbed her arms, his flesh sizzling on hers, and shook her. "You're killing yourself."

"So what?" she sobbed. But the light around her flickered, and her skin cooled by a few degrees.

"Lucy." He wrapped his arms around her tightly, ignoring the sting of her magic. Goddess, she was powerful. "Baby, stop. Just *stop*."

She was crying, but he could feel her acquiescence. The light flickered and dimmed, and then it was gone. The night closed in around them, and Gray had to blink away the dots dancing in front of his eyes. The heat dissipated, too, steaming away as though water had been thrown over coals. He held on to Lucy tightly, even though he felt as though he were hugging a porcupine, until he was sure she'd released all her magic. Eventually, the burning sensations faded, and she wilted into his embrace.

She shuddered, weeping, and he leaned back just enough to see her face. Her eyes had returned to normal, and thank the Goddess, it seemed as though she'd stopped bleeding. The streaks of red on her face and neck looked like warrior's paint. "Are you okay?"

She smiled grimly. "I will be in three days."

"What?" He looked at her, frowning.

"I used my gift," she said. "Now I have to pay the price."

"Price? Lucy, what are you—"

She seized in his arms, and screamed.

Chapter 4

Gray felt the stiffness of Lucy's muscles, the tremors of pain worming through her. She pushed herself out of his arms and rolled to her knees, leaning over to vomit in the grass.

He reached for her, but she fell to the ground, racked by another seizure.

Then Gray understood.

He was witnessing Bernard Franco's curse. No, he'd been witnessing it. All the damage Lucy had caused to herself using her power was also because of Franco. He'd never seen magic turn on its master like that. He'd thought Franco was a worthless bastard before, but he hadn't realized what a sadistic fuck he really was. He knelt down next to Lucy, who quivered on the ground, moaning. He grasped her shoulders, and she screeched as if he'd poured acid on her.

Gods-be-damned! He immediately let go, and she rolled away, curling into a ball.

"What can I do, Lucy?"

She didn't answer.

Marcy had been a virtual stranger, and Lucy had tried to save her anyway, even knowing how high the cost would be. He felt sick to his soul.

Staying as close as possible to Lucy without touching her, he looked around for a conduit for a communication spell. A cell phone would've been a damned sight more convenient, but there were no cell towers around—most companies avoided towns with too much magic. What was the point? Magic and technology couldn't be friends, although plenty of magicals and mundanes were trying to figure out ways to bond them.

To communicate with the sheriff, he needed aqueous material, and spied a puddle close by. He didn't want to leave Lucy, but it wasn't like he was doing her much good. He'd never felt so helpless before. . . . Okay, not true. Nothing would ever make him feel more helpless than waking up chained to a stone slab with his wife pressing a knife to his chest.

But this was damned close.

He wanted to touch Lucy, to console her, but it would be worse for her if he did. Franco had covered all the angles with his curse, bringing Lucy not only physical torment but apparently the inability to accept any gestures meant to comfort or allay her pain.

Gray stood up, strode to the puddle, and then knelt next to it. He gathered magic, created the communication spell quickly, and sent it toward the water. The muddy liquid accepted the red sparkles, absorbing the purpose of the magic, and within moments, he saw Taylor Mooreland's face peering at him. Gray spotted a coffee cup and spoon off to the side and realized the spell had found the sheriff doing dishes in his kitchen.

"What's wrong, Gray?"

"Marcy's dead," he said. "And Lucy . . . Lucinda Rackmore is injured."

"Where are you?" Taylor's expression was all business. Only his eyes revealed the ghosts of his concern.

"Off Cedar Road, near the highway exit ramp."

"There's a portal near there," said Taylor. "It'll take me less than ten minutes to get to the one at the office."

Gray nodded. The transport portals were old magic, created by the Dragons to help the people of Nevermore travel quickly between their farms and town. No one really used them much anymore, and some locations had even been lost over time.

"Hold tight," said Taylor. "I'll be right there."

Another thought had been circling, and Gray's instincts urged him to go with the odd idea. "Taylor?"

Impatience flashed across the sheriff's face. "Yeah?"

"Bring Ember."

Taylor's eyes widened a fraction, but he didn't argue. He nodded, and disappeared from view. Within moments, the image floating on the water faded.

Gray returned to Lucy. She was soaked, from both rain and sweat, her body shaking, her teeth gritted. Her eyes were closed, too, but there was no escaping her torment. Franco had made sure of that.

"Gray?" Her voice was a mere whisper.

"Here, baby. I'm here." He sat down, not giving a shit about the uncomfortable ground or wet earth. God, he wanted to touch her. Just to pluck one strand of hair, or to brush his thumb over her cheek.

Her eyes flickered open. The shadows smudging the delicate skin underneath those pain-filled orbs bespoke exhaustion and starvation. Looking at her now, he could see how frail she looked, how thin and pale. She'd been near collapse when she'd reached him this afternoon, and still she'd managed to soldier on.

How could he have turned her away?

"I'm so sorry." Tears leaked from her devastated gaze. She shuddered, and he realized the effort to talk was costing her more pain. Guilt battered at him. He'd been such a self-centered prick.

"Don't be sorry," he said tightly. "For anything."

"I shouldn't have come here." Her body jerked, and she hissed, her hands clenching into fists.

"Don't talk!" he demanded roughly. He gentled his tone. "Don't make it worse."

She actually laughed. She stared up at him, her body contorted with pain, but a sliver of humor glinting in her gaze. He was amazed. Lucinda Rackmore was a survivor. He would've never guessed the spoiled girl he'd known so long ago had a core of steel.

"Look what I've done," she said. "Marcy . . . she was just a kid." She swallowed, hard, and he saw her legs twitch. Was she serious? Lucy herself was only twenty-five. But he knew both the great reckoning and Franco had aged Lucy far past her years. She spoke with a bitter, resigned tone no one should use, least of all a girl with so much power, so much potential. Mostly, though, he heard the overwhelming exhaustion dripping from her words. She was close to giving up—he could feel it.

Even steel melted under the right conditions.

"This isn't your fault," he said, but even he heard the doubt in his own voice. He didn't know what had happened. Maybe it was her fault. He didn't think she would do anything to harm Marcy on purpose, but what if Marcy had suffered because Lucy had brought tragedy with her?

Her blood-streaked face turned away, and he felt as though he'd failed her again. He tried to drum up the old indignation at her audacity of seeking him out—he even tried for the apathy that had previously served him so well—but he couldn't. Damn it all. Lucy had no one.

Not even him.

"Gray!"

He looked up and saw the sheriff and Ember striding across the road. Behind them sparkled the oval doorway of the portal, which closed like a big winking eye. Relief washed over him. He wasn't alone dealing with this mess anymore. The sheriff offered Lucy a cursory glance, then turned and strode toward Marcy's body.

Ember knelt beside Lucy and looked down at her with such compassion, Gray was reminded yet again of his own emotional inadequacies.

"Don't touch her," he said. "It worsens the pain."

"I know dis curse," she said softly. "It's demon juju."

Gray felt as though she'd struck him. *"What?"*

"You don't tink dey Goddess give such magic to us, do you?" She shook her head. "Magic neutral, Guardian. You know dis. Dat's why dey's got to be balance." She sniffed. "But da Dark One don't play by nobody's rules but his own."

Demon magic. *Shit.* Fear slicked his spine. "You're sure?"

"I don't say such tings lightly."

It had never occurred to him that Franco had tapped into the powers of hell. Of course, it made sense. It explained the complexity and horror of Lucy's curse. If Franco was messing with Pit magic and Gray could prove it, he'd have the bastard by the balls.

"Can you help her?" he asked.

Ember looked pensive. Then she slowly, sadly shook her head. "She got to do the sufferin'."

He blanched. "She said it would take three days."

"I'm sorry, Guardian. Ain't no fix for dis."

"Gray," called the sheriff.

He looked over his shoulder and saw Taylor crouched near Marcy. He waved him over. Gray hesitated, reluctant to leave Lucy.

"Go on," said Ember. "I'll stay."

The sheriff and Marcy's corpse were only a few feet away, but as Gray crossed the distance, it felt like miles.

He didn't want to examine his need to stay near Lucy. It felt too much like giving a damn.

Gray felt even more like a failure as he stared at the crumpled form of a girl who hadn't really had a chance to live. If only Marcy had trusted him, he might've been able to save her. She'd been so scared. Scared of the person who'd hit her—and likely the same person who'd finished the job. *Save the witch,* she'd said. Then she'd gone and tried to save Lucy all by herself.

"The witch do this?" asked Taylor.

Gray's head shot up. "What?"

"Your friend." Taylor's expression revealed nothing and his tone was as flat as the Texas panhandle. "Marcy's dead, and she's not."

"Go take a real good look at Lucy," said Gray, fury boiling through him. "Tell me if you believe she had the strength to beat a girl to death. And then, you sanctimonious ass, tell me her motive for hurting the person trying to help her."

The sheriff was too professional to let Gray's animosity get to him, but he couldn't stop the surprise widening his gaze. Yeah, well, he wasn't the only one surprised. Gray's rusty protective instincts had been roused.

Taylor tipped his hat back in the aw-shucks move Gray knew was calculated. "Sorry," he said with that country-boy sincerity, "but I'll have to question her."

"Sure," he gritted out. "If she fucking survives, you can fucking question her."

Taylor said nothing. Instead, he reached out and clasped Gray's shoulder. Gray didn't appreciate the attempt to calm him. He pulled away from his friend's grip.

"You didn't see her—what she did. Lucy almost died trying to bring Marcy back. She's a thaumaturge."

This time the sheriff couldn't stifle his shock. "Holy shit. Why didn't it work?"

"Because Marcy was already gone. Bernard Franco used demon magic to curse Lucy," said Gray. "She used her thaumaturgy, and now she'll be in agonizing pain for days. You think she'd risk that if she'd murdered Marcy?"

"Maybe she didn't mean to kill her, and was trying to bring her back." But the sheriff didn't sound too sure.

"I have an idea. Why don't you look for some evidence before coming up with your theory? And try not to let your prejudice against Rackmores get in the way."

Taylor flushed, his gaze narrowing. "You think I'd arrest her just because she's a Rackmore?"

"Isn't that what you're trying to do?"

Taylor's nostrils flared, and he took a step forward, his hand resting on his gun belt. Gray wanted the sheriff to try and punch him. He'd like nothing better than a low-down dirty fight, because he really wanted to hit something.

"Dat enough!" Ember popped up and marched toward them. "Dis ain't no playground, and you not children. We got tings to do. Important tings." She knelt next to Marcy and muttered something incomprehensible, a prayer maybe, then closed the girl's eyes. Her gaze flickered to the sheriff. "Don' tell me not to touch da evidence, neither. Child all crumpled up on the road like a used tissue. And what you do? Throw temper tantrums like spoiled boys. Shame on you both!"

Taylor looked away, and cleared his throat.

Gray felt the heat of embarrassment crawl up his neck. Ember was right. He was acting like a jerk. Again. Taylor was good at his job, even if he had a blind spot for Rackmores. At the end of the day, he trusted his friend to do the right thing.

"Don't call her 'the witch' in that snide tone again," Gray said. "Her name is Lucy." He turned on his heel and returned to his pain-stricken charge. He crouched down, studying her. She was a mess—a shivering, filthy, courageous fucking mess.

After a short conversation with the sheriff, Ember joined him.

"Use the portal," she said, her accent nearly gone. It seemed the stronger her emotions, the more her Jamaican showed. She was getting back in control of herself, and Gray needed to do the same. "I'll drive your truck back to your house."

"Thank you." Goddess above, he didn't want to pick up Lucy. How much agony would that cause? He glanced at Ember and knew from her expression she understood his dilemma. "Isn't there any other way?"

" 'Fraid not." That one dark eye peeking from behind the purple lens studied him. "You a dream walker, aren't you?"

Startled, he stared at her. "What?"

Her smile was full of secrets. "What *what*? You are a Dragon, aren't you?"

He got the strange feeling she wasn't talking about his House designation. A cold sweat broke out, and he shook his head. Then he nodded. Of course, she meant his House. What else could she mean?

Not many wizards outside of the Dragon Order of the Moon, a strict, religious order of magicals devoted to dream walking, even tried it. It wasn't an easy thing to do, which was why most Dragons didn't bother with trying to learn the intricacies. He'd tested well on dream walking for his high school entrance exams, and the summer before he started ninth grade, his mother had sent him to one of the order's temples in California to study the art of entering another's subconscious. It had been years since he had done it—it was too easy to get lost inside dreams, to forget about the real world.

"I can't stop my chickie's pain," she said softly. "But soon, her body will give out and she'll sleep. Not for long. That curse too strong to give her much relief. You dream walk with her, give her strength, hope."

Gray nodded, though he was unsure if he could manage it. Yet, if he could alleviate a little of her torment, give her something to hold on to as she suffered through Franco's curse, it was worth a try.

"Pick her up, and go," said Ember. "Nothing gonna make it better 'cept to do it fast." She aimed her palm toward the field across the road. He felt a shift in the atmosphere, the tingle of powerful magic, and the portal opened. How the hell had she managed that? Portals required keys, and she didn't have one. Or hell, maybe she did. It was just another nail in the coffin of his own apathy.

I'll make it up to Nevermore. To everyone. Especially to Lucy.

Sucking in a steadying breath, he leaned down and scooped up Lucy. She wailed, and his stomach clenched. *Please, give her succor, Goddess.* He couldn't stand that he was hurting her. He ran across the road, trying not to jostle her, but failing miserably.

Her shrieks turned to choked sobs as he stepped through the portal. Magic tingled around him and he felt a rush of wind and then, almost instantly, light. He hadn't even considered that he might end up at the sheriff's office and have to transport her farther. But somehow, Ember had managed to send them to his house. She'd known his home had a portal—actually it had several—but he couldn't worry about Ember's uncanny knowledge. He almost cried himself when he stepped through into his bedroom. He hurried to his big, unmade bed, and as gently as he could, he put Lucy down on top of his black coverlet. She looked like a broken

ceramic doll tossed into a tar pit. He risked tucking a
pillow under her head. She flinched and moaned, but at
least she didn't issue one of those heartrending screams.
He didn't dare risk trying to tuck her in. He didn't want
to add any more pain.

He'd done enough damage.

Her eyes fluttered open and zeroed in on him. "Why
does it smell like feet and bologna in here?"

Then she passed out.

Gray couldn't stop the laugh. He sat on the edge of
the bed and curled his hand into the black sheets so he
wouldn't stroke away the damp strands of hair clinging to
her face. *Feet and bologna.* He took a sniff, and grimaced.
It definitely smelled guylike, and not in a sexy kind of way.
Hell, he'd paint the room pink and light vanilla candles if
she wanted. But for now, he had to dust off his dream-
walking skills. He didn't know how long she'd be out, and
he wanted to do something that actually helped her.

Gray crawled onto the bed, very careful not to touch
Lucy. He lay on his side less than six inches from her
soaked, ravaged body, and stared at her. Even though
she still twitched and shuddered, she had, just as Ember
predicted, fallen into unconsciousness. Her chest rose
and fell rhythmically, and he was halfway to appreciating
the loveliness of the sight before he caught himself. She
had a damned fine rack—and he was a jerk for noticing.

You're going to burn in hell, Gray. Worse than before.

He moved his gaze to her face, thinking about those
sad green eyes, that stubborn tilt to her chin, the pride
that somehow still clung to even her most desperately
uttered words. Slowly, his breathing deepened, and he
murmured a prayer to his Dragon ancestors, asking for
protection as he ventured into the world of dreams.

Within moments, he was asleep.

*   *   *

The sky was pearlescent pink, like the underside of a seashell. Lucinda couldn't see a sun, or any source of light. Huh. Maybe the pink was the light.

She was lying on the softest material she'd ever felt. Something silky covered her body, but she didn't want to move her head, not even the couple of inches to look down.

The pain was gone.

She focused on the endless seashell sky. After a while, she realized she was floating along on some kind of current. She feared if she moved at all, or even breathed too deeply, Bernard's curse would strike her, turning her blood to fire and her bones to acid. The gentle motion of the water lulled her. She felt safe in this odd place.

I'm dreaming.

Oh. That made sense. Slowly, she rolled to her right and looked out over a purple sea. Her "boat" was a rectangle of thick moss. The silk was a blanket designed more to soothe than to warm. When she slid it off and looked down at herself, she chuckled. She was wearing a silver bikini.

Her moss raft moved toward the bay of an island with an endless white beach. Yards beyond was the lush greenery of a jungle, its perimeter dotted by palm trees. Then she saw a man standing at the edge of the water, a hand shading his face as he watched her float closer and closer to the inlet.

"Swim," he called out. "The water's great."

Gray? Startled that he was in her dreams, waiting for her, she hesitated. Why would she dream about him?

Deciding it didn't matter who shared the beach with her, she slid into the warm, lapping water and started swimming.

Oh, the purple sea felt glorious around her, a thousand massaging fingers guiding her toward the shore, toward the man who waited there.

In no time at all, her feet touched sand and she walked out of the water to join Gray. He had no scar or tattoos. He almost looked like the man he'd once been, and she had a flutter of regret for all that happened. To him. To her.

She studied him. He was fit and healthy, ropes of sinewy muscle displayed, and she had the strangest urge to run her hand down his washboard abs, tickle the line of dark hair darting into his black swim trunks.

She stopped less than a foot away, unable to pull her gaze away from his gorgeous body. *He could be mine. Right now.* She was unnerved by the erotic nature of her own thoughts . . . and excited, too. She twisted her hands, biting on her lower lip, unable to give voice to her turmoil.

"You asked me to marry you," he said, as if she'd spoken. "Did you think you would escape my bed?"

"You said no."

"To marriage," he said. "But not to sex."

"I didn't offer sex."

He grinned, and the wicked smile sparked a fire in his changeable blue eyes. She felt something give way in the pit of her stomach—a tingling warmth that stole down to the apex of her thighs. If her suit bottom weren't already wet from her swim, it would be now in response to her own lust.

For Gray Calhoun.

It was a shocking, titillating idea.

Gray crossed the distance between them and took her hands into his.

"Where are we?" she asked. Something felt weird about this place—and she realized that it wasn't her own creation. She was visiting someone else's mental landscape.

Gray's?

"Yeah. It's mine." He looked around, a small smile of satisfaction flirting with his lips. "It's peaceful. It requires nothing from me." His gaze returned to hers. "I'm glad you accepted my invitation to join me."

Invitation? She frowned, but he shook his head, as if trying to ward off her concerns.

"Don't worry so much, all right?"

His large warm hands cupped hers and he pulled her closer. Her heart skipped a beat. He smelled like the sea, and mingling with the sharp salty tang was a musky, masculine scent. The pit in her stomach widened and dipped and twisted, and she felt as though she'd gotten onto a roller coaster. But she liked the sensations.

"How do you feel?" he asked. His voice was tender, and so unlike him, she shifted uncomfortably.

She shrugged. "Okay, I guess. What happened to—"

"Shush." Gray released one of her hands so he could put a finger to her lips. "We'll talk about everything later, I promise. I want you to relax. Are you hungry?"

Oh, yes. She was hungry, but not for food. Her gaze flicked to his, and she saw the desire glimmering in his eyes. He wanted her, and she could let him take her. Right here on the white sandy beach with the purple ocean lapping at their legs.

She couldn't stop the image from forming. Gray's mouth on her breasts, his big, tanned hand slipping between her thighs, stealing underneath the triangle of fabric . . .

Before she could wipe it out of her mind, Gray pulled her into his embrace and held her close. Being in his arms felt foreign, but she melted against him anyway. It had been too long since she felt the touch of another, too long since someone had cared about her. Even if it wasn't real, she wanted it.

Gray's lips caressed the shell of her ear. "Is that what will make you feel better? You want me to give you pleasure, baby?"

Dark thrills shot through her.

This is Gray, she thought wildly. *He would never want me. Nobody wants me.*

"Stop," he murmured. "This place is different. There is no hiding. No secrets. No lies. We don't have to protect our hearts here. Please, Lucy. Tell me what you want, and I'll do it. I'll do anything."

Somehow, he was reading her thoughts. Maybe being in his dream had given him access to every part of her. She felt too vulnerable. She didn't want a pity fuck, but even that would be better than his unbearable kindness. Tears seeped out of her eyes. She felt pathetic for wanting something simple, and that she had to ask Gray of all people to do it. She couldn't stop the words, though. She had no pride left.

"Hold me, Gray."

He sat down on the beach and pulled her down with him. Then he scooped her into his arms and settled her onto his lap. She curled up like a purring kitten, pressing the side of her face against his chest and listening to the rhythmic pounding of his heart.

"Lucy," he whispered, leaning down to kiss her temple. "Sweet Lucy."

"If you call me Juicy Lucy," she muttered darkly, "I will punch you."

He laughed, and the rumble of sound in his chest sounded like happy thunder. "I won't call you Juicy Lucy today." He tightened his arms around her. "But tomorrow I might just risk it."

"It's your funeral," she said, hiding her smile.

For the first time in a very, very long while, she felt safe.

Then lightning zigzagged out of the pretty pink sky, and shattered her into a thousand, molten pieces.

She heard Gray's anguished shout, but she was already floating free of his grip. He tried to keep her with him—she could feel the strength of his will as well as the strength of his arms. But she was a ghost now, drifting upward, every inch of her on fire, burning, burning like retribution.

Gray jolted awake, and sat up, turning toward the writhing form of Lucy beside him. Her eyes were open, but glazed over, and he knew she couldn't see him. But she was seeing something. Visions? Did the curse include screwing with her mind, too? Her lips trembled, tears streaming like tiny rivers, as she whispered, "No. No, don't hurt her. I'll do anything. Please."

"Gods-be-damned!" He scrambled toward her, wanting so badly to take away her pain he couldn't breathe. "Lucy."

She stiffened, and then her body arched and started to undulate. The seizure was so violent that he had to pin her shoulders down to keep her from flopping onto the floor. The moment she stopped, he let go and backed off. Her throat worked as if her screams were trapped there.

He had never seen anyone suffer like this before. Not even he had endured this kind of agony when Kerren had plunged her dagger into his heart and offered his soul to her demon lover. He'd known nine minutes of unbelievable torment as he fought for his life. *Nine minutes.* And Lucy had hours, days ahead.

No. He hated to leave her, but he had to talk to Grit. The old man was wily as hell, and if anyone knew how to circumvent this curse, he would. "I'll be right back, baby."

She didn't respond, but he hadn't really expected her to.

Grit and Dutch were in the kitchen right where he'd left them, but he cut off their complaining, and hurriedly explained what had unfolded over the last few hours, including all the details he had about Franco's curse.

"Cain't undo demon magic, son," said Grit. "It's like Ember said—she'll have to do the suffering."

"Shouldn't have turned her away, your royal douche-ness," said Dutch. "Bet you're sorry now."

"Shut your mouth, or I'll shut you." Gray glowered at the surfer's blue cover. Neither of the books actually had eyes, but they could still see. He didn't need to be reminded that he'd been a dumb ass. True, he might've spared Lucy the decision to enact the curse if she'd been tucked safely inside his house. But Marcy would still be dead. All he could do now was try to help Lucy, damn it.

"The dream walking worked?" asked Grit.

"Yeah. Except she can't sleep for long. No doubt Franco made it part of the curse—keeping her awake to suffer."

"All we got to do, then, is put her in a deeper sleep." Grit sounded thoughtful. "Magic one-oh-one, boy. Every spell has limits, and so do curses. Cain't account for every little thing when you're creating spells, right? Yep. Gotta be a place Lucy can go in her subconscious that the curse cain't reach."

Hope surged through Gray. Franco's curse was heinous, but it couldn't self-correct. No spell could. All spells had parameters, and no magic could do more than directed. Magic was alive, but it wasn't intelligent. It didn't have morals or ethics. It relied on its master to tell it what to do, how to behave.

"I prefer Sugandi root," Grit was muttering, "but we don't got any. Shoot. Have to make do with Holy Basil."

Obeying his grandfather's instructions, Gray took precious time to create incense from Holy Basil and a few other ingredients. He added the spellwork Grit insisted on, too, which took even more time. Every so often, he heard Lucy scream, and his heart would skip a beat.

Finally, it was done.

"Burn it as close as you can to her so she's breathing it in," said Grit. "And you gotta do the dream walking with her. Otherwise, she might not come out of it. This is comatose stuff, boy. Don't forget you're dreaming, neither! You and that girl could be trapped in your own minds if you stop payin' attention." His grandfather's worry was evident in his sharply delivered words.

"It won't be like that again," said Gray. "I'll come back. And so will she."

"Good luck, son."

"Yeah, dude," chimed in Dutch. "See you on the flip side."

Gray took the bowl of incense and hurried back to his bedroom. He hoped that Lucy would remain unconscious for the duration of the curse's effects. He had no doubt she'd feel like she'd been trampled by elephants when she woke up, but he'd worry about that when the time came. All Lucy had to do was get through the next three days.

All she had to do was survive.

Chapter 5

Ember never doubted her Goddess, but sometimes she didn't like Her methods. "So much sufferin'," she murmured as she lit the fragrant candles on the altar. She felt an answer deep within: *Necessary.* "I know," she whispered as she watched the flames dance, her heart heavy. "I know."

Figuring out how the world worked was complex and often confusing. Many cultures had come up with different explanations of what was essentially the same thing. The magicals had even gone so far as to claim lineage to immortal beings, because people born with powers needed explanations, too.

The Creator Mother, the Goddess, was the best part of everybody. She inspired wisdom, compassion, nurturing, courage, and kindness. She had called Ember into Her service, and Ember had gone willingly, honored to be one of Her prophets.

The Goddess's gift had cost half of her human vision. She'd taken off her glasses before she'd entered the sanctuary, a chapel created in what had once been a walk-in closet in the master bedroom. Now she traced the skin under her blind eye, and wondered if she was strong enough to do what must be done.

Yes, my Chosen. The surety of the Goddess lifted the burden of her worry.

Ember's grandmother had taught her that the destination wasn't as important as the journey. *Don't matter what road they use, chil'. All paths lead to the Divine.*

Well. Not all paths.

Everything in the universe had its opposite—a requirement to maintain the balance. What was joy if you'd never known sorrow? And how could you experience peace if you'd never been troubled?

This world was a learning place. There were worlds beyond this one offering tranquillity and enlightenment. Absolute, continuous joy could be attained, if that was what a soul truly wanted. Humph. Ember thought nirvana would be a boring way to spend eternity.

The Dark One was the opposite of the Goddess. His nature was as unchangeable as Hers, but because He was impatience, greed, selfishness, violence, and hatred, He always wanted what He couldn't have. And He inspired others to feel the same way.

The balance had shifted dangerously in Nevermore, right under the nose of the Guardian. Gray Calhoun had his own journey to take, but he and Lucinda were integral to the drama that would soon unfold.

They would need her.

But for now, she was just the owner of a tea shop, which had gotten a surge in business thanks to the Guardian closing the café.

Ember blew a kiss to the silver statue of the Goddess and rose. Then she gathered energy and used it to blow out all the candles. *Return,* she told the magic, *and thank you.* She ambled out of the chapel and into her bedroom.

Rilton sat on the bed, waiting for her.

He was a tall glass of milk, her husband. Rilton Sanders was as pale and soft as white bread and nearly half a foot taller than her, but thin—almost like someone had tied willow branches together and slapped a cardboard face on top. He was younger than her by nearly a decade, his blond hair pulled back into a single braid that hit him midback. He was immensely kind, was handsome in his own way, and loved her without question.

Rilton was her other half.

Once she devoted herself to the Goddess, she put aside all her other dreams. She never thought she would fall in love. And she certainly wouldn't have believed anyone who tried to tell her that her soul mate was an overeducated white boy who'd grown up on a wheat farm in Kansas. Sometimes, Ember suspected the Goddess was a romantic. Or She liked a good joke.

"You all right?" he asked softly.

"No," she said. "Dis one gonna be difficult."

"What can I do?" He stroked her hair. That was Rilton. He offered instant support free of reservations. He was a thoughtful man, and whenever she asked his advice, he never gave a quick answer. It could be frustrating, waiting for him to examine all the angles before coming up with a suggestion. He'd told her the quickest decision he'd ever made was to marry her—and that decision had been made within the first minute of meeting her.

Rilton never lied, either. He didn't like hurting people, so he often kept truths to himself. He was a man who had no secrets of his own, but he could be trusted to keep those of others. He knew all of hers, and loved her still.

Ember leaned against him, and he slipped an arm around her shoulder. "We should get back," she said, unable to keep the sigh out of her voice. "Lots of people need tendin'."

"So do you."

The smoky tone of his voice told her what kind of

tending he wanted to give her. She looked at him, her right eye seeing his physical body, and the left seeing his spiritual form. He was a whole man, in sync with himself and the world. It was why she could look at him, but not others. Some people were so out of balance with their spirit side, it hurt to look at them. Rilton had the glasses made for her, so that her left eye would be protected from all the ugly of people's souls.

He kissed her tenderly, and lowered her to the bed. Ember wrapped her arms around his neck and kissed him back.

Life was about living . . . even in the tiniest moments. And life without love . . . Well, that was no life at all.

Lucinda woke up on the silky, white sand, the pearlescent pink sky above, and the purple sea tickling her feet.

For a moment, she did nothing but enjoy the steady beat of her own heart, and the rhythm of her own breathing.

She was safe. The absolute knowledge of that wrapped around her like a fuzzy, warm blanket. She embraced the feeling because it felt so good, and it had been so long since she'd felt anything except exhaustion and fear.

The great thing about a dream beach, she decided as she sat up and stretched, was that the sand didn't creep into unwanted places. In fact, this sand didn't cling to her at all. She noted she was in the silver bikini again—only it had been modified quite a bit. The tiny triangles of the top barely covered the areolas of her thirty-six-C breasts. And the bottoms were a joke. The teeny front triangle was all the coverage she got—the sides looked like floss, and nothing covered her booty. She had no doubt Gray was responsible for this ridiculous outfit. Even in dreams, men were men.

She rose to her feet and looked around.

She was alone.

Disappointment wiggled through her. She wasn't sure how Gray had managed to bring her into his dream again, but she was glad. Then she had another thought: Was she dead?

The last thing she remembered was the alternating sensations of being dipped in freezing water and then feeling as though she'd been stuck in a microwave on the high setting. After being forced to endure the horrible, painful process of the cursing itself, she'd thought she understood the hellish torture in store for her for accessing her thaumaturgy.

No. Not even close.

She shuddered. How long did she have here? How much respite could she drink in before being yanked back into her tormented body?

Her gift had saved a life once. For a few precious minutes. Still. What made her think she could save Marcy, especially with a curse-warped ability?

Sadness prickled her contentment. She shouldn't be on a beach enjoying the feel of warm sand beneath her feet, and inhaling the languid, sweet-scented air. Marcy was dead.

Why would someone want to kill her?

For whatever was in the red bag.

Her heart skipped a beat. What had happened to it? Was it still tucked into her jean pocket? She wasn't sure she'd be able to honor her promise to Marcy. Nevermore wasn't her concern. In fact, being here for any length of time would eventually draw Bernard's notice—and there'd been enough casualties of his wrath. Anguish crept through her. She had enough secrets in her keeping.... She wasn't sure she could accept the burden of one more.

"Hey!" called out a male voice.

Gray strode toward her, wearing a pair of black swim trunks and a cocky grin. Even here he emitted strength, virility, danger. Her knees threatened to buckle, and her stomach pitched.

In lust with Gray.

She really was dreaming. There was nothing she could do about Marcy, or the mysterious red bag, or even her own possible demise. All she had was now, here, with a man who had no reason to give her the time of day, much less share a dream state with her. He was a Dragon, she remembered, and of course, he'd be a dream walker, too. *Overachiever,* she thought grumpily.

He stopped and gave her a slow look that set her blood on fire. Oh, Goddess. He knew how he was affecting her. In fact, he was doing it on purpose. She didn't know what to do about that. Or about him.

He widened his grin. "How ya doin', Juicy Lucy?"

She put a hand on her cocked hip and pretended annoyance. "I told you not to call me that."

"Yeah? What are you gonna do about it?"

She stalked toward him, eyes narrowed. He stood firm, legs apart, arms crossed, gaze sparkling with challenge. When she finally got up close enough to poke him in the chest, he scooped her into his arms and, with one big heave, tossed her into the purple ocean.

She came up spluttering. By then, he'd joined her, and as she gulped in some air, he dove under, grabbing her ankle and dunking her again.

He darted away, doing a backstroke, and laughed.

Why, that—

Lucinda forgot about everything. No more worries about Bernard's curse, her crappy luck, poor Marcy, the red pouch, or her stupid attraction to Gray. It all left her mind. She knew only *one* thing: She was sooooo going to get him.

It took a while—an hour, an afternoon?—but Lucinda finally managed to dunk Gray. She swam up behind him and, using all her weight, shoved him down hard. He sank into the purple water with a satisfying splutter.

Even though she was sure he'd let her get the best of him, she still felt triumphant. But not stupid. She headed toward the shore as fast as she could. By the time she'd gotten out of the water, he was splashing onto the shore right behind her.

Lucinda turned to run, but she wasn't fast enough. She squealed when she felt his fingers snag the bikini bottoms. Then he swiped at her ankles and she fell into the sand, laughing. She rolled onto her back and stared up at Gray. He stood above her, his chest heaving, his eyes sparkling.

"Gotcha," he said. Then he fell on the sand beside her. He rolled onto his back, too, and they lay on the warm sand shoulder to shoulder and enjoyed the view above them.

"It's so peaceful here," she murmured. "How could you ever go back to the real world?"

"I almost didn't."

Lucinda turned on her side and looked at him. His gaze remained on the sky, but she could see the turmoil in his eyes all the same. "Tell me."

For a moment, she didn't think he would tell her anything. Why should he? He might be helping her now, but she was under no illusion there wasn't a price to be paid. He wouldn't have changed his mind if he hadn't thought of a way he could use her. It was just the way the real world worked.

But this place was not the real world.

"After Kerren . . . after what happened . . . being alive *hurt*. I wandered for a while."

"Five years?"

He shrugged, but the casual gesture belied his tension. She knew he wouldn't reveal anything about the time he'd disappeared.

"After I moved to Nevermore to help my grandfather, I needed somewhere to go. I felt . . . confined. So I went deeper and deeper into my dreams. I created this place, and started sleeping the days away. I'd wake up long enough to go to the bathroom or grab something to eat, but after a while nothing seemed more important than being here. My grandfather . . . I guess you could say he managed to yank me back into reality."

Lucinda felt her heart clutch. "Oh, Gray."

"Don't," he said softly. "I don't deserve your sympathy." He turned toward her then, his expression deliberately polite. "Are you hungry?"

He seemed to like asking that question. He was pulling back from her, and she wondered if he regretted sharing so much about himself. But she knew a lot about self-protection. Trust was a precious gift.

"Who needs to eat in a dream?" she asked.

"We can do anything we want," he said. "We can have all-dessert dinner. Or eat lobster drenched in butter. Or gorge on steaks." He eyed her. "You're not a vegetarian, are you?"

"Goddess, no," she said. "Hundred percent carnivore."

"Good. I won't have to pretend to like carrots. C'mon." He got to his feet and then held out a hand to help her up. "I'll make you the best dream meal you've ever eaten."

Gray was as good as his word. He created a platform made of old planks and, in its center, a fire pit. Then he made huge, soft floor pillows for them to lounge on. He cooked her lobster and steak, wished up cheesecake and ice cream and chocolate. They talked about everything—visiting the Great Library, being at the Grand Court in Washington, a place Gray had known well. There were only two Grand Courts—one in the United States and the original one in Europe. Once a year, representatives from both Courts would meet to renew, rework, discard, or create new worldwide policies for magicals.

They talked a little about politics, including the rumors about the Grand Courts reenacting laws that prevented marriage between magicals and mundanes.

"It's not the first century anymore," said Gray. "Even if it were true, those laws wouldn't hold up. The truth is that the world holds a lot more mundanes than magicals these days. We'd run out of prospective mates very quickly."

"It's probably the Ravens," said Lucinda. "So many of them tend to be purists."

"There's no such thing."

"I know."

Their conversation turned to the magical-testing legislation being discussed in the U.S. Senate. The proposed law wanted to use new technology to test whether a fetus had magical DNA, so mundane parents could prepare appropriately.

She saw Gray look her over and sigh. She'd asked him to create a robe for her, and he seemed to regret that he had. She didn't need the warmth, but being half naked around him was too much a temptation. Unfortunately, Gray seemed to care less about his own half nakedness. In fact, she suspected he knew quite well the effect he was having on her. "Wouldn't it be nice to think that parents would love their baby no matter what? Whether it was a boy or girl? A magical or mundane?"

"You're right," said Gray. "It shouldn't matter."

He started talking about Nevermore, about what it was like to grow up in such a small town. But Lucinda had heard the grief in his tone, and realized Kerren's betrayal had cost him more than just a dream of love everlasting—but of fatherhood, too.

Lucinda pushed away the thoughts. Regrets worked like a slow poison, creeping through her veins, stealing life drop by drop. She couldn't think too much about the past, or about the future.

Instead, she listened to Gray talk about his childhood, about the town that was as much a part of him as his own soul, and drifted contentedly in the currents of his voice.

Taylor Mooreland swallowed the last of his cold coffee, then leaned back in his chair. His desk faced the picture window that overlooked Main Street.

It was just past eight a.m.

He liked mornings. He was usually behind his desk before seven a.m., a good two hours before regular office hours and before his assistant Arlene showed up. The fifty-six-year-old mother of four grown children was annoyed to no end by Taylor's energy and efficiency, which too often curtailed her urges to mother-hen him to death.

He smiled. Arlene reminded him of his own mama. Even though Sarah Mooreland had been gone for five years now, he still found himself picking up the phone to call her. He could never get used to it. Five years felt like five minutes.

Heart aching just a little, he shifted his gaze to the report on his desk. He'd already opened the folder and studied the file. He'd seen autopsy photos before—even ones of people he'd known. Nevermore was too small a town to have strangers in it. But it galled him to see Marcy splayed out like a Christmas goose. Poor, sweet Marcy. She'd been beaten down already by her step-mama. Oh, Cathleen had never laid a hand on her. She punched at Marcy with her cruelty, whittling down the girl's self-esteem until she had none left.

Gray had been right. There was no way Lucinda Rackmore could've administered the beating. When he'd seen her at Ember's, he noticed how gaunt she was—and that look in her eyes, well, it reminded him too much of how his mother looked after Dad took off. It was the look of a woman who'd been broken. She didn't have the strength, much less the will, to hurt Marcy.

He sure as hell would've liked her for it, though. Because if she wasn't responsible, that meant one of Nevermore's own had done the deed. Unless there was some stranger lurking around and he hadn't noticed. He snorted. No one could hide in Nevermore. Folks were too nosy to keep quiet about anything, especially out-siders wandering around. Hell, three people told him about the woman trudging up to Gray's house before she'd even thought about walking into Ember's.

Lucinda Rackmore would have to cough up some straight answers to all his questions. Why was Marcy headed out of town with nothing but the clothes on her back? Was she just giving the witch a ride to the high-way? Had they planned to leave together, or was Lu-cinda hitchhiking and had Marcy stopped to pick her up? Why were Marcy's pockets emptied, and who had done it?

He'd bagged and tagged everything, even the wet napkins that had been scattered next to the body. Wa-ter had ruined everything—he wouldn't be able to get prints for damned sure. He had several magical items that he could use as a law enforcement officer. Mundanes couldn't manipulate the energy needed to create spells, but they could activate objects with magical purpose. However, once the magic was triggered, the object became useless. Law enforcement had its pick of valuable magical tools, but not one of them included the ability to lift off degraded prints from rain-soaked order pads and pencils.

"I got nothing," he muttered. He pushed the file away, disgusted. Then he pulled it back and squared the edges to align with his desk planner. Messy wasn't in his DNA.

It had been two days since Gray disappeared with the witch. Taylor had gone by the house a couple times, but the bastard wasn't opening his door. Gray could be moody and distant, but his integrity was solid. A sense of foreboding stirred, and he wondered if something bad had gone down in the Guardian's house.

Taylor never ignored his instincts, but he also didn't jump to conclusions. He realized his own prejudices against Rackmore witches easily fed his desire for Lucinda to be responsible for anything wrong. The likeliest scenario was that Gray was ignoring him to take care of Lucinda. The very idea boggled his mind because Gray had more reason than he did to be pissed off at the Rackmores. He'd been sent to hell by the girl's sister, for Goddess' sake!

The foreboding deepened.

Had Lucinda done something to Gray?

He couldn't reconcile the pain-stricken female writhing on the side of the road with a woman who could do the Guardian any damage. Gray said the curse lasted three days. And if it was demon magic . . . shit. Empathy stirred. Despite what Gray had accused him of, he wouldn't arrest Lucinda just to soothe the wounds of his childhood. He knew it was his father who'd made the decision to abandon his family. It was easier as a kid to blame the other woman. No child wanted to believe his own father didn't want him. That had been his first lesson about betrayal. And cowardice. Edward Moore-land hadn't had the balls to tell his wife to her face that he didn't want her or their family anymore. He'd left a gods-be-damned letter.

Bastard.

He switched off those thoughts, and returned to the problems at hand.

Was Lucinda as cold-blooded as her sister? He didn't know. She'd done something to get on the wrong side of Bernard Franco. Now, there was a certified asshole. What had Lucinda done that pissed off the Raven so much he'd worked a demon-magicked curse against her? Why not just kill her? Goddess knew, enough of his enemies had disappeared over the years.

There was too much he didn't know, and he wasn't the type of man to let a situation fester. Lucinda Rack-more had to be dealt with, and if Gray refused to handle her, then Taylor would—even if it meant sticking her in magical quarantine.

The bad feeling was beating like a primal drum in his gut. Screw it. He'd drop by again. He'd knock un-til someone answered or the door gave way, whichever came first.

He stared morosely into his empty coffee mug and debated about whether he should wait for Arlene to make a batch of coffee or drag his lazy ass to the break room to make it himself. He always made a thermos of coffee at home that usually lasted until Arlene arrived, but he hadn't slept last night—or the night before that. He needed all the caffeine he could get right now.

He put the mug down and returned his gaze to the view outside. Not much traffic. Every now and again a truck rattled by. Across the street was the old Sew 'n'

Sew. The owner, Mrs. Thelma Clark, had died less than a year ago. Supposedly her estranged daughter, who'd moved to California the day she turned eighteen to chase movie-star dreams, was going to come in and take over the business. His mother had grown up with Mary Clark and had once told him that "her head was full of stuffing." He'd seen neither hide nor tail of Ms. Clark, though the bills on the place were getting paid every month on time. He figured she'd make her way back to Nevermore eventually.

He had fond memories of the dress shop. His mother had worked there during the days, and in the evenings, she worked at the café, at least until Cathleen Munch took over. Not even his softhearted mama could find anything to like about that woman. After that, she took on extra jobs wherever she could, and he'd started working for Ol' Joe, the cranky bastard who owned the farm next to theirs. Mama wouldn't let him quit school, even though he was the oldest and the strongest. Ol' Joe pushed him hard, but it didn't take too long to figure out that man was a marshmallow. He was ninety-two when he died, and Taylor had worked for him all through high school. The summer after Taylor graduated, he buried his boss. He wept like a baby, crying all the tears for Ol' Joe that he could never cry for his own father.

Still, Taylor had been surprised to find out that he was the sole heir to Ol' Joe's estate. He got the farm, the huge house, the barn, the animals—everything. He sold their pitiful land and its too-small house and moved his family into the spacious home. Everyone got their own bedroom, and the big, open kitchen had thrilled his mama something fierce. She spent weeks scrubbing clean every stick of furniture, every wall, every floor. And did she ever bake! Chocolate-chip cookies, sour-apple pie, brownies, blueberry muffins. He sighed, remembering how good it all tasted.

After the family had gotten settled in, he'd made himself an apartment in one of the abandoned outbuildings. He refurbished the whole place himself. He liked things simple. And quiet. He loved his brothers and sisters, but they drove him crazy. The chaos in the Mooreland household never ceased.

Thanks to Ol' Joe's generosity, his mother no longer had to find extra work, and Taylor was able to take online college classes. It took a while, but he managed to get his degree in police science. Then he went to the academy and got his proper training. When he'd returned to Nevermore, he went straight to Grit to announce his intention to become Nevermore's sheriff. Grit dusted off the deputy position that had been vacant for the last thirty years, and gave it to him. He had to wait out the current sheriff, who'd been pleased as pudding to hand over the crap assignments to the newbie.

Taylor hadn't cared. He loved the job.

Five years ago, everything changed. Life went along in a nice, neat line, the kind he liked. His brothers and sisters moved out of the house one by one, until only his fourteen-year-old brother, Anthony, and his seventeen-year-old sister, Carrie, were left. Annalise moved to Denver with her partner, Onna, and they opened an art studio. Kenneth married a local girl and took over his father-in-law's farm on the north side of town. Doreen married right out of high school, got divorced a year later, and remarried a year after that . . . and wash, rinse, repeat. He'd lost track of the number of times she'd gone down the aisle, but she eventually figured out she was in love *with* love, and moved to Vegas to be a wedding planner.

Dominoes started to fall.

Gray Calhoun returned to Nevermore and moved in with his grandfather. *Click.* Sheriff Billings decided to retire and move to Florida. *Click.* That same week Grit's illness took a turn for the worse and Gray took him to Leticia's house in Washington, where she called in some big-time healers. Gray returned a few days later, looking haggard and soul-sick, and informed everyone he was the new Guardian. *Click.* One of his first acts was appointing Taylor as the new sheriff. *Click.* Less than a month after he became sheriff, his mother fell and hit her head. She died alone on the floor of the kitchen.

Boom.

The doc compared it to dropping a glass. If it hit at its weakest point, it shattered. His mother had been baking, and dropped an egg. Slipped in the yolk. Hit her skull at just the right angle on the edge of the counter, and was unconscious before she hit the linoleum. The fall, that second blow to her head, did her in.

After the funeral, Carrie asked to go live with Annalise and Onna, and he helped her pack. She'd stayed in Denver and eventually became manager of Annalise and Onna's art gallery. He didn't blame her, or any of his other siblings, for not visiting too often. Hell, he couldn't walk through the kitchen without thinking about his mother lying on the floor breathing her last. To this day, he avoided going in there as much as possible.

Anthony still lived with him. He was nineteen now, and really liked working with the land. Ant created gardens, all kinds of wild landscaping. It was like living in Wonderland. Of course, the farm was no longer a farm. Taylor sold off most of the land and the cattle. They had the big house, a small barn, and several acres, and that was enough. Good thing they had the barn. Ant collected strays. The more wounded, sick, and ugly, the better.

Yeah. It was just him and Ant in that big ol' house. It was quiet most days, and calm. And lonely as hell.

"Shit." Taylor rubbed a hand over his face. What was with all the going down memory lane? The past was the past. He couldn't change it. His belly twisted. He couldn't get rid of that bad feeling, and he knew it meant something was gonna happen that fucked up his world.

He got up from the desk, and went to the window. Thanks to Arlene, everything in the office sparkled. She hired out for the windows, and she could spot a smudge from a mile away. So he resisted the impulse to lean against it. He stared at the empty streets. Most days were like this . . . days filled with small disputes, the occasional ticket, lunch at Ember's, and paperwork.

The sheriff's office had been in the same building since the founding of the town, though there had been updates and changes every now and again. Other than his part-time deputy, Terrence—whom everyone called Ren—he was the only law enforcement in town. Both magicals and mundanes had held the position over the years.

Taylor was proud to be sheriff of Nevermore.

His gaze shifted down the street to the darkened windows of the Piney Woods Café. It was diagonal from his office, bearing the cornerstone of the first building erected in Nevermore. Thanks to Cathleen's neglect, it was looking its age. He couldn't believe that Gray had closed it. He didn't like Cathleen Munch—although he wasn't sure shutting down the café was the right action to take. Just another point of business he needed to discuss with Gray.

The door of the café swung open and Cathleen, dressed in a blue sweat suit and white sneakers, marched across the street. He tensed, watching to see if she would have the raw nerve to go into Ember's place and cause a ruckus.

The woman didn't even glance at the tea shop. She strode down the sidewalk, a woman on a mission, her gaze fixed on her destination.

The sheriff's office.

Damn it. Taylor turned away from the window, and returned to his desk. He picked up his empty coffee mug, and sighed. No Arlene. No coffee. No time to go hide in the bathroom.

He heard the front door bang open, and the squeak of Cathleen's shoes on the hardwood floors.

"Sheriff!" she screeched from the small lobby. "I demand justice!"

Chapter 6

Gray sat on the beach, and watched Lucinda walk out of the water. The lavender drops dotted her pale skin like candy sprinkles on white frosting.

He wanted to lick her.

Just a dream, he told himself. When he woke up, he wouldn't feel anything except pity for Lucinda. That was all he could afford to feel for her. It wasn't like they could be anything to each other.

Here, he would make her feel special, feel safe. When they returned to reality, he couldn't give her anything but protection. He would ask Ember to give her a job, and he would find Lucy a place to live. If Bernard Franco stepped a toe into Nevermore, Gray would be happy to show the heartless bastard the meaning of true power. Bernard would never bother Lucinda again.

"It feels like we've been here forever," said Lucinda. She sighed contentedly and sat next to him.

His gaze dipped into the cleavage of her tiny bikini top. The water had already dried, leaving only acres of pale, perfect skin. Was she really this beautiful? Or had he created her dream body to satisfy his desires? He hadn't been able to resist giving her a sexy bikini—and she hadn't protested. And, thank the Goddess, she'd ditched the robe.

"They don't talk."

Gray blinked and looked at Lucinda.

"What?" he asked.

She cupped her breasts, which of course made him look—and want—again. "They don't talk. You looked as if you were hoping to have a conversation with them."

Just a dream. He dragged his gaze from her boobs to her face. "I do," he said.

The humor in her gaze faded. He saw the wariness first and, underneath, the desire. She wanted him. He knew it from the first time she entered his dream. He could hear her thoughts . . . and oh, he could feel the way lust burned through her when she looked at him.

"It wouldn't mean anything," she said. Her tone was uncertain, as if she couldn't decide whether she wanted it to mean something or not.

"I'm conflicted," he admitted. He should drop it. Toss her in the water again, but . . . Shit. He wasn't a stand-up guy. "Nice" wasn't an adjective that had been used to describe him in a long while.

He cupped her heart-shaped face and looked into her eyes. "Eventually we'll wake up, and it won't be same. We won't be the same. I can't be with you. I can't give you anything."

She studied him, her expression softening. He wondered what she'd seen in his face that could merit such a look of compassion. What secrets had she discerned? What pain had he not hidden?

He dropped his hands, but she wouldn't let him move away. One of her small hands grasped his knee and stopped him from getting to his feet. He wanted to run away from whatever was unfolding. He wasn't in control of it. And it pissed him off that she made him feel this way.

Her fingertips danced over his jaw. The light touches held him hostage, as did the intention that glittered in her green eyes.

She leaned in, and then she kissed him.

That small, intimate brush of her lips sent fire racing through his veins. She was so gentle, so careful, he felt humbled by her. How could she give him even this small part of herself? She treated him like she could care about him. Like . . . maybe she already did.

He leaned back, his heart thundering. It couldn't be like this. Not so fucking sweet. Hard and mean, yes. Lust burning and bruising . . . tangle of limbs . . . sweat and moans . . . oh, hell yeah.

Then he wouldn't have to listen to his conscience.

He didn't resist when she kissed him again. She held his face carefully, as though he were fragile glass. Her mouth was a butterfly, flitting, flirting, landing oh, so briefly before moving away. She flicked her tongue against the corners of his lips.

"Let me in," she whispered.

He opened his mouth, and accepted the slow sweep of her tongue. He felt undone by her tender regard. He'd wanted to tumble her, to take her . . . and she was giving something to him. Something he didn't even realize he needed.

No. He wouldn't let her do this. He wouldn't feel this way again. Gods-be-damned! Betrayed by his own body . . . manipulated by another Rackmore witch.

Disgusted with himself, he pulled away and stared at her. He saw nothing calculating in her eyes, only warmth and need. A need he could fulfill. Her berry mouth was swollen and ripe. He wanted those lips on him, everywhere. She still cupped his face, and he liked how she held him. He liked how she treated him—he just didn't deserve it. Worse, he couldn't trust her actions were genuine, and not designed to elicit a particular response.

However, he knew one thing right down to his soul.

She wanted him. And he wanted her.

He wouldn't pretend it was anything but sex.

"What are you doing?" he asked sharply.

Her eyes widened, and he felt like a jerk when she let go of him. Her gaze shuttered. "I thought I was kissing you."

"Well, don't." He shoved a hand through his hair. "I want you. But I want you hard and fast. I want to be inside you, driving you wild, making you scream. I want us tearing each other apart."

I'd like that, too. Her thought drifted through his mind. Triumph flashed through him, and he leaned forward, ready to pounce. *If he cared, even a little. But I've been used enough.*

Gray stopped cold. He felt like she'd punched a hole through his chest. "Lucy."

"I'd like to take another swim." She rose to her feet, and offered him a small, trembling smile. "This dream will be over soon."

Translation: It was over now.

He watched her walk into the waves until she was hip-deep, and then she dove under the purple water and swam away.

Way to go, prick. Why didn't he just give her what she wanted? Was she so different from any woman who wanted a little romance, a little tenderness? It wouldn't have been real, but she understood the rules here.... Didn't she?

He was scarred and bitter and distrustful. He couldn't drop his guard long enough to make love to a beautiful woman. He'd told her there were no secrets here, no need to protect their hearts.

He'd been wrong.

*　　*　　*

He owed the witch his thanks.

Her pathetic attempt to save Marcy had been an un-expected boon. The Guardian was thoroughly distracted now, and that was good. He needed time—to find the object, to create the spell, to fix his mistakes.

Ah, but the witch had given him another gift, as well. She was on the run from Bernard Franco. He could easily trade her location for the Raven's help should he need it. However, Franco's gratitude might turn to treachery, and he couldn't risk having anything else out of his control.

Even so, he was so pleased by this new development that he'd decided Lucinda's death would be quick. Yes, she deserved his mercy.

And his pity.

He stood next to the table and stared down at the magical items. Only one, the most important, of course, was missing. Marcy had stolen it. He'd underestimated his timid little lover. When he found out she'd been in the basement of the café spying on him, he'd lost his temper. He thought her sufficiently cowed, but instead he'd made her bold.

Too bad Lennie had been fended off by the witch and hadn't retrieved the eye. Oh, how he'd whined about getting scalded. The man had no tolerance for pain at all. On the upside, all it took to shut him up was a bottle of Jack Daniel's.

While his friend nursed his wounds, he'd managed to get into the old clinic long enough to search the body and the items the sheriff had bagged as evidence.

The eye wasn't there.

The good news was if Marcy didn't have it, that meant Lucinda Rackmore did. The bad news was that she was in the Guardian's house, and not even he could break through the protections there. He had to plan for multiple scenarios. If the witch trusted Gray with the eye, the man's ingrained sense of duty would surely make him give it to the sheriff. But if the witch kept the eye a secret . . . well, that was another issue altogether.

Despite his confident prediction, the portal had not opened. He'd sensed the frailness of the barrier and he'd been so sure it would peel away and allow him to call forth Kahl. Gray Calhoun was like all the others in Nevermore. Everything just fell into his lap—he wasn't Guardian because he deserved it. He'd been born a Calhoun, been raised a Dragon, and simply waltzed into town to take his rightful place.

I have a birthright, too. No one had known the truth, and those with an inkling—like those old-bat librarians—buried it. Everything had been taken from him. His parents. His magic. His identity.

Fury lashed at him.

It was too bad the portal hadn't opened. It probably would have if he'd gotten all the objects in place and the spellwork finished. Instead, the barrier had solidified, and now he would have to start over.

He beat back his anger, tamped it down flat until every wisp of it was gone. Nothing worked smoothly the first time. Or even the second. There was more work to be done—which included getting his little treasure back from the Guardian.

But first, he had to do some cleanup.

Taylor wished his head would just explode already. The pain pulsing in between his eyes went up a notch every time Cathleen spoke. She sat in his office across from his desk, lolling in one of the leather wingback chairs that creaked every time she moved. And she moved a lot.

"He didn't show up for the inspection, no sir. Says right on the town books that I got rights. If the Guardian don't keep his word, his word is no longer law. Says it right there." She leaned forward and tapped the page with her sharp, pink nail.

Taylor squinted down at the old ledger with its yellowed pages. It was one of the books written by the first sheriff, a series of laws enacted by the original Guardian to ensure the protection of the town and its people. How Cathleen had known about the tome when he hadn't stuck in his craw. She didn't read anything that might have truth in it, and she sure as hell wouldn't have the attention span or interest to dig through arcane law books.

Still, she'd marched right to the floor-to-ceiling bookshelves that lined the left side of his office and pulled it out from the first column, third shelf. It was among a bunch of oversized, thick law books Taylor had thought of as fancy dressing for his office rather than contributions to his work.

"You see, Sheriff?" She lifted her chin and sniffed, thoroughly playing the offended party. "I made sure everything was right and proper. And he didn't even bother to show up. What kind of Guardian is he?"

"Would you like to ask him?" Taylor leaned back in his chair and pinned her with a hard stare. "I'm sure Gray would be happy to give you a demonstration—just so you're real clear on the kind of Guardian he is."

Cathleen's face mottled, but she took the hint and shut her mouth. Taylor might have his own issues with the way Gray handled his Guardian's duties, but that didn't mean he deserved anything less than Taylor's loyalty and public support.

Taylor read the ledger again. Law was law. Gray would be pissed, but it was his fault. He should've remembered the damned inspection. Taylor had no choice. He had to let Cathleen reopen the café.

"Hey, Taylor. There's a—"

Deputy Ren Banton stopped in the doorway, and took in the scene. His dark gaze moved from Cathleen to Taylor. He quirked an eyebrow at Taylor, and then he had the nerve to grin, just a little.

"You need something, Ren?"

"Accident off Brujo Boulevard, up near the fork to Old Creek."

Taylor's gaze went to the phone on his desk, and then to the bowl of water he kept for communication spells. He couldn't enact one, but he could receive them. Ren saw the direction of his gaze, and shrugged. "That's up near our farm. Dad called me when he found the wreck."

Ren's dad was Harley Banton—a widower who'd had to raise his son alone. It was a sad fact that Ren's mama, Lara, had committed suicide. Ren had been only a few months old, about the same age as Ant when it happened. His wife's suicide had nearly broken Harley, and he became something of a recluse. A note had never been found, either, which Taylor had always thought odd. Lara was quite a bit younger than her husband, the niece of the Wilson twins who came to live with her aunts. The Wilson twins ran the library, Tuesday through Friday, eight a.m. to four p.m. They were both in their seventies and as persnickety as ever. Goddess help you if you kept a book past its turn-in date. They'd loved their niece dearly, and they'd been devastated when she'd taken her life by overdosing on Valium.

It had been a double blow to the town. First, to see one of their own abandon his kin to chase a skirt, and second, to see a vibrant young woman take her own life. The two events had been only a couple weeks apart— and both had fed the gossip mills for months.

So, yeah, Ren was young, barely twenty, but solid. He'd graduated from high school with Ant and he was one of the few kids who'd stuck around. Most of Nevermore's children left. Some stayed and some came back, but most wanted to pursue lives outside of small-town living and backbreaking farmwork. He and Ant had once been close, but as their interests diversified, they'd drifted apart. Seemed to Taylor that his little brother cared a lot more about plants than he did people.

"Taylor?"

Taylor blinked and found both Ren and Cathleen staring at him. Shit. He'd been drifting again, losing his focus.

"All right, then," he said wearily. "Let's go."

"What about me?" asked Cathleen in a high-pitched voice. "What about my rights?"

"You can reopen the café." He needed coffee, and aspirin. Ren saluted him, and walked out, probably to go start up their only law enforcement vehicle, an SUV that had seen better days.

Taylor watched Cathleen pop up from the chair. She looked like a vicious little bird hopping from tree branch to tree branch, hoping for the opportunity to peck out someone's eyes. He was sick that she hadn't asked about her stepdaughter. Not once. When he'd told her about Marcy two days ago, all Cathleen could do was lament about not being able to find good help. *Who's gonna be my waitress now?* she'd wailed. She acted like Marcy had gotten murdered just to inconvenience her.

"Will the wake be tomorrow?" asked Taylor pleasantly.

Cathleen stopped in the doorway and turned toward him, her eyes narrowed. "What wake?"

"For Marcy," said Taylor. "The autopsy's done. Her

body's ready to be released. I assume you've made arrangements for her burial?"

Cathleen said nothing for a moment, and he knew she was calculating all the money she'd lose giving out free food to mourners. Anger pulsed through him. He wanted to take out his gun and shoot her.

"Wakes are tradition in Nevermore," said Taylor, as if she needed reminding. She'd outlived her father-in-law and her husband, both of whom had wakes at the café. He'd be damned if he let her wiggle out of giving Marcy one. "Everyone will want a chance to say their good-byes."

Apparently Cathleen decided she'd won enough battles today. She grudgingly nodded. "Of course, I'm having a wake. She was my kin." She regarded him, her lips curled. "I can open the café right now, though, right?"

"I can't stop you."

That pleased her. She offered a tepid smile, and then she spun and marched out.

"Goddess, forgive me, but I hate that woman." Taylor checked his weapons belt and made sure all was in order. Then he plucked his hat from his desk and put it on.

Arlene was coming in as he was going out.

"What in the world did Cathleen Munch want?" she asked. Then she took one look at his expression, opened her big red bag, and out came a thermos of coffee and a bottle of aspirin, which she pressed into his hands.

Taylor leaned down and kissed her cheek. "I think I'd like to marry you, Arlene."

"Already taken," she said. "But if things don't work out, I'll let you know."

Since she'd been happily married for thirty-five years, he doubted he still had a shot. "Jimmy's damned lucky."

"He sure is."

Taylor left, feeling a smidge better.

Arlene stood in the lobby and looked around. "I really need to come in earlier," she said to the empty office. "I always miss the good stuff."

Gray sat on the shore and watched Lucy swim. She seemed to never tire of the water, or maybe it was just that she was tired of him. Okay. She hadn't exactly been avoiding him. She still had an easy enough manner, even when she asked him to create a one-piece bathing suit, which he reluctantly did. Unfortunately, having more of her covered up did nothing to soothe his raging libido.

Guardian.

Startled, he glanced up at the pink sky. "Ember?"

Oh, dere you are. Time to come home now. We got work to do.

"What about Lucy?"

Her suffering over, now she got to recover. Her body weak from all dat pain.

"Maybe it would be better to stay here until she's fully healed."

Or maybe it better for you.

Gray sighed. "I'll send her back first." He paused. "Are you in my bedroom?"

Me an' the sheriff. Sorry 'bout the door.

"The door?"

But Ember's voice was gone. Once again he was awed by her power, and he wondered just what kind of magical she was.

How long had he and Lucy been dreaming?

Suddenly worried, he called Lucy to the shore.

It was time to go back to reality.

Where his regrets lived.

When Gray woke up, his eyes felt like sandpaper and his throat was as dry as a Texan's sense of humor. His hand clutched the pillow next to him, right where Lucy's head should be. He shot up, panicked.

"Whoa, pardner," drawled Taylor. He stood next to the bed holding a glass of water. "Ember took Lucinda into the bathroom to clean her. She was a mess." He handed Gray the water, and wrinkled his nose. "You could use a good dunking, too."

Gray gulped down the cool liquid. "How long have we been out?"

"Three days. Grit's been worried about you."

"It wasn't like that," he said. Taylor had known about Gray's dream forays—and that Grit's sudden, awful decline had ended those journeys. He'd barely gotten his grandfather into his mother's care before he'd crashed. "I swear it."

"I believe you."

Gray's limbs felt achy and numb. And he had to piss bad.

Taylor seemed to read his mind. "It's a wonder you both didn't pee the bed."

"I was dream walking with her. The body practically shuts down when you go that deep."

Taylor jerked a thumb over his shoulder. "Ember took her to the hallway bathroom because the tub's bigger."

Gray got out of bed. His limbs prickled as blood rushed into places that had been still and numb for three days. Being upright made him dizzy, and he dropped the empty glass onto the floor. It rolled under the bed and clinked against something. He had no idea what was under his bed. He just hoped he wouldn't have to clean out any science experiments.

"You need help?"

"I got it." Gray stumbled into the master bath and took care of business. As he washed his hands, he looked at himself in the mirror. His hair was greasy, his face covered with stubble, and his eyes were bloodshot. He smelled like he'd fallen into horse manure. His clothes were stained with Lucy's blood and his own sweat, not to mention wrinkled and smelly from soaking up all that rain.

When he exited the bathroom, Taylor was standing by the bedroom door. "I figure you wanna check on her first."

Gray wanted to see Lucy with his own eyes, even though he knew Ember would take good care of her. Something about that woman inspired compassion and trust. As he got to the door, he paused. "You going soft on me, Mooreland?"

"Your fingers were tangled in her hair," he said. "The back of her hand was resting against your cheek. Don't know if you'll like it, Gray, but you two have a connection now. She's yours." He eyed him and tipped his hat back. "Or is she?"

"Mine," agreed Gray.

The door to the bathroom was closed, but this was his house, damn it, so he opened it and strode inside.

Ember knelt on the tiled floor next to the claw-foot tub. She murmured as she wiped Lucy's face with a washcloth. Lucy's eyes were closed, and he realized she was still unconscious. She was in her own dreamland now, and he wished he could be there with her.

"I got a spell holding her above da water," said Ember. "She won't drown."

"I'll take care of her."

"Will you, now?" Ember draped the cloth over the rim of the tub, and stood up. She turned around, hands on her hips, and stared him down.

Once again, Gray felt like a novice in the presence of a master Dragon.

"She's mine," he offered simply.

Ember was unimpressed. "Don't you claim her 'cause you need to clear your conscience. You can't have it both ways, Guardian. You can't feel guilty you doin' da wrong tings, then accuse her of manipulatin' your feelings."

Gray's mouth dropped open. "How did you know I was . . . that was only in my own head!"

"Da Goddess told me. She say you can't hide no more." Ember touched the edge of the black side of her glasses. "Everyting got a price. Sometimes good tings require sacrifice, and sometimes bad tings give you gifts. You went to hell, but you got a gift, too."

"No," said Gray. His blood ran cold. That was his secret, his burden, and his alone. "This isn't about me."

"Will be soon enough. But dat's your journey to take, oh stubborn one." She crossed her arms. "You gonna go?"

"It's my damned house!"

Ember shrugged, and Gray saw that he'd have a better chance of moving a mountain than getting that woman out of his bathroom. She had the audacity to *shoo* him. "Go take care of yourself. Den come back and tell me how you gonna claim dis woman."

She waved her hands at him again, and Gray gave up. His own smell was making his eyes water. And now that he knew Lucy was okay, he supposed it wouldn't hurt for him to take a shower.

Taylor stood in the hallway, smirking.

"Shut up," said Gray. "Just shut the hell up."

Lucinda woke up in a tub of lukewarm water. Just as she realized magic was keeping her afloat, it popped like a soap bubble, and she slid under the water.

"Lucy!" She heard Gray's yell, then felt his hands underneath her armpits. He yanked her out of the water, and then swung her into his arms.

"I'm n-naked," she protested.

"I'm trying not to notice," he said. "It's not really working, though."

"Did you notice I was c-cold, too?"

His gaze swept over her breasts, lingering a tad too long on her beaded nipples, and he grimaced. "Yeah. Definitely cold." He leaned toward a cabinet, and she reached out to open it. It was filled with fluffy blue towels. She grabbed one and tried to cover herself, but her limbs were trembling too badly. The towel fluttered to the floor like a wounded bird.

"I can't." She squeezed her eyes shut. "I'm sorry."

He strode out of the bathroom, down the hall, and into a bedroom. The walls were painted white and had a border of delicate pink flowers. The furniture was all white, too, including the full-sized wrought iron bed.

It was lovely.

The bedspread matched the border—white with delicate pink flowers. The sheets were pink, and the multitude of pillows all different shades of pink, too. The covers had been pulled down, and Gray put her into the bed, even though she was still wet from the bath. He grabbed the corner of the bedspread, but hesitated.

His gaze roved her flesh, but this time not with desire. Lucy turned her face away as he examined the scars that riddled her skin. *Don't ask,* she silently begged him. *Please, don't ask.*

"You need to eat something." Gently, he pulled the covers up to her chin, and pushed her wet hair away from her face. "Ember's making soup. You think you can stomach it?"

"Yes," she said. "But I'm not sure I can hold the spoon."

"I happen to be an excellent spoon holder."

She smiled. She wished she could accept his kindness

without question, but she remembered far too well the look in his eyes when she'd knocked on his door. Nor would she ever be able to forget their dream together. If she could've accepted his terms and just given in to their passion, it would've been something nice to hold on to for a little while. But she knew he was wary of her, even though he was trying to be honorable.

"This is much better than your room," she teased.

"I would've taken you here instead, but the portal opened into the master suite. I was afraid to carry you any further."

His serious answer quashed any further attempts at levity.

"Why did you change your mind, Gray?" she asked. "I'm grateful. . . . I really am. But you didn't want to help me. Why should you?"

"What your sister did wasn't your fault," he said. "It's not fair to hold that against you."

"Thanks," she said drily. "You're a saint."

He shoved a hand through his damp hair. "I was a prick, okay?"

"Yeah," she agreed, "you kinda were."

He laughed, and the sound went right through her. It reminded her of the old Gray, the one she hadn't appreciated as a self-centered brat. She knew better than anyone that sometimes people were changed so substantially by tragedy, their very cores were reshaped.

Gray could never go back to who he was.

And neither could she.

Carefully, he sat on the bed next to her. For a moment, she got the impression he wanted to hold her hand or touch her face, but he did neither. "I'm going to help you, Lucy. You can stay in Nevermore. I'll give you official sanctuary. Ember's willing to let you work at the tea shop for room and board. There's an extra apartment above hers—it's part of the same building. It'll take a little elbow grease to clean up, but I'll help you."

"I can't risk it."

His gaze snapped to hers. "You can't risk what?"

"You. Ember. The town. Bernard will come for me, and he will level this place to get me."

"The hell." Gray's expression turned thunderous. "I'm a Dragon. A Wizard of Honor. The Guardian of Nevermore. He won't dare."

"I'm sure all your titles will scare him to death."

Gray's brows slashed downward. "If you thought you were risking Nevermore, why did you come here?"

"To ask you to marry me." She sighed. "If you'll recall, I was on my way out of town when . . ." She felt the blood drain from her face as the memories all came rushing back. "Marcy."

"Cathleen already buried her." His tone suggested he wanted to bury Cathleen. Alive. "This morning, apparently, without notifying anyone. But she's having the wake tonight."

"I'd like to go."

"All right." He rubbed his jaw. "I can't believe Cathleen reopened the café."

"She didn't close it to mourn her stepdaughter?"

"Worse. I shut it down for inspection, but since I was dream walking with you, I didn't show up. She found some arcane law on the books that basically gave her the right to reopen the café, and I can't nail her with another inspection for thirty days. She'll have her act cleaned up by then, and I won't be able to do jack shit."

Lucy reached out and grasped Gray's hand. "I'm sorry. The café seems like an important part of Nevermore. It's too bad it's being run by someone so selfish and cruel."

Gray looked down at her fingers, and she suddenly

felt foolish. She tried to pull away, but he placed his other hand over hers so that her hand was trapped between both of his.

"You lay there weak from that damned curse, one you suffered because you tried to save a girl you barely knew, and still you seek to comfort me for something so small."

"It's not small to you."

He stared at their hands, and then he looked at her. "Marriage is the only way to protect you."

"If anything truly can," she said. "Bernard can't break the marital bond between magicals. Being your wife would give me protections not even he could tamper with." She needed him to understand how little she could bring to the table. "Marrying me won't break the curse. Nothing will do that. My thaumaturgy is practically useless."

"We'll find a way to free you."

Lucy stared at him, her heart stuttering. "Gray, what are you saying?"

"I'll marry you."

Stunned into silence, she couldn't do much more than gape at him.

"It's not a love match," he warned. "But I expect us to share a bed. And the responsibilities of guardianship—what magic you have must be used to protect the town, same as mine. You'll be my wife in all ways, Lucy."

Except in his heart, she thought sadly. This was definitely not a romance. She needed him, and though he might not admit it, he needed her. And if their dream meant anything, they had the kind of sparks that would make sex spectacular. That was more than she could expect—and it was more than she had with Bernard. At least Gray was up-front about his intentions, and letting her know he did not love her. She'd rather have a loveless marriage with equality and respect than be the mistress of man who claimed he loved her, even as he was beating her unconscious.

"And if we find a way to lift the curse?" she asked.

"If we break the curse and we nullify Bernard as a threat," said Gray, "I will give you marital absolution."

Relief flowed through her, shadowed by that same, aching sadness. He didn't want her, not really. Ah, but safety was within reach—she wanted to weep, but she'd shed enough tears already. "I agree to your terms," she said. "Thank you, Gray."

He nodded sharply, and then he let her hand go and stood up. "I'll talk to Ember and Sheriff Mooreland about the arrangements."

"When?"

"Right now," he said. "They're downstairs fixing the back door. Mooreland didn't remember the key under the mat before he busted it down."

"How long were we dreaming?" She studied the tiny pink flowers dotting the bedspread.

"Three days. Lucy?"

She looked at him. He gestured around the room, frowning. "I know a ceremony where the bride is prostrate isn't exactly romantic, but—"

"I will stand up for my vows," she said firmly. "I just need a little rest. And that soup you promised."

He nodded. "Taylor can perform the ceremony."

Lucinda understood. Gray wanted a legal, perfunctory transaction. She couldn't blame him for not wanting the dressings of a wedding—it would remind him too much of when he'd taken vows with her sister. That had been a love match for him, if not for Kerren. And for Lucinda, picking out a dress and flowers would perpetuate the lie that their relationship was more than a means to an end. He was her protector, and for his commitment to her, she would give him her loyalty and what little power she had left.

She preferred the obligation stripped bare, as well, just as a reminder that the truth, no matter how ugly, was better than a pretty lie.

"My clothes?" she asked.

"They're in the bathroom. I'll wash them for you."

"No."

He looked at her sharply, and she flinched. For all her self-talk of truth and lies, she was reluctant to share the secrets that motivated her. Bernard wanted her back for many reasons, not least of which was to get back what she had taken. And now she had Marcy's secret to keep, too.

She wanted to trust Gray. But what if she told him . . . and he decided not to marry her? What if he told her she wasn't worth the trouble?

Then he's not the man I believe him to be.

Gray was staring at her, waiting for her to make up her mind. She realized he understood she was wrestling with her conscience, and he was waiting to see what she said. Trust was a two-way street. She couldn't keep circling Gray, hoping for him to give in, or give up, before she did.

She would make the first gesture.

"Marcy asked me to keep something for her. She told me to take it and leave Nevermore."

"Take what?" he asked.

"In the pocket of my jeans," she said. "There's a little red bag. I don't know what's in it."

He studied her face, frowning. "You didn't want to tell me."

"She died for it, Gray. She gave it to me to protect, and now I'm trusting you with it, too. For her." The rest of her words remained unspoken, but she knew he'd heard them all same: *Don't let us down.*

"I'll take care of it." He hesitated, then walked back to the bed and leaned over her, brushing a light kiss across her lips. "And I will take care of you."

It was almost better than a wedding vow.

Almost.

Chapter 7

Gray sat at the kitchen table with Taylor and Ember, munching on a batch of Ember's chocolate-chip cookies. He'd just finished telling them about Lucy's predicament and their solution: marriage.

"Are you out of your ever-loving mind?" asked Taylor. "You're gonna marry another Rackmore witch? And not just any Rackmore, but the sister of your ex-wife? Someone cursed by a Raven?"

"Well, when you put it like that," said Gray sarcastically. "Yeah." He knew how it sounded. He knew it was crazy, but he also knew deep down in his gut that he was Lucy's only chance. Eventually Franco would catch up to her, and more than likely kill her.

Or maybe he'd just torture her some more.

Gray thought about all the tiny scars that dotted Lucy's pale flesh and he wanted to destroy Bernard Franco inch by inch. Bastard. He had no doubt Franco had cut her, had made her bleed, and suffer. Why the hell would she put up with that kind of shit?

"Ember, I hate to admit it, but these are as good as my mama's." Taylor sighed contentedly, and grabbed another cookie from the plate.

"That's a kind thing to say," said Ember. "Thank you." She wasn't eating the cookies, though. She was too fascinated by the pair of books in front of her. One was big and leather, reminiscent of saddle leather, and the font of the title screamed Old West. The other was much smaller and slim, like a poetry book. It was as blue as the ocean and the title font looked like waves.

"You mind scratching my binding again, Ember?" said the leather book. "My own grandson won't do it."

" 'Cause it feels weird to tickle my grandfather, even if he is a book," said Gray.

"I need a scratch, too, Ember," said the blue journal. "Gray's stingy with the touches."

" 'Cause you're a dude," said Gray, feeling defensive. "Quit flirting with a married woman."

"Flirting's not cheating," insisted Dutch.

"I can't believe you have two soul books." Ember scratched the bindings of both books and they practically purred. "Once, I got to visit the special soul collection in the Great Library. So many people talking, telling their stories. I could've stayed there for weeks listening."

"I know why you have Grit," said Taylor. "The old man requested it. But how'd you get Dutch?"

Gray didn't really want to talk about the books. He wanted to check on Lucy, but after the fifth time of seeing if she was "okay," she actually snapped at him to leave her alone. At least with a nap and a belly full of Ember's chicken soup, she was feeling stronger. He'd managed to dig up some old garments of his mother's. Most were too big for Lucy's thin frame, but he'd take her shopping and buy her anything she wanted.

In his upstairs magicked safe was the red bag he'd dug out of Lucy's front jean pocket. He hadn't looked inside it because he didn't want to know. Not yet. He was sure whatever Marcy was attempting to smuggle out of Nevermore was about to add another complication to his life. Taylor would be pissed at him for not handing over evidence in an active investigation, but frankly, Taylor could kiss his ass. Gah! He felt like a curmudgeon—a big old, grumpy, crusty curmudgeon.

Damn it all. He was turning into Grit.

"I asked him to bring Dutch with us," said Grit.

Startled out of his thoughts by his grandfather's whiskey voice, he looked at Taylor. "I don't know how they got to be friends, but honestly, the librarians were happy to see them both go."

"We were too much for them to handle," said Dutch. "Too righteous."

Ember laughed, and gave the journal another tickle.

"How long will it take?" asked Gray. "Do you need anything special?"

Taylor dusted cookie crumbs off his hands. "For what?"

"For marrying me and Lucy."

"Now?"

That got Ember's attention. Her one dark eye zeroed in on him. Gray resisted the urge to look away. He refused to feel ashamed about not giving Lucy a dream wedding. She had agreed it should be simple and quick. They were not in love. They'd made a . . . a business deal. With perks for them both.

"You not gonna give the girl a chance to plan?" Ember snorted. "She need a dress, and some flowers. You got her a ring, already?"

Gray flushed. He hadn't thought about a ring. At the very least, the Guardian's wife should have some sort of symbol signifying his bond to her. He had no jewelry, at least none that he wore, and none that he could give her. Shit.

"You agree they should be married?" asked Taylor. He looked at Ember as if she'd grown a second head. "Seriously?"

"If'n my grandson thinks he ought to get hitched, then that's that," said Grit.

"Specially if she's a gorgeous babe," added Dutch.

"Excuse me a minute." Gray scooped up the books.

"Whoa, dude. Easy on the binding."

"Dagnabit! Where are you takin' us?"

"To the library."

Both books started complaining. Grit said the other books rubbed his cover the wrong way, and Dutch thought the library was stuffy and creepy. Gray put them on the desk, which was crowded with other books, old papers, and trinkets he'd never found a place for. Like every room in the house, it was crowded with lives past, his and other Calhouns', and he wondered how everything had gotten so out of control.

"How long we gotta stay in here?" asked Grit.

"I have to get married," said Gray. "And then my first outing with my wife will be to say good-bye to the girl she almost died to save. After that, we're going to bed."

Dutch snickered. Gray thumped his cover. "Enough, you. Lucy needs rest."

"Uh-huh. She's pretty, right?" asked the surfer. "Bet she looks good naked."

"You'll never know."

"That's harsh, dude. Way harsh."

"I'll be back for you tomorrow. If you both behave."

"I hate being a book," said Grit. "Why'd I ask for a soul imprint on a *book*? Shoulda asked to be a chair. Or a wind chime."

"Good night, Grit. Be good, Dutch."

They muttered their good-nights, and Gray returned to the kitchen in time to hear Ember say, "It's meant to be. But I don't agree with dis coldhearted method of sayin' da vows."

"Lucy and I agreed to keep things simple," said Gray. "We're both very clear that this is a mutually beneficial arrangement."

"So she get protection," said Ember quietly, "and what you get?"

"A wife who won't sell me to a demon to save her own hide."

Ember rolled her eyes to heaven. Then she sighed. "I can perform the ceremony. I am a priestess of the Goddess."

"No, thank you, Ember." Lucy's apologetic voice drifted from the doorway of the kitchen. "Gray and I would like Sheriff Mooreland to do it."

Gray stood up from his chair, his gaze on hers. It felt like his heart had turned over in his chest, and he rubbed the spot absently as he hurried to meet her. She leaned heavily against the frame, looking frail and beautiful in his mother's light green dress. It was far too big for her, but the color was stunning. Her hair hung down in ringlets that caressed her shoulders. "Brown" wasn't a good enough description for her hair color—it was streaked with caramel and auburn. It looked shiny and soft, and he couldn't resist winding a curl around his finger. Her skin was creamy smooth, her mossy gaze fringed by long, dark lashes. Her cheeks were a little too hollow, but not even illness could dim her beauty. She wore no makeup, but she didn't need any adornment. His gaze dropped to her lips, pillow soft and the color of pink wine.

"Hello," she said.

He dropped the curl and drew her into his embrace. "I would've come for you."

"I know," she said, pride edging her tone even as she clung to him, still too weak, "but I had to try."

"You're strong," he agreed. "I imagine you'll be carrying boulders by tomorrow."

"Someone has to do the heavy lifting around here."
He grinned at her.

"I don't believe it," muttered Taylor.

"What did I tell you?" asked Ember smugly. "Meant to be."

Gray ignored the peanut gallery. Lucy felt so small and light against him. Not only was he going to take her shopping; he was going to fatten her up. He felt like if he moved the wrong way, she might crumble beneath his fingertips.

She looked him over, smiling. He'd taken the time to put on a dress shirt and black pants. He was wearing his fancy boots, too, the black ones with the silver trim. She looked pleased with his appearance, and that made him glad he'd gone to the effort.

"Are you ready?" he asked.

"Yes."

He knew she wouldn't appreciate being treated like a weakling. The woman had struggled down two flights of steps and across the mess-strewn living room so she wouldn't have to ask for his help. He would allow her the dignity of appearing as though she could stand.

He turned, and she placed her hand along his arm. He put his hand over hers, trying to pour his strength into her. She stood close, leaning against him. He felt her quivering, and he knew it was costing her great effort to keep upright.

"Wait, now," said Ember. "Mooreland, get over dere and say your hellos to da bride. Gray, you let me straighten you out. Goodness, you look a sight."

Gray glared at the woman, but she calmly ignored his ire, fully expecting both men to do what she said. Taylor gave in before he did. He watched his friend stomp over to Lucy, completely unthrilled with the whole situation. Still, he was gentle as he put his arm around the bride.

"You've been busy," he said.

"Yes," said Lucy. "I really need a day planner."

Taylor laughed, and Gray had the sudden urge to bash his friend's face in. They might have a marriage of convenience, but Lucy was his, damn it. And he didn't like Taylor getting all . . . funny with her.

"Guardian, c'mere."

He followed Ember to the corner of the kitchen, casting looks over his shoulder as Taylor and Lucy had a low conversation. It seemed as though his bride was melting the icy exterior of the lawman. He wasn't sure he liked it.

"Here."

Gray looked down at the delicate ring Ember offered him. Three strands in various shades of silver had been woven together to create the circlet. He'd seen it on Ember's forefinger, one of several rings she wore. He knew immediately that Lucy would love it. "How much?" he asked.

Ember reached up and smacked him on the back of the head.

He blinked down at her, stunned.

One dark eye shot daggers at him. "You got no manners. You don't ask to pay for a gift."

"Okay, already. Sorry."

"Go get married, you jackass."

Feeling thoroughly chastised, he pocketed the ring, and returned to his bride. She was looking pale, but holding steady.

Gray and Lucy stood before Taylor and spoke their vows.

The ceremony took less than five minutes. Legalizing a marriage between magicals wasn't that complex, especially in a town where wizards made most of the rules. In no time at all, Taylor turned to Gray and asked, "What do you offer your bride to show your faith in the bond you now share with her?"

Gray pulled the silver circlet from his pocket. The look on Lucy's face made him immensely grateful that Ember had given him the ring. "I offer this as my promise to be faithful, and to cherish you."

"I accept your gift." She took it and slipped it on her finger. She smiled at him, and the glow of happiness in her eyes made him feel like he'd done something right. They could make this work. It would be far better than his bond with Kerren because they were entering into their marital agreement with eyes open and no expectations for a future together. They could enjoy each other—and when it was time, they'd walk away.

Taylor turned to Lucy and asked, "What do you offer your groom to show your faith in the bond you now share with him?"

Gray opened his mouth to say he expected nothing, but he was surprised to see Lucy reach into the folds of her dress and pull out an object.

In the center of her palm, she showed him a small circle of braided hair. "I offer this humble ring as my promise to be faithful, and to cherish you."

She'd cut and braided her own hair to make him a ring. Somehow she'd woven a blue ribbon within it. He sensed the magic, too, and noticed how smooth and shiny it was, like it had been lacquered. She had nothing, but she'd still managed to create something. He was touched by the gesture. No, more like he was rocked to the core by it.

He stared at it for too long.

Lucy's fingers closed over the ring. "I'm sorry. I don't know what I was thinking. You probably wouldn't want to wear such a silly—"

He grasped her hand and pried her fingers open. He

picked up the delicate braid and placed it on his finger. "I accept your gift."

Then, because he couldn't give voice to the emotions crowding his heart or to the fears that somehow this was more than it should be and perfect all the same, he leaned down and kissed her.

"Guess I don't have to say this part," said Taylor drily.

Ember sniffled. "Oh, shush, you big idiot."

Lucinda sat at the kitchen table, a bundle of nerves. She hated feeling feeble. It seemed she had felt that way ever since the great reckoning. Like she couldn't catch her breath. Like she couldn't see into the darkness. Like she couldn't step in a single direction without falling into a spiked pit.

And all the while, helpless.

Weak.

Stupid.

But now? Holy Goddess. *I married Gray.*

A few minutes before, Ember hugged her until her spine cracked and then gave her a great smacking kiss on the cheek. Taylor had been much more circumspect in his congratulations. A firm handshake and "Good luck to you both."

The sheriff was probably still annoyed with Gray. He'd tried to ask her about Marcy's death, but her new husband had cut him off. She'd promised to answer his questions tomorrow, and then Gray had insisted she sit down, and frankly, she was relieved to do so. He walked the sheriff and Ember to the front door.

After Ember left, she heard Gray ask Taylor to wait and then his footsteps pounded up the stairs. When he returned, they'd gone outside. She wondered what they had talked about. Her?

Her stomach clenched and she pressed a hand against

her belly. Oh, what did it matter? It was taking refuge as
Gray's wife or in Mexico, and at least here she wouldn't
be looking over her shoulder as much. Even Bernard
would hesitate to challenge Gray outright.

But she was just as sure he'd figure out a way to get
to her.

He always did.

"Are you all right?" asked Gray. He stood in the
doorway, studying her. "That's an idiotic question.
Never mind. Ember made some special tea for you. I'll
pour you some." He crossed to the stove, and she saw
the teapot on the front burner. He started opening cabi-
nets, which were either empty or piled with all sorts of
objects—none that actually belonged in a kitchen. "I
just have to find you a mug."

She was surprised he could find anything. Every room
she'd been in was a ceiling-to-floor mess. The front room
had big, bulky furniture piled with clothes and books
and boxes. It spilled over the tables and onto the floor.
She'd spotted cobwebs in every corner and dust coated
everything—including the family photos, mirrors, and
clocks.

What on earth did Gray do every day that he couldn't
be bothered with even minor housekeeping? Maybe his
Guardian duties kept him so busy that he didn't have
time to pick up. She glanced around the kitchen, and
grimaced. Dishes towered on both sides of the ceramic
sink. Spellbooks, spice jars, bowls of herbs, and crystals
littered the counters. The stove needed a good scrubbing; she shuddered to think what the oven looked like.

Lucinda determined right then and there the first way
she could help Gray. She would get his house in order.
That was something that a wife did, right? She didn't
have a lot of experience with housework. She'd never
had chores as a child—and her mother certainly hadn't

known a dishrag from a duster. After her mom died, Lucinda spent a lot of time struggling to survive—and hadn't lived anywhere long enough to clean it. When she became Bernard's mistress, she never had to lift a finger—not even when she'd been relegated to the penthouse harem. Still. How difficult could it be?

She glanced around the kitchen, feeling even more inadequate. She wasn't much of a cook, but she could do some basic recipes like lasagna and stew. Determination straightened her spine. She could learn her way around the kitchen. It was a goal—a goal that didn't involve figuring out how she was going to eat, where she was going to sleep, what else she had to do to escape Bernard's very long reach.

Clean house. Learn to cook. Be a good wife.

Simple, right?

"You're pale," said Gray. He stopped searching for a mug and crossed to her, kneeling at her feet. His gaze roved over her face, and he looked so concerned. Why? She knew the truth of their marriage. He'd made it clear that feelings were not involved in their relationship. She had to remember that. She knew too well how easy it was to fall into the trap of the heart—though Bernard had never truly held hers. He was a master manipulator, a puppeteer who knew which strings to pull. She was ashamed that she'd fallen for his tripe, that she'd allowed herself to become snared in his silky web.

"What must I do," Gray asked as he cupped her face, "to chase away those shadows in your eyes?"

Lucinda met his gaze and realized he was driven too hard by his own guilt. So ingrained were the concepts of duty and integrity in his conscience that he would fulfill every vow he made to her. In being her husband in all ways, he might make her forget her promise to remember nothing real lay between them.

"I'm merely tired." She ran her fingers through his hair, thrilled that she had the right to do so. Her husband. Had anyone told her she would one day marry Gray Calhoun, she would've called them crazy. But it seemed she was the crazy one.

His gaze had darkened, from blue sky to stormy sea. He pulled her hand from his hair and kissed her knuckles. Did he realize how romantic such gestures were? Probably not. It was his nature to treat women with such care. Not even Kerren's betrayal could erase his respect for females and his innate need to protect them.

"Can you sit at the edge of the chair?" he asked.

She didn't ask why; she simply scooted to the edge, and waited. He seemed pleased by her acquiescence, and grasped the bottom of her thin but voluminous dress.

"What are you doing?" she asked.

"It's phase one in my plan to change that look in your eyes." He gazed up at her. "Just for a little while, I don't want you to feel sad."

"Oh? And you can do this how?"

"I'll show you, wife." He gathered her dress, laying the folds across her thighs. "Hold on to this. And open for me."

"I didn't . . ." She clutched the material and licked her lips. "There wasn't any . . ." Her face went hot. Gray's eyebrows went up as he waited for her to finish a sentence. "Panties," she managed.

"Show me," he said, his voice husky. "Now."

She did so, revealing her lack of underwear. The ones she'd been wearing hadn't been washed, she had no idea where her duffel bag was, and she'd been too embarrassed to ask Gray about procuring undergarments. She hadn't even put on a bra, a fact made obvious by the thin material.

For a moment, Gray said nothing as he took in his fill

of her nether regions. She felt vulnerable and nervous. It was strange showing him her . . . *goods* like this. What was he doing?

He leaned down and planted a kiss on her clit.

She gasped. "Gray!"

"What?"

"You can't think you're going to"—she sucked in an unsteady breath—"do something. Down there."

He straightened and looked at her. "You've had lovers," he said. "You're telling me not one man has ever explored such a delectable spot?"

Embarrassment flooded her and her whole face felt as though she'd dipped it in lava. She glanced away from him. "No."

"Lucinda. Look at me."

It took effort—she still had *some* pride—but she managed to meet his gaze.

"I don't care how many lovers you've had," he said. "We are only for each other now. That's all that matters."

She didn't want him to think that she'd slept with a bunch of men. Maybe he didn't care, but she did. She wasn't a whore, even though Bernard had made her feel like one. And he had never, not once, put his mouth against her like Gray just had to bring her pleasure. In fact, she rarely received any pleasure at all from their couplings, which he'd squarely put on her. *You're frigid, darling. But don't worry. I will always love my little ice queen.*

"How many men do you believe would sleep with a Rackmore?" she asked softly. "After the great reckoning, no one would talk to me, much less date me. I never knew a man until Bernard." She couldn't resist touching Gray's hair again. He didn't seem to mind at all. She'd always had to be so careful with Bernard. He didn't like to be touched—and she had craved it. She always had to check her impulses to seek affection. To give affection. "He never made me feel the way you did in our dream."

"And how was that?" His gaze was enigmatic, his hands resting on her thighs, his thumbs rubbing circles.

"Like I was on fire and you were the only one who could put out the flames."

"That's how it should be," said Gray. He studied her, and she couldn't name the emotion glittering in his eyes. "You've only slept with him?"

"I wish I hadn't," she said, her tone bitter. "I wish I had never met him."

"I know that feeling well enough."

"Aren't we a pair?" She laughed hollowly. "So much baggage between the two of us it's a wonder we can walk anywhere at all." She stroked the scar on his temple. "What are we doing, Gray? Have we made a mistake?"

"We've chosen our path together, Lucy." He turned his head to kiss her palm. Then he looked at her. "I won't abandon you."

She hadn't realized she was going to cry until the tears fell. How had he known what she hadn't quite realized? She did feel abandoned—by her father, who committed suicide, by her mother, who catered to a lover until her heart literally gave out, by her sister, who was a callous bitch. Every relationship she'd ever had reinforced a single painful truth: *Nobody wants me.*

Was it any wonder she ate the crumbs of affection that Bernard tossed her way? He'd been a cruel man, lavishing her with presents one week, beating her senseless the next. It didn't matter than he'd used his magic to make sure she was malleable.

She was so ashamed. Even now when she felt safe and she was free, she felt unworthy of Gray's protection—and she hated that she needed it. Needed him. Because she wasn't strong enough on her own.

"Lucy."

She looked down at him. "I'm sorry," she said. "I can't seem to stop crying."

"Open for me, baby. Let me make you feel good."

It was all he could offer her, she realized. Physical pleasure was the comfort he could give, and she would take it. She didn't want to feel sad anymore, either. So, she opened her thighs and gripped his hair as he leaned forward.

"You are luscious." She felt the sweep of his tongue along her labia, first one side, then the other. A pause to tease her clit with short, rough strokes. Then he rained small, sweet kisses along her swollen flesh.

Pleasure sparkled—champagne bubbles, sunlight dancing on spring flowers, the unexpected eddies in a clear stream.

She let her head fall back and her eyes drift close.

He took his time, went exquisitely slow. Tasting. Licking. Kissing. He lapped the evidence of her desire like a man savoring a rare dessert. Her skin tingled, and her nipples were hard and aching. She couldn't quite catch her breath, and she felt like her heart would beat right out of her chest.

The coil of bliss tightened . . . and tightened.

"Gray." His name was a plea.

He rapidly flicked his tongue over her clit, bringing her closer and closer to the peak.

She moaned.

His fingers dug into her thighs.

Then he suckled her, hard.

She imploded.

She nearly fell off the chair, but Gray held firm, not complaining as her fingers yanked at his hair. He pressed his face against her, allowing her pulsations to suck at his tongue.

The sensations were ... Goddess, *incredible* wasn't even a good enough word to describe how she felt. It was wind-rushing, ocean-crashing, star-falling beautiful.

Eventually she floated back into her body.

When she opened her eyes, Gray was still kneeling at her feet. She saw the satisfaction in his gaze, and of course, there was the lust. The same lust that echoed within her. At least they had this connection, if nothing else.

"I think I died," she said.

"I was the one in heaven."

She laughed, feeling lighter than she'd felt in ages. Physical release wasn't a bad way at all to lift a bad mood. In fact, it was now her number one favorite way to feel better.

Gray placed one last, lingering kiss on her, and then he pulled down the dress. He stood up, his gaze still on hers. What now? she wondered. She felt awkward, and unsure. She'd never initiated sex with Bernard. He would've never tolerated anyone else being the aggressor in such things.

"We should go upstairs," she said. "Unless ... you prefer it here, as well. We could change places." She wished she felt more confident. Slowly, she reached out to touch the very obvious hard-on in his pants.

"Lucy." He moved out of her range. "It doesn't work like that."

She frowned at his crotch. "I'm pretty sure they all work the same way."

He snorted with laughter. "That's not what I meant. C'mon." He offered his hands, and she took them. Then he helped her stand.

Her legs were like noodles, and she crumpled.

Gray scooped her up. "You need to rest before the wake."

"But we're not finished. At least, you're not. Hey!" She glared at him. "Are you bossing me around?"

"Yes." He kissed her. Fully. Deeply. She tasted her own essence on the sweep of his tongue. "I plan to take you to bed. A lot."

"I suppose I shall just have to tolerate your animal lusts," she said primly.

"I appreciate you suffering through it," he responded. "Perhaps you could keep the screaming to a minimum?"

She smiled. "Not a chance."

Chapter 8

By the time Taylor got back to his office, he had little more than an hour to get ready for the wake. Word traveled fast in Nevermore, and he had no doubt everyone would be at the café to pay their last respects to sweet little Marcy, especially since no one had been invited to the actual funeral.

Cathleen was one of the most worthless human beings he'd ever had the displeasure of knowing. He couldn't believe Leland Munch had the stomach to date the woman, much less marry her. Half the town suspected Cathleen had somehow caused her husband's death, and Taylor did, too. Oh, not on purpose. He figured Leland died just to get away from her. He sighed. The world could be damned unfair. He unlocked the office and didn't bother turning on the lights. He knew the place well enough he could navigate it blind. He sat down heavily at his desk and turned on the lamp. The circle of light revealed the photos of the accident he and Ren had worked yesterday.

The Mustang had been a classic, a real beaut, or would've been without those flames painted on the hood. The car and its driver had been totaled, which was what happened when idiots drank too much whiskey and got into pissing contests with immovable objects—like the two-hundred-year-old oak tree that marked the fork in the road. Folks could continue right up Brujo Boulevard and to the Daisy Estates, which was really just a big ol' square of ten hundred-year-old houses, some fancy, others not, or go left up to Old Creek, which led to Harley and Ren's farm, the cemetery, and, at the end, the lake.

The driver was the Archers' youngest son, Lennie. Henry and his wife, Maureen, maintained a home in Daisy Estates. The Archers had five children; four had moved to other states. Lennie hadn't been the most motivated young man, choosing to leech off his parents in between drunken bar fights and losing jobs. Still, no parents should have to bury their child. And the Archers had been devastated . . . even if they hadn't been surprised.

Everyone would be attending another wake soon, and it was a damned shame.

Unlike most folks around Nevermore, the Archers had never been farmers. Once upon a time, Nevermore used to have Archer's Dry Goods and General Store. It had closed down decades ago because Henry's grandfather had a gambling problem, and he managed to throw away his family's fortune on the ponies. All the Archers had left was their family home and some investments that paid out enough for them to cover their bills.

April through October, every Saturday, there was a farmers' market in the town square. That was how everyone supported themselves and the local economy. Whatever couldn't be grown or bought in Nevermore was ordered online. Sometimes, folks got together and took a trip to Dallas, loading up on bulk items for anyone who put in a few dollars.

It was just the way things were, even though he wished they were different. Having a local store again would be nice. Maybe folks would come to town more often, and Nevermore would start to feel like a community again, rather than a refugee camp.

Taylor studied the pictures, but he couldn't put his finger on what was bothering him. The tires were brand-new, which struck him as odd. He didn't know why. Lennie took really good care of that car, treating it better than he did his own mother. No, something else niggled at him. He didn't like the timing of the two deaths. No doubt that Lennie's stupidity had finally killed him. But so soon after Marcy's murder? Probably wouldn't mean much, but he'd still check with Thomson about the tires. Like most other families in Nevermore, the Thomsons could trace their roots all the way back to the founders. There had been a Thomson in charge of the local garage since the days of horses and carriages—from blacksmiths to mechanics and all in the same location.

Poor Lennie. Nevermore didn't have a doctor, not anymore, much less a coroner. They had a mage healer—Miss Natalie, but she was getting on in years and had no kin or apprentices. It was rare she came to town anymore. Most folks who needed her services went to her house in Daisy Estates, or they waited to talk about their complaints during Dr. Green's monthly visits. Next door was the old clinic, which still had working cold storage and a surgery. Dr. Green rotated among the smaller towns, and he couldn't come back to do the death certificate for Lennie right away. The doc had been surprised to be called so soon after doing Marcy's autopsy, and promised he'd try to return in the next day or two. So, Lennie was tucked into the clinic's freezer.

And Marcy was in the ground in a plain pine coffin.

His head started to throb, and his eyes hurt. He pushed the photos along with the report into a crisp, new folder. He put it on top of Marcy's file and aligned them both with his desk planner.

Then he pulled the red bag out of his front pocket.

He was annoyed that Gray had withheld evidence from him.

"I found it on the ground that night. I'm sorry, Taylor. I forgot about it. It must've fallen out of my jeans when I took off my clothes to shower."

He knew Gray wasn't quite telling him the truth, but he wasn't sure which part was the fib. He also wanted to know why the hell the Guardian would intentionally interfere with an ongoing murder investigation. Not even Gray was that damned arrogant.

"She died for whatever's in here," said Gray. *"I figure this is the reason she was leaving Nevermore."*

Then Gray had told him about finding Marcy in the alley crying in the rain. She'd had a black eye and split lip, and she'd run away rather than take the help Gray had offered. She must've been scared as hell—and who could terrify her more than the Guardian? Gray had been like an absentee father around Nevermore, and everyone knew it. Hardly anyone relied on him to do more than what was required to keep the Dragon protections. It was a sad fact, one he hoped Gray would rectify. Nevermore needed its Guardian. All the same, he was a powerful wizard, and everyone knew that, too.

"She told me Lucy was in trouble, that everyone was. What the hell is going on?"

Taylor didn't know. All he had were bad feelings making mincemeat out of his guts, two people dead inside a week, and a mysterious bag that obviously didn't belong to Marcy. And he hadn't asked Lucinda a single question because he'd been too busy marrying her off to Gray—and then getting hustled out the door.

He opened the bag and dumped the contents.

It was an eyeball.

At least, it looked like one. It was oval shaped, made from smooth, clear glass, or maybe a crystal of some kind. In the center was a red circle, and within that, a black dot.

He didn't like holding it. Or even looking at it. He knew the thing was magical, because it made his fingers tingle. That bad feeling worming around inside him turned into a nest of rattlesnakes.

How had Marcy gotten hold of something like this?

And why had she taken it?

He'd show it to Ember. At this point, he should deputize the woman and be done with it. For now, he'd lock it in the floor safe. Gray himself had added the protections to the metal box inlaid beneath his desk. Only the sheriff could access the safe. Until he had a better idea what it was—and what it did—the eye was better off being locked up.

He stuck it back in the bag. It took less than a minute to secure the object within the safe, and if his back twinged and his knees creaked as he got up from spinning the dial . . . that didn't mean he was getting old, did it? He was only thirty-five, but some days, he felt ninety-five.

Taylor promised Gray that he would finish the marital paperwork tonight. Gray sure was eager to close up every loophole. Even though all newlyweds required a certificate to legalize their union, marriage for magicals worked a little different. When magicals declared their vows, their powers wove together. It worked almost like a spell except it was automatic. Some scientists thought it was a primal response, an ancient code that activated to strengthen the bond between mates and increase their breeding potential. Yep. It was always about perpetuating the species. They could get divorced just like anyone else, but it was called "absolution," and unbinding oneself from another magical took the help of other wizards and witches. It was only magicals marrying each other that sparked the response, too. A mere century ago, there were still laws that made marriage between magicals and mundanes illegal, even though it was widely known that magic-bonding didn't occur with mundanes. It didn't mean people didn't get married in secret or buck the traditions of their societies. That was the human race for you, always seeking to bridge the gap . . . and then burning down the bridge.

It still stunned him that he had married Gray to Kerren's younger sister. Kerren was Kahl's go-to girl for getting his dirty work done, and word was, she relished every depraved act. It wasn't like people hadn't tried to stop her, but being half demon had made her immortal. Attempts to kill her never worked and the few times she'd been captured, she'd escaped.

Taylor wished he knew the whole story between Lucinda and Gray, but he doubted he was gonna get it anytime soon. He imagined when Gray's mama found out what her son had done, they'd be able to hear the explosion all the way from Washington, D.C. He wasn't sure what he might have done in the same situation. He had no doubt that Lucinda was in trouble, 'cause, hell, she was a Rackmore, but there was something else, too.

Damn, he was getting tired of puzzles.

He heaved himself up from the desk. If he laid his head down like he wanted to, he'd probably sleep the whole night. Criminy. He really was getting old.

He needed to rifle through Arlene's desk for the marriage certificate, because she kept the originals. She was just as organized and anal as he was, and he didn't mind if she wanted to rule over all those headache-inducing forms.

Yawning, he walked from his office to the small lobby with its black-and-white checkered floor, and flipped on the light. He stared at Arlene's desk.

It was a mess.

Paperwork overflowed her in-box. Files were left open. A half-filled mug sat on the corner.

Arlene's purse was under the desk, where she liked to keep it in case she had to get at her gun. He didn't like it, but she wouldn't give up her .45. He made her get certified with the weapon, and had gotten her a concealed permit.

She would never leave that monstrosity. The woman kept a rolling pin in it, for Goddess' sake.

But someone had shut off the lights and locked up.

He unholstered his Colt. His office was the largest room in the building, unless you counted the jail cells on the basement level, and the single magic-dampening room used for either short imprisonment or magical quarantine. He hardly ever had to use them, though. Behind Arlene's desk was the hallway that led to Ren's smaller office, the break room, the supply closet, and the archives.

The bathrooms were at the very end, right next to the emergency exit.

What had happened to Arlene? His heart was thudding in his chest as fear ghosted through him. His training kicked and he began checking the building. He couldn't help but think about Arlene unconscious or . . . No. She was too stubborn to die.

Ren's office was empty, and the break room clear. In each room, he flipped on the lights. No intruder. No Arlene. He knew the supply closet was too full to hide anyone, but he checked it anyway. Nothing but a tower of toilet paper, shelves full of cleaning supplies, and seven more brooms than they needed.

As he moved toward the back door, he noticed the chair butted underneath the old iron doorknob to the women's restroom. Relief trickled through him.

He knocked. "Arlene?"

No response. Had she hit her head? Or had someone taped her mouth and tied her up? He moved the chair out of the way and reached for the knob.

The door swung back.

Arlene stood there, her clothes wrinkled, her face puffy with sleep. Only she could take a nap while waiting for rescue. "About time you got here. I've been locked in here for hours!"

He was so relieved she was alive and ornery he swept her into his embrace and squeezed the breath out of her.

"C'mon, now," she huffed as she squeezed him back. "I'm all right."

"What happened?"

He hustled her into the break room, and made her sit down. Then he got Arlene a cold bottle of water from the fridge and started rustling her up a sandwich.

"It was almost four o'clock, and I decided I wanted some jasmine tea. Made myself a cup, but it tasted funny. Hoo-boy, I got sick. Barely made it to the toilet before I almost barfed up my lungs." She looked at her watch. "Nearly seven o'clock. Goddess! I haven't gotten locked in a bathroom since Little Jimmy put superglue in the keyhole. He was eleven."

She sounded proud. Arlene had always appreciated the cleverness of her children, even if it was to her own detriment. Little Jimmy grew up to join the military. He was in some special ops unit doing missions that he couldn't talk about, but no matter where he ended up in the world, he called his mama every Sunday night.

"Who the hell would lock you in the bathroom?" asked Taylor.

"Kid's prank more than likely." She didn't exactly sound convinced, and neither was Taylor. He couldn't think of a single kid stupid enough to come in his office and do something like that to Arlene. If it was a prank and he found out who the moron was, that person would be cleaning up every piece of trash off Cedar Road for the next month.

"Anyone come in before four?"

"Ren. He dropped off those photos on your desk, checked his e-mails, and left. I fielded some phone calls about Marcy's wake. Folks weren't happy Cathleen didn't invite no one to the funeral."

"I don't think there was one," grumbled Taylor. "Bet she just put her in the ground without any prayers at all."

"Humph." She frowned. "Trent came by, too. Atwood sent him over to file a complaint about Cathleen's illegal disposal of her garbage." She waved her hand. "Ant stopped by to talk about my new rose garden. That was much earlier, though."

"You hired him to do a rose garden?"

"Sure did. That boy has a real talent. And I've always wanted a rose garden."

Taylor resisted the urge to roll his eyes. His brother's obsession with gardening was the least of his worries. Taylor knew about the café's overflowing Dumpsters, because Gray had told him. And he knew Cathleen had pissed off Atwood by refusing to pay the service fees. "What'd she do with the garbage?"

"He doesn't know. He says she got rid it of somehow and it wasn't his boys who'd done it."

"You got a form for that?" He put the plated ham sandwich in front of Arlene and she dug in with gusto.

"Of course I do. Gave it to Trent and told him Atwood would have to file a formal complaint in person. He runs that nephew of his ragged 'cause he's too lazy to do his own work." She eyed him. "All right. What happened?"

"Gray married Lucinda Rackmore." Taylor blew out a breath. "Goddess help me, *I* married them."

Her eyes went wide and she nearly spit out the bite she'd just taken. She managed to get it swallowed, but not without a few gulps of water. "I never thought Gray would marry again—and to a Rackmore! I'm surprised you agreed to it."

"Like I had a choice." He rolled his shoulders trying to work out the knots. "She's in trouble. And cursed something fierce. I guess he figures being her husband is the best way to protect her." He paused, thinking about the way the Guardian and his new wife had looked at each other. *Business transaction, my ass.* "How long do you think it takes for people to fall in love?"

"A minute and a half," said Arlene. "You think Gray's in love with Lucinda?"

"Even if he was, he'd deny it six ways to Sunday. Eh. What do I know?"

"That is a question, all right," said Arlene with a smile. She dusted bread crumbs off her shirt. "I better go check in with Jimmy. He's in Dallas helping Allan with that hot rod of his. I swear men never grow up."

"We never do," agreed Taylor, grinning. That explained why Jimmy hadn't called worried about Arlene. He wasn't around to know she hadn't gotten home on time. And knowing him and his son's love for cars, they were probably arms deep in an engine block.

Taylor watched her pick up the plate and head toward the sink. He stood and plucked it out of her hands. "Don't you worry about cleaning up. It'll keep."

"I'll do it all tomorrow. I don't have time to go home and get myself presentable for the wake," she said. "I'll just have to see what I can do with myself here."

"You're beautiful," said Taylor. He leaned down and kissed her cheek. "I'm glad you're okay."

Arlene actually blushed. Then she slapped him on the

chest. "Get out of my way, sweet-talker. I'll meet you in the lobby."

Taylor did another sweep of the offices, even took a look around the empty cells in the basement, but he didn't discern a single thing that looked wrong or out of place. Maybe it really had been a prank. Or maybe whatever the intruder wanted wasn't here.

Just one more puzzle for him to figure out.

Arlene took only a few minutes to fix herself up. Then she retrieved the marriage certificate and Taylor filled it out and signed his name. All the form needed now were the signatures of the bride and groom.

"C'mon," said Arlene, wrapping her arm around his, "let's go say good-bye to Marcy."

The first thing Gray noticed when he and Lucy walked into the Piney Woods Café was the huge donation jar on the counter. Folks around here didn't have a lot of money, but they took care of their own, so the jar was already half full of change and dollar bills. Cathleen could have asked for help in a million other ways, but no, she expected Marcy's friends to part with their hard-earned cash. Not a cent being put into that container would be devoted to Marcy.

"What a coldhearted bitch," said Lucy.

Gray looked down at her and saw fury in her eyes. She glared up at him. "Can she do that? Trade on her stepdaughter's death to make money?"

"I won't let her."

His promise seemed to mollify her. Unable to resist, he put his arm around her thin shoulders and held her close. The sheriff hadn't yet released her duffel from his custody, so they'd ended up washing her soiled clothes. He could tell she wasn't comfortable wearing a shirt, jeans, and tennis shoes to the wake. It was obvious, too, that her clothes were old and threadbare. She told him that she'd left Bernard without a thing except what she was wearing—which had been silk pajamas and cashmere socks. Then she'd admitted that she procured food and clothing through charities. If she couldn't find a shelter serving a meal, then she usually went without. Even when she managed to get some cash, thanks to being a Rackmore, she never kept it for long—certainly never long enough to spend it.

His heart broke for her, but he knew she wouldn't appreciate his pity. He'd gone upstairs to put clean sheets on his bed. He had every intention of sleeping in it with Lucy. The bedroom itself would take hours to set in order. It needed a good scrubbing. Instead of resting in the guest room like she was supposed to, he found Lucy in the kitchen doing the dishes. And she had already started lists for cleaning supplies, missing utensils, and gardening equipment. She said she was his wife, and she would keep her part of their bargain and her vows.

Obviously, she had a whole different set of expectations than he had. He'd been thinking with his dick first, blinded by those berry lips and dewy flesh. Beyond sex, and protecting her from Franco, he hadn't much thought about how they'd live together. He hadn't considered how she'd fit in his home—or within what had been a solitary, and selfish, lifestyle. He hadn't had a chance to adjust to the idea of Lucy invading his space, much less jumping into the role of wife with such . . . enthusiasm.

Well, more like bared-teeth determination.

He decided he'd sort out how he felt later. Right now, he just wanted to pay his respects to Marcy and get Lucy home. She was pushing herself too hard, and he didn't like it. He'd made her leave the kitchen, but she told him in no uncertain terms she would get the dishes done before bedtime. Ha. That was what she thought. If she even *looked* toward the kitchen, he'd put a sleep spell on her.

He guided Lucy deeper into the café. People were clustered in small groups, talking in low voices. On the counter, Cathleen had arranged saltines and glasses of water. Then there were the offerings of the attendees. Pies. Pasta salads. Casseroles. Food for a woman who didn't care at all that her stepdaughter had been beaten to death.

"I should've realized," murmured Lucy. She looked at him, and he was surprised to see the shame in her gaze. "We should've brought something. Isn't that what people do? I remember you said no one made a good funeral casserole better than Nevermore women."

"You remembered that I said that? When did I . . . ?" He lifted his eyebrows. "At the reception after my . . . the other . . . um, wedding. We talked for a while. Outside on the terrace."

"I guess that conversation kinda imprinted." Color rose in her cheeks.

Goddess, she was lovely.

"This is my failure, Lucy. I'm the Guardian."

"And I'm the Guardian's wife," she whispered.

"Which you've been for less than two hours. Give yourself a break." He pulled her in closer and tipped up her chin. Her eyes looked too big for her face, and she was so pale. Like moonlight. "You nearly gave your life for hers. That's better than a gods-be-damned casserole."

He'd spoken too loudly, and the room went quiet.

People glanced at them, expressions varying—from puzzled to suspicious. Gray met those curious glances, daring a soul to say a word against him or Lucy. Soon enough the conversations restarted. It seemed, too, that people made an effort to give him and Lucy space.

Bridging the gap between himself and the citizens of Nevermore was going to take a lot of work, especially now that he'd married a Rackmore witch.

"Gray." Taylor joined them. He took a moment to shake Gray's hand and then he bussed Lucy's cheek. Gray knew it was a public show of support, and he appreciated it. He kept screwing up—and damn it, he felt like he was trapped in quicksand. How was he ever gonna make things right for the town? He kept sinking under the weight of his idiocy.

"Oh, you!" Arlene busted through their tight circle and gave Gray a hug that nearly bruised his kidneys. Then she turned toward Lucy. "Aren't you sweet? I could eat you up with a double scoop of ice cream, I could." She hugged Lucy with just as much gusto. Then she leaned back. "I'm Arlene. You need anything at all, honey, you just call me."

"I . . . um, okay. Thank you?" Lucy sounded confused and looked dazed. Being around Arlene could do that to a person. She was energetic and bighearted—a human whirlwind that came at you with soft arms and warm words.

"Well, then. I gotta keep making the rounds." She gave Lucy another hug and then smacked Gray on the arm. "I better see you more often round here. We miss you."

"Yes, ma'am."

Lucy leaned into him, and he held her close. Every so often, he felt a shiver go through her. Was it the aftereffects of the curse? Or just nerves about being in the café's negative space? Or maybe she wasn't looking forward to seeing Cathleen. Goddess knew he wasn't. He kept his wife close, and she seemed content to remain next to him, her arm around his waist, as she studied the people around them.

Gray took in the mourners, too. He'd known these people his whole life, and yet they were all strangers to him now. He didn't see Ember and her husband, Rilton, but he didn't blame them for skipping. No doubt Cathleen had made it clear they weren't invited.

He knew just about everyone. There was Harley, who'd been friends with Gray's parents. At least he had been once. After his wife committed suicide, he stopped coming around. He still ran the same small farm up near Old Creek. Taylor had asked Gray to give Ren the part-time deputy position a few months ago, even though the boy was only nineteen. Well, twenty now. A friend of Ant's, if he recalled correctly. Still, Gray had done so without question because he'd trusted Taylor. And yeah, he didn't want to be bothered with thinking about anyone other than himself and his own pain.

His gaze landed on Henry and Maureen Archer, who'd managed to come pay their respects even though they'd just lost their son. Taylor had told Gray how the kid had wrapped his Mustang around the oak tree. Damned shame.

His gaze snagged on Trent. He hadn't known him at all, not until the boy had stood up to Cathleen. He was talking to Ren intently, and Gray wondered what their conversation entailed.

"What's the deal with Trent?" he asked Taylor.

"Troubled, but mostly a good kid. Just turned seventeen. He's Atwood's nephew. You remember his younger sister Sandra?"

"Yeah. She moved to Oklahoma. Got married, right?"

"Fell in love with Tommy Whitefeather. He was Cherokee. Worked for the casino up in Durant."

"Oklahoma," Gray clarified for Lucy. "The casino's 'bout the only thing out there." ·

"Tommy made a good living. He was a decent guy," said Taylor. "Few months ago, Tommy and Sandra got T-boned by a drunk driver."

"Shit," said Gray. He grimaced. "Cathleen called Trent a half-breed." He nodded toward Ren. "How'd they get to be friends?"

"Don't know if they are," said Taylor. "You know how it is here, Gray. Everyone knows everyone."

"I don't see Cathleen," said Lucy.

"She's in the back," said Taylor casually. His gaze bounced around the room. "Probably figuring out how to make gruel because saltines and tap water isn't enough of an insult."

Gray snorted. "She's a blight on Nevermore."

"I was gonna go with 'wart on a gremlin's ass,' but your description has more class."

They looked at each other, and grinned.

Cathleen came through the swinging kitchen door. She stopped behind the long Formica counter, her gaze sweeping over the people like that of an executioner surveying death row inmates. Her concession to mourning was to don a black jogging suit and black Nikes.

The second her beady eyes alighted on them, her expression turned mean. She stomped around the counter and made a beeline, her arctic gaze zeroed in on Lucy.

"Don't make her explode," muttered Taylor. "It's messy, and I'll have to arrest you."

Gray could do worse than zap the woman with a fireball, or even a bolt of lightning. *Much worse.*

Cathleen arrived and planted herself right in front of Lucy, hands on her hips. Before she could even open her mouth, Lucy offered her hand and said, "I'm terribly sorry for your loss, Miss Munch. I didn't know Marcy well, but she seemed like a lovely girl."

Gray was amazed at the calm, sincere way Lucy

spoke to the crone. She held the woman's gaze, emanating nothing but sympathy.

Cathleen backed up a step from Lucy, looking at her as though she were plague-ridden. "Don't need the well-wishes of a Rackmore," she snarled. "Get out!"

People gasped, and others muttered darkly. Coming from a grieving stepmother, Cathleen's rudeness might've been overlooked, but her inhospitality . . . No, that was an unforgivable offense. Even the Rackmore witches deserved a chance to mourn.

Lucy dropped her hand. Her face had gone red with embarrassment, but when she looked up at Gray, she had that stubborn tilt to her chin—and a look about her as if she were a deposed queen who refused to give up her crown. "I'll meet you at the house," she said quietly.

"The hell," said Gray. He tucked Lucy next to him and glared down at Cathleen. "Apologize to my wife."

"Y-your . . . *wife*?" Cathleen went white. One chubby hand fluttered against her throat.

"I married them myself," said Taylor pleasantly. He pushed up the brim of his hat. "Go on, now, Miss Cathleen. Offer the Guardian and his lady your congratulations."

She reared back so violently, she bounced off a table, and thudded to the floor.

Gray shared a look of astonishment with Lucy, and then they looked down at the prostrate woman.

"Well," said Taylor. "Don't that beat all."

Ren and Trent stood a couple feet behind Cathleen, but only the deputy bothered to come to the woman's aid. Gray didn't want to touch the crazy woman, much less help her, and it seemed as though Taylor felt the same way. Ren's expression suggested he'd rather be shoveling manure than helping Cathleen Munch into a nearby booth.

"You need some water?" asked Ren. "Maybe a saltine?"

She wouldn't meet his gaze. In fact, she didn't look around at all. She seemed to have shrunk in and wrinkled, like a prune left out too long in the sun. "Just leave me alone," she said.

Ren stepped back, and Cathleen suddenly scooted out of the booth. She stood in the middle of the café, her eyes wild. She turned and pointed at Gray. "There's the demon! And the demon's bride." She spit at them, but the globs of saliva fell harmlessly to the floor. "The Calhouns killed my daddy! And now they got a Rackmore witch to do their dirty work. I hope you both burn in hell!"

Silence was so thick Gray felt like he could choke on it. He was stunned by Cathleen's breakdown—and the expressions of the townsfolk revealed the same shock. Cathleen trudged behind the counter and went into the kitchen. The oppressive atmosphere deepened. Gray felt like he was gonna suffocate, and no doubt everyone else felt the same.

He'd had enough of this farce.

"We'll miss Marcy," said Gray. "She was a good girl who deserved a much longer life. Sheriff Mooreland assures me everything is being done to find the person who killed her. I swear to you, as your Guardian, she will get justice. Thank you all for your donations. The sheriff will ensure the funds go toward a proper headstone for Marcy's grave."

People took the hint and headed toward the exit. A few stopped to offer their congratulations to Gray and Lucy, including Trent and Josie Gomez, but most folks shuffled by without a word. In no time at all, Gray, Lucy, Taylor, Arlene, and Ren were the only ones left.

Cathleen's weeping had quieted, but she seemed to

be pacing. Her shoes squeaked against the linoleum in a consistent, endless pattern.

"I'll stick around," said Ren. "Make sure everything gets locked up and she gets home okay."

"Thanks," said Taylor, clapping his deputy on the shoulder. "I appreciate it."

Taylor scooped up the donation jar. Gray took Lucy's hand and followed him and Arlene outside. It was a clear night, the moon bright and full. The air seemed clean, and so much lighter than what they'd been breathing in the café.

"Got your marriage certificate," said Arlene. "Just need your signatures. Then I'll make you a couple of notarized copies tomorrow." She dug inside her gargantuan purse and pulled out a folder and a pen. "Here. Let's use my car."

Like most folks in Nevermore, Arlene had a truck. Hers was a 1986 short-bed Toyota, just the right size for its hood to serve as a desk.

The moonlight was enough to illuminate the paper. Gray signed his name above "Name of Groom, Magical," and handed the pen to Lucy. She actually took the time to read the whole thing, and as it was a document created by magicals, its language was formal and in some places archaic.

She pointed to the sentence above where she was supposed to sign. "What does that mean?"

Arlene leaned in and read, "'I hereby relinquish the name of my father's lineage and take that of my husband's, which I will henceforth honor and use as my own.'" She snorted. "Well, so much for women's rights. I think the magicals need to update their paperwork."

"It's just a formality," said Gray. "And you don't have to take my name. Whatever you decide, our marriage will still be legal."

She nodded, and looked down at the certificate, still apparently unsure about which name she wanted to use. It reminded him how Kerren insisted she remain a Rackmore. She'd marked out that same sentence. He didn't blame Lucy for not taking his name—after all, one day their marriage would be dissolved and it would probably be better for her to keep "Rackmore" anyway.

She leaned down and scrawled her signature: *Lucinda Therese Calhoun*.

Gray tried to tell himself he wasn't pleased by her choice, but . . . well, he was. Yeah. It made him old-fashioned and maybe a chauvinist, as well. She picked up the paper, and then flinched. "Ouch."

"What?"

"Paper cut," she said. "Crud. I got blood on the certificate."

She showed it to him, and he watched the red smear fade into the paper. *What the—*

Both their signatures turned silver and one by one the letters lifted from the page. They swirled together in a dance of bright, merry magic. Then slowly returned to their original positions and faded to the black ink.

"What the hell kind of magic was that?" asked Gray.

"The marrying kind." Arlene gently took the certificate from Lucinda and placed it in her folder. "I have to get these babies directly from the Grand Court 'cause of the spellwork. Magical notaries do that stuff themselves, but don't you worry, even though I'm a mundane, my seal will work just the same. It's why I order the certificates special."

Gray frowned. "That didn't happen when I signed the certificate with Kerren."

"Well, maybe you had the wrong kind of paper," huffed Arlene. "You damned sure had the wrong kind of wife." She patted Lucy on the cheek. "This one's perfect. I suggest you keep her." She stuffed the file back in her purse and shooed everyone away from her truck. "I gotta get home. Y'all do, too. G'night!"

They all backed away from the truck.

Taylor tipped his hat. "I'm tuckered out. I'll see you tomorrow." He patted the jar he still held. "I'll make sure this all goes to Marcy's headstone."

"Get her the best," said Gray. "I'll pay whatever's left."

Taylor nodded. "Good night."

Gray and Lucy said their good-nights, and then Gray took his wife's hand. They had walked to town because Lucy insisted she wanted the exercise. It wasn't that far, but he still regretted not bringing her down in Grit's truck.

"I feel so strange," she said.

"How do you mean?"

"I don't know. Like I was tied down and someone cut me free from the ropes." She smiled up at him. "I feel like I'm floating."

"Sounds like a good feeling."

"It is," she said. She stopped, and he did, too. She stepped into his embrace and stood up on her tippy-toes to brush a kiss across his mouth. Her small hands drifted down his chest, fluttering along the edge of his pants.

His balls tightened.

"I don't feel like doing the dishes after all," she said.

"Oh?" he asked. He brushed her hair back and let his fingers drift down the side of her neck. "What do you feel like doing?"

"You."

He scooped Lucy into his arms and hurried up the hill toward the house.

Chapter 9

Anticipation buzzed through Lucinda as Gray carried her all the way up the stairs and into his bedroom. Ever since she'd signed the certificate, she'd felt an odd sort of freedom. Maybe it was only that she knew she was safe—that Bernard couldn't touch her again. Not ever. Oh, he might try, but it wouldn't matter. Not now. And if she had to live with her curse for all her days, then so be it.

Gray put her down onto the freshly made bed and then rolled in beside her. He gathered her close, and her heart started to pound. He was so gorgeous. She traced the line of his jaw and dragged her forefinger across his lower lip.

"What now?" she asked.

His breath skirted her lips as he leaned down and took her mouth. It was a tender assault—but one that made her ache. Made her want more. His hand slipped through her hair and cupped the back of her head. He deepened the kiss, thrusting his tongue inside to mate with hers.

Heat flared. Oh, yes. There was the lust that Gray inspired so well. Need was an ache that he both encouraged and fulfilled. She had never felt this way before, and she reveled in her first true tastes of passion.

His lips moved down her throat, lingering at the base.

His tongue dipped into the concave between her collar-bone, followed by the soft brush of his lips.

His hands slid under her shirt, and she shifted so that he could reach the back strap of her bra. He easily un-snapped it.

"Sit up."

She did as he asked, nerves plucking her stomach, her skin tingling, her body aching for his touch. Everywhere. She wanted to feel him everywhere.

He took off her shirt, her bra. Then she lay back on the pillow and let him. His stroking fingers made her want to purr. Oh, how she loved his touch.

"What happened?" he asked. His fingers danced along her scars—and there were so many. He'd made her forget that she was flawed. That Bernard had dam-aged her.

Shame filled her. She tried to sit up, to push away his hands, but he pressed a kiss to her belly, and she stilled.

"You're beautiful, Lucy." He looked up at her. "We all have scars. Some you can see. Some you can't."

She reached down and put her fingers on the scar that twirled down his temple. "I don't see your scars," she said softly. "I just see you."

"Let me love you."

Her breath caught at his words, and for an aching sec-ond, she wanted to know that Gray really did love her. How wonderful it would be if their marriage was real, and she was truly his bride. The woman who held his heart.

But that could never be.

Instead, she gave herself over to his tender minis-trations. He kissed each and every scar, and with every bestowal of affection wiped away her shame. Though Bernard's marks remained on her flesh, the memories of his cruelty faded. Bernard's final hold on her crumbled away—shattered by the man who worshipped her now.

There was only Gray.

Touching.

Kissing.

Loving.

He trailed a path to her breasts, raining tiny kisses over each of them, cupping them in his hands and squeezing lightly.

Then his mouth closed over one turgid nipple.

"Oh," she said. "Oh, Gray."

He paused and looked at her with a heavy-lidded gaze. "I love when you say my name."

"Gray," she offered. "Gray."

He kissed her, this time with rough possession, to show her that his control was snapping. She wanted him so much. She felt the same unleashing of her desire, hot and slick and wild.

"More," she said. "More."

She tangled her fingers in his hair. He gave her nipples torturous attention, suckling them so hard, the pain turned to pleasure.

Her heart pounded.

Her blood raced.

Her body burned.

His hand coasted down her stomach and wiggled beneath her jeans, her underwear. He infiltrated the nest of curls at the apex of her thighs. He lightly pinched her clit between his thumb and forefinger, released the tiny nub, and pinched again.

Lucinda moaned.

Not content with those small torments, Gray slipped two fingers inside her and curled them up slightly.

He began to stroke.

Pleasure spiked. Raw electricity, flaring bright and hot.

"How are you doing that?" she panted. She arched,

trembling. Her eyes rolled back in her head as sensations built in intensity. She lost the ability to breathe, to think. He made her feel so good. And however he'd managed to find such a sensitive spot within her ... oh, she was glad.

He was looking at her, his eyes dark with passion as he penetrated her. "Yes, baby. Like that."

Lucinda grabbed his shirt and twisted the fabric. Her heart pounded and pounded—waves against the shore, stars crashing to earth. She moved her hips in rhythm with his strokes. She couldn't look away from those blue eyes, the sky on fire, the sea raging.

"Come for me," he whispered.

"You," she managed. She shuddered, sucking in air. "Not without you."

"We have all night," he promised. "This is for you."

He leaned down and laved one taut peak ... then lightly bit.

Lucinda felt the world shatter all around her. She cried out, giving herself over to the rolling pleasure, riding wave after wave. She held on to Gray tightly as she fell endlessly into light and heat and beauty.

She collapsed against the bed, thoroughly sated.

But Gray wasn't finished with her. *All night,* he'd said. She managed to open her eyes. "Again?" she asked.

"Damn straight." He yanked off her jeans and underwear, and then dragged off his own clothes. She caught a flash of his gold dragon tattoo on his pectoral, and the scar that covered his right shoulder.

"Lucy," he said as he moved on top of her. "You are beautiful."

"You make me feel as if I am," she said. "That's enough."

He parted her thighs, and she knew it cost him to be gentle. Maybe later they could take each other like ravenous beasts—tearing and clawing and screaming. But now, she wanted this slow conquering.

With one hand, he captured her wrists and raised her arms above her head. With the other hand, he steadied himself over her. His cock filled her, his motions steady, and tender. Oh, so tender.

"I'm not going to last," he said. "It's been too long for me. And you . . . I can't resist you."

"We have all night, remember?" She scored his buttocks with her nails. "More, Gray. Give me more!"

He pounded into her, his strokes deep and sure. Still he held her wrists, his thumb pressing against her erratic pulse. She bucked against him, her clit throbbing as pleasure built swiftly once more. He was panting, trying to hold on, but she didn't want him to. He'd given her enough. . . . Now she wanted to give to him.

"Come inside me," she begged.

His eyes flew open and he stared down at her. He sucked in air between his teeth. Sweat dripped off his brow. "Lucy," he murmured. "Lucinda."

His face went tight and he stilled, groaning as he buried his cock deeply. She wrapped her legs around his waist and clung to him as he spilled his seed within her.

Her body was awash in need, desire. A buzzing climbed her spine, then zipped down again—sensation after sensation vibrated from her core.

Gray let go of her wrists and held himself up. "You're close again, aren't you?"

She nodded. "I can't seem to help myself."

He grinned as he sat up and knelt between her legs. "Touch yourself."

"What? Where?"

"Hold your breasts. Play with your nipples."

Even though they were both naked and sweaty, and all kinds of messy, Lucinda felt her face go hot. She'd never touched herself intimately like that . . . not with someone looking at her with such anticipation. Gray wanted to watch her, and the idea that he wanted to . . . unexpectedly turned her on.

Everything about Gray turned her on.

She was beginning to realize what a terrible and self-ish lover Bernard had been.

"I'm not frigid," she said.

Anger flashed in his eyes. "Did Bernard tell you that?"

"I never had an orgasm with him. He told me it was because I'm . . . broken."

"You are not broken," he said evenly. "Touch your-self, Lucy. Let me take you over the edge."

Tentatively, she cupped her breasts and squeezed.

Gray groaned. "I'm getting hard again already."

"You like it."

"Hell, yeah."

She grasped her own nipples and experimentally pinched them. Twin bolts of lightning arrowed straight to her core. She looked at Gray, dazed. "That feels good."

"Keep doing it, baby."

He leaned down between her thighs and suckled her clit. Little fireworks started going off right then.

Lucinda rolled her nipples between her fingers, tugging on them, while Gray alternately sucked her clit and rapidly flicked the swollen nub with his tongue.

Pleasure exploded, and she screamed Gray's name as she fell into the glorious fire once more.

He crept out the back door of the sheriff's office and shut it quietly. The lock snicked in place—and he smiled. No one would ever know he'd been creeping around inside after office hours.

He'd set up a spell trap on the sidewalk in front of

Gray's house. If anyone left the house carrying the eye, he would know who. It had galled him to buy the trap from an online vendor when he should've been able to make his own. Even with the amplification of the objects and constant practice, he could barely tap into the energies. *Soon,* he promised himself, *very soon.*

Still. Nothing pleased him more than to see it in the sheriff's possession.

It was just past one a.m. The alley was a through and through, and even though it was the long way, he didn't want to walk past Ember's. She was too damned smart, and far too sensitive to the shifts in the balance. He couldn't chance her looking out a window, or even stepping outside. She wasn't predictable, and that made him uneasy. It wasn't that he couldn't control the situation. He was in *complete* control. No, it was only that he was careful.

Always.

So, he went left and took a stroll. He patted the front pocket of his pants, reassured.

The eye was his again.

It was worth the risk he'd taken earlier in the day—dosing Arlene's tea and locking her in the bathroom. He liked the old gal, and he didn't want to hurt her, not unless he had to.

Again, he'd purchased the magic he'd needed to turn off the safe's spellwork. The slow-degrade add-on had been expensive, but he'd needed the protections to fade over twelve hours so that no alarms, or Mooreland's uncanny senses, were triggered.

He grinned. Getting into the sheriff's office to retrieve his possession had been a cakewalk. He'd placed a marble into the bag and left it. Oh, the oversized glass orb wouldn't fool the sheriff if he opened it, but if he just checked the safe, he'd have no reason to believe the eye wasn't in its bag. There was no way to replace Gray's protections, either, but hopefully Mooreland wouldn't notice. If he did, he'd probably just ask the Guardian to reinstate the protections, and that would be that.

He had no idea how long it might be before the sheriff realized the object was gone. A day. A week. It didn't really matter. He'd covered his trail. No one would be able to follow.

It was time to start his work again.

Thirteen days until the new moon. The portal would be frail again, and this time, he would call forth Kahl and make the bargain. Gray Calhoun in exchange for his magical birthright.

He would have the power he deserved. What good was knowing all that he did about magic and yet not having the fullness of it to work with? All the objects he'd spent years gathering, unlocking, coaxing into his possession. All the time and effort he'd used up learning about things he could never do.

But soon . . . soon he would come into his powers. And then he could right the wrongs of his past. An injustice had been done, and he would make sure the debt owed was paid.

The alley spilled onto Silver Lane, which connected to Main Street and, farther down, Dragon's Way. On his right was the town square. In the middle of the paved circle lined with its moldering benches and overgrown bushes was the full-sized bronze statue of a dragon, its wings extended as it stood on its hind legs, snout pointed toward the sky.

On the other side of the circle, several yards beyond the statue, was the Temple of Light, which was locked up most of the year. Gray opened it only for his grandstanding. He remembered how the place used to be open year-round, available to anyone who wanted to go inside and commune with the Goddess. The temple had gotten vandalized several times, and Grit finally shut its doors. Faith was a tricky thing: hard to gain, easy to lose. No one had faith in Gray—especially now that he'd married a Rackmore.

He frowned. Then he turned away from the town square and headed toward Dragon's Way.

He hadn't expected the marriage. Not that he was particularly worried. He'd done his research and learned how Franco had cursed his mistress's thaumaturgy. The witch was weak. Hardly a threat at all—not even as the wife of Nevermore's Guardian. No, he didn't need to worry about them. And he always had his ace: Franco. One call to the Raven and he'd give the newlyweds all kinds of headaches.

Might come in handy if things didn't work out with Kahl. Oh, he had no doubt he could call the demon lord forth. He knew the spells, had the right kind of objects, the necessary tributes. But having a backup plan was never a bad thing. Franco had contacts. He could open doors into all sorts of places. It wasn't the same as having the gratitude of a demon, but it was close.

Even so ... it might not be a bad idea to give the sheriff and the Guardian something else to worry about. Mooreland was too smart for his own good. And relentless as hell. There wasn't much crime in Nevermore, so the sheriff had plenty of time to devote to Marcy's murder. Of course, her murderer was already dead, so in a way, Mooreland owed him for taking out the trash. Then again, the damned fool hadn't seemed satisfied about Lennie's death. His intuition was too finely tuned. The sheriff was the kind of man that followed hunches, no matter how strange.

Yes. He definitely needed to send them scurrying off

in another direction. Keep 'em busy so they didn't have time to think about Marcy or Lennie.

His footsteps clicked against the brick street as he went down Dragon's Way. A block later, he turned right onto Brujo Boulevard, passed the dark and empty Archer's Dry Goods and General Store, and entered the alley between it and the Piney Woods Café. Five years ago, he'd financed Cathleen's new brick wall, which cut off access from the Sew 'n' Sew and the building that housed Atwood's offices and apartment. Not only did the fat ass run the town's waste-removal services; he also put out *Nevermore News* every month. Like the world needed to know about another calf birth or the plight of the school's FHA program.

Sometimes, he felt suffocated by the smallness of Nevermore. It was disgusting how satisfied some people were with so much nothing.

The alley was too narrow to fit a car, so no one really cared about the addition, except Atwood, of course. He'd complained about it interfering with pedestrian convenience, but since the café owned the land, Atwood couldn't do much about it. *Old windbag.* Whatever. He'd needed to discourage folks from taking shortcuts and noticing things that they shouldn't.

Soon, he wouldn't have to hide anymore. Everyone in Nevermore would be grateful for what he'd done. They would be happy he was the Guardian. And they would be amazed by all his magic.

He entered the café using his own key. He knew the place well enough that he didn't need lights to maneuver around the tables and chairs. In no time at all, he was behind the counter and in the kitchen.

He thought about the way Cathleen had acted at the wake. He knew she hated the Calhouns—almost as much as he did. Her reaction to Gray marrying Lucinda was unexpected. Why did she care? Eh. The cover of the café was too good to give up. Cathleen's vitriolic personality and revenge-mindedness suited him just fine, especially since no one would believe he'd have anything to do with her. He needed to control her better, that was all.

After he opened the door to the basement, he flicked on his penlight and walked down the rickety wooden stairs. He pulled out the key to unlock the entrance to his special place.

He turned on the lamp on the worktable. He carefully replaced the eye in the empty middle space, the honored gem among all his treasures. "You're home," he said.

It glowed.

He pulled up a barstool and sat, looking at all the magic. Placed in a certain order, with the right spells in the right location, the items would work together to unlock the planes between earth and the underworld. It wouldn't last very long, but it would be strong enough to summon Kahl.

Then he'd take his revenge on those who'd denied him his true birthright. And his power—oh, he'd take that, too.

My magic, he thought as he touched the objects one by one, *mine.*

Gray awoke in a cavern. His heart nearly heaved out his chest as he recognized the lair of Kahl, the very place where Kerren had stabbed him in the heart and offered his soul to her new master.

It took him a moment to realize he wasn't chained to the slab. No. He was standing next to it, dressed in a black robe, the same as Kerren had been that terrible night. In his hand, he held a silver dagger.

"Sacrifice her."

The darkly sensuous male voice echoed through the cavern. Gray looked down at the slab and saw Lucy bound there. She was naked—her wrists and ankles clasped in enchanted irons. His heart thudded dully. No. He didn't want to be here. Not ever again. "It's okay," he told her. "It's okay."

Her wide green eyes stared at him, filled with betrayal and hatred.

"You know how it works," said the voice. "Remember? It's your turn now. You have the power."

Fear chilled his blood. The knife felt cold in his hand, like he was gripping a shard of ice. "No!" He spun around, looking for the owner of the voice. "I won't."

"You are bound to me, servant. You took something that was mine to regain your life. Now you must pay your debt."

"I owe you nothing!"

"She would kill *you*," he offered slyly. "Has she not the same foul blood as her sister? Would she not do anything to save her own life? What a fool you are, Gray Calhoun, to give your heart to another Rackmore witch."

Doubt flickered. Gray looked down at Lucy, at the tears that tracked her cheeks and dripped onto the bloodstained stone. Her chin cocked in that stubborn tilt of hers, her gaze determined. She wouldn't ask him for mercy, he realized. She would take the knife to her chest rather than beg for her life.

Not like him. He had begged Kerren. He'd even wept. She'd killed him anyway.

"Sacrifice her!" demanded the voice. "Take your revenge, Dragon. Become what you must to serve me!"

"No!" He dropped the dagger and clawed at Lucy's chains, but he didn't have the strength or the magic to free her.

"You bastard," she whispered. "Now you've killed us both."

Pain exploded in his shoulder. He felt stringers of heat crisscross his flesh, crawling up his neck to throb at his temple. He tore off the robe and looked down at his shoulder. It glowed with magic.

The scar caused by Kerren's treachery pulsed with light, with pain.

His skin started to flake away.

Horror swelled like poisoned flowers, blooming in his gut, exploding in his head. *No. Not this.*

Red scales glittered.

His secret revealed; his fear unleashed.

He screamed.

Lucy's heart slammed against her chest as she watched Gray struggle with his nightmare. She'd tried to shake him awake, but he was too far gone. Being a dream walker made him more vulnerable to his subconscious travels.

He shouted, "No!" and tossed off the covers.

His scar was glowing. She felt the pulsing magic, and the strange heat emanating from his twisted flesh. Fear slithered through her. Sweat slicked his naked body as he writhed and moaned. He was in such pain. What was happening to him?

She had to wake him up, and she could think of only one thing to do.

Lucy crawled on top of him and slapped him as hard she could.

He roared and his eyes flew open. Even though he was staring straight at her, she knew he was seeing something else. He tossed her off and rolled on top of her. He held her down by the arms, fury etched on his features. "I will never hurt her," he cried. "I do not serve you!"

"Gray!" she yelled. She didn't struggle, but it took effort. She was terrified. "It's me, Lucy. Gray! Wake up!"

He stilled, and his eyes cleared. He was breathing hard, his body quaking as he shook off the vestiges of whatever vision held him hostage.

He blinked down at her. "Lucy?"

"It's okay," she said. He had her pinned, so she couldn't move. She very much wanted to stroke away the lines of worry creasing his brow. "You're all right, Gray."

"Goddess!" He readjusted his weight and let go of her arms. "Did I hurt you?"

She touched his face and leaned up to kiss his chin. "You could never hurt me."

He blanched. He shifted as though he might move off her, but she grabbed his shoulders. "Stay," she murmured. "I'm cold."

"You want to use me for a blanket?"

"Do you mind?"

He closed his eyes briefly. He moved down just enough to keep his weight from crushing her completely, then laid his head down on her chest. She stroked his hair.

"Do you want to talk about it?" she asked.

"No," he said. Then he sighed. "Sometimes I dream about the night Kerren killed me."

"I'm sorry," she said. "I'm so sorry. I wish I could make it better for you."

He lifted his head and looked up at her. "You do, don't you? All that you've been through and you still seek to help others. To help me when I turned you away."

"Temporary insanity," she offered. "Understandable when you were faced with the sister of the woman who sent you to hell."

"I don't want to think of you like that. You're Lucy. My beautiful wife."

Her pulse leaped. "Don't forget talented, sexy, and flexible."

His lips cocked into a sexy grin that sent frissons of awareness through her. "All those things, too. Though I may need a demonstration to prove your flexibility."

"You know," she said as he rose above her, "you are a very useful blanket."

He kissed her lazily, building the passion between them slowly. She stroked the corded muscles of his belly, fingertips gliding down to his cock, which hardened even more under her tentative touches. He was velvety smooth, and warm. She gripped him and squeezed.

He groaned. "You're killing me, baby."

"I'm unmerciful, too," she said. "I live to torture." She squeezed him again.

He slid an arm underneath her. She gave a startled yelp as he flipped over, reversing their positions easily. She found herself on top of her very aroused husband, and suddenly in control of their lovemaking.

"Go on," he said. "Torment away."

Uncertain about this new game, Lucinda looked him over while she decided what to do next. Bernard had never let her on top—he would've never let anyone take a power position in bed.

Yet Gray offered himself to her without reservation. He was a patient man, and he was kind. Rough, too, and blunt, but very much a man she liked.

She tapped her bottom lip and tilted her head. "Hmmm. What first?"

Gray's eyes glittered, and his fully erect penis pressed intimately against her wet heat.

He flexed his cock, and it hit her right in the sweet spot.

"Hey!" She sucked in a breath. "No tormenting the tormentor."

He grinned.

She leaned down and peppered his chest with kisses. Her fingers skimmed the ropes of muscle, tracing his rib cage, scoring his hips.

He moaned, and feminine satisfaction curled through her. More confident now, she flicked her nails against his flat brown nipples, and then she suckled each tiny nub. He shuddered.

Her body ached for his. She lifted herself above him, and positioned herself so that she could rub against his cock. She moved in long, slow strokes, tormenting them both. Gray's eyes were dark with lust, and she was quivering.

How long could she last against her own need?

Against his?

Leaning forward, she offered her breasts for him to feast on, and he did, cupping and kneading them, pinching the turgid peaks.

She gasped.

And so, he did it again.

His gaze never left hers. He skimmed the undersides of her breasts, teasing her areolas with light touches. Then he suckled one nipple, letting go to blow softly on the crinkled flesh. He did the same to her other nipple. All the while, those blue, blue eyes dared her to go further, to do more.

But she was done with torture.

"Help me," she said, panting. "I want you inside me."

She got onto her knees, moving back, and hovered over his cock. He held on to his shaft while she pushed down, taking every inch of him. He filled her up completely. For a moment, she could do nothing else but sit there, hands flexing against his stomach, and try to remember how to breathe.

She was, at first, tentative. Gray merely watched her, his hands fisted in the covers, as she tried out different ways to move.

She sat straight, bouncing, while clutching his stomach to stay upright.

Then she stopped, deciding to lean forward and place her hands on either side of his rib cage. She slid up and down. Gray seemed to enjoy it, but she wanted to find the optimum position to pleasure them both.

She stopped again, and Gray groaned. "Seriously. You're killing me."

"Well, I promise you'll die happy. Now hush. I'm thinking."

"Can you think *and* move?"

"No." She grinned at him. "I have an idea."

"I love ideas," he said.

"You sit up, I wrap my legs around your waist, and we . . . you know. Together." She frowned. "Do you think that would work?"

"Yes," he said fervently, "yes, I do."

"You'll have to really put your back in it," she warned.

"I'll do more than that," he promised.

He sat up while still embedded inside her, which she found a rather impressive move. Her body trembled with Gray-inspired need, and she knew he felt the same urgency. Anticipation went only so far.

He sat in a cross-legged position, and she wrapped her legs around his waist and pressed close against him. Her distended nipples rubbed against his chest, sending little lightning bolts of pleasure zapping through her.

"Ready?" he asked.

"Yes," she said, licking her lips. "Oh, yes."

They both started to move together. Eventually they found a rhythm that left her breathless. There were no more words, no more teasing. She clung to him, eyes closed, awash in the pleasure of their connection. He held her tightly as he thrust, his lips pressed against her shoulder.

"I can't hold on," he whispered. "Come for me, Lucy."

She shattered.

She cried out, her nails digging into his back as the orgasm rocked her to the core.

Gray groaned, impaling her as he came, his body shuddering. His hands gripped her back as he filled her up, his teeth scraping her collarbone.

For a long moment, they held each other.

Lucy reveled in how wonderful it felt to be with Gray. This was how it was supposed to be between lovers. But it was more than just great sex. It was that connection she'd never had, not with anyone. One day she would have to leave. Not just because he didn't want a permanent marriage—but because she could love him. Goddess above. She could love Gray and stay his wife forever, and be happy.

How was she going to walk away?

Chapter 10

"Where've you been?" asked Taylor, watching Ant tramp into the house, dragging dirt in his wake.

Taylor sat on the stairs drinking his second cup of coffee. He didn't like being in the kitchen, and the formal living room with its big, antique furniture and oversized hearth made him feel too lord-of-the-manor-ish. It was Saturday, and he didn't want to go to work—even though he would. He went into the office every day.

What else was there to do?

Ant eyed him. "You still here?"

"You're looking at me, aren't you?"

His brother was a couple inches over six feet, just a hair shorter than Taylor. He supposed the kid would be considered handsome even though he was covered in dirt and what all ninety-nine percent of the time. Ant didn't actually date much. The pickings around Nevermore were kinda slim. Either the girls wanted to get married, or they wanted to leave. Very few of Nevermore's children stayed. There weren't a lot of opportunities for jobs, much less careers. Not to mention how family farms were dying out one by one.

Ant was almost twenty now.

Criminy. His baby brother was a grown man. Taylor felt old all over again. He sipped his coffee and watched Ant stamp the mud off his boots. His brother was good about cleaning up after himself, so he didn't worry too much about the mess he was making.

"Didn't see you at the wake."

"That's 'cause I wasn't there. I went to Marcy's grave site this morning and planted geraniums. You know she doesn't even have a headstone? I asked Mordi about it. Said Cathleen didn't get her one."

"The town's buying it," said Taylor. "I'll drop by the cemetery today and make the arrangements."

Mordecai Elizabeth Jones was the undertaker of Elysian Fields, Nevermore's only cemetery. Every first child in the Jones family was named Mordecai, boy or girl, because that was the tradition—as was training that first child to take over the family business. A Jones had been in charge of Elysian Fields since the day Nevermore became a town. Mordi liked her job, a little too much, if you asked Taylor. She graduated high school a year early and went to Houston to go to funeral college. After she'd gotten her two-year degree in mortuary science, she'd returned to take over the business. Her parents retired, bought an RV, and were currently roaming the United States visiting famous grave sites. Mordi was their only child, and she was the youngest undertaker in the history of Elysian Fields. She was always hanging out at the cemetery. She said dead folks were more reasonable than the living. This, from a girl who wasn't a magical. But it didn't seem to stop her from talking to the dead folks.

She was kinda weird.

Then again, it was hardly her fault she'd been born and raised in a cemetery. She was about Ant's age, a couple months older, but neither one seemed too interested in each other.

"What's going on in that brain of yours?" asked Ant. "I don't like it when you look at me like that."

"Like what?"

Ant took off his hat and slapped his thigh with it. His curly brown hair was too long. He needed a haircut. And he needed to stop messing around with those plants of his and go get a decent life somewhere.

"Like you think I should be married with kids or taking over a corporation or something. I like it here. I like what I do. And I do make a living with my gardening."

"I know."

"Sometimes it's better if the world's not so big," said Ant. "There still coffee?"

"Yep."

Ant went into the kitchen and poured himself a cup. Unlike Taylor, he didn't mind being in the kitchen. Taylor couldn't understand why it was so easy for Ant to be at peace with their mother's death. Or maybe he wasn't. They didn't exactly talk about it.

Ant returned to the foyer. "Any word about Lennie's funeral?"

"The doc's coming in on Monday to do the death certificate," said Taylor. "Then I can release his body to the Archers. You talk to Lennie much?"

"Not really," said Ant. He plopped down a couple stairs below where Taylor sat. "There were what? Twenty-two of us in the senior class? Mordi would've been, too, if she hadn't done accelerated studies." He blew on the hot coffee. "You got any idea who hurt Marcy?"

"Not a damned clue," said Taylor.

"Gotta be someone in town."

Taylor grimaced. He didn't like thinking about who might have motive to kill Marcy. Not a person came to mind, other than Cathleen. Had the old bat paid someone to do it? As despicable as she was, she needed Marcy, not only to be her slave waitress, but to pick on.

Making other people miserable made Cathleen happy. And she was too selfish to oust the person she had any control over. Marcy was the only waitress at the café because nobody else would work there.

Who else would have a reason to kill the girl? He thought about the magical item locked away in his safe, the one that Marcy had been trying to smuggle out of town. Was that the reason she'd died? Or did it have something to do with Lucinda Rackmore? Shit. Calhoun. She was Lucinda Calhoun now. He needed to question her. Damn it! Gray couldn't shield his wife forever.

"Not many magicals left around here." He stared down into his empty mug. "Just us mundanes."

"So?"

He shook his head. "Just seems important is all. I don't know why. Not yet."

"You'll figure it out," said Ant. "You always do."

"Maybe." He put down his mug. "You know Trent?"

"Atwood's nephew? Yeah. I see him every now and again. He's okay, I guess."

"He ever hang out with Lennie?"

Ant shrugged. "You know how it is around here, Taylor. People can't be too picky about their friendships. We don't have a lot to choose from. I've seen him at Dragon's Keep on the weekends. Lennie spent a lot of time there, but hell, so does everyone else. You know, he used to date Marcy."

"So did Ren, as I recall, back in high school."

"I did, too, for all of a minute. She was nice," said Ant. "She deserved better."

"She damned sure did." He sighed. "Don't suppose Bran's serving alcohol to minors?"

"You mean does Trent have a beer?" Ant laughed. "C'mon, Taylor. Bran serves everyone."

"Doesn't mean that it's right. The drinking age in Nevermore is eighteen."

"And you waited till then?"

Taylor looked away, trying to hide his smile. He'd been sixteen, an arrogant kid with too much swagger and not enough sense. He'd gone straight for tequila. Ended the night puking his guts up in the bathroom and passing out on Bran's couch in the back room. Bran shook him awake the next day and made him drink a god-awful concoction that wiped away the hangover. Bran was a magical—a powerful aquamancer, one who had not claimed a House. He'd built his home and his business on an old river barge. Dragon's Keep was anchored off the shore of Lake Huginn.

Bran never seemed to age, either. He looked like a strong, fit, silver-haired fifty-year-old. He always had, and Taylor suspected he always would. He couldn't prove it, and the old man had never admitted it, but Taylor believed Bran was immortal. Magicals usually lived longer, perpetuated by the energies they could so easily tap into, but most weren't immortal. In fact, very few were.

"Truck coming." Ant nodded to the windows that flanked the front door. "Looks like Ren's."

Taylor carried his coffee out to the porch and waited for Ren to arrive. To his surprise, Trent was with him. The boy was obviously off work today because he was head-to-toe goth—from kohl rimming his eyes to the black shirt with safety pins around its collar.

Ren rolled down the window. "Figured you'd be at the office already."

"Nope. What is it?"

"Gremlins." He slanted his gaze toward Trent. "At-wood's place is crawling with them."

"Does nobody remember how to use a phone?" asked Taylor. "The whole town has landlines set up."

"I tried calling here before I left the office," said Ren. "Got a busy signal."

Trent leaned out the opened passenger's-side window. "My unc's pissing himself. Ran to Ember's screaming like a little girl."

"Ember go down to his office and work some juju?"

Trent shook his head. "She said—and I quote—'Oh, no, chil'. I don't mess wit da gremlins.'"

Taylor snorted a laugh. "All right. I'll meet you at Atwood's. And somebody call Gray. We'll need his magic to seal up the crack that let those little bastards in."

"Gremlins," said Lucinda. She lounged in bed, feeling almost boneless. She'd have to get up, though. She had wifely duties to perform. "Really?"

"Yeah. I was hoping something like this wouldn't happen. The town's so out of alignment, it's a wonder we haven't gotten 'em before." Gray hunted through his dresser. He'd taken a shower, so his hair was still damp, and he pulled on a pair of faded jeans. The bedroom, like every other room in the house, was a terrible mess. How he'd found the jeans was a mystery to her.

"Ha!" Triumphant, he drew out a blue shirt and put it on. He turned toward her, grinning.

Her heart tripped and she felt something soft and bright wrap around her. He made her feel safe. And strong. And . . . loved.

"Hey, what's wrong?" He strode toward the bed and sat down, putting a hand on her thigh. "You feeling okay?"

"More than okay," she said. Not love, she thought desperately. Just great sex. Great sex and safety felt like . . . well, she didn't really know, now, did she? Her gratitude mixed in with everything else was just making her feel good. Gray didn't want the L word anywhere near their relationship.

She'd be damned if she would ruin her marriage by falling in love with her own husband.

"I was thinking that I could get the house in order. At least, I could start somewhere. The living room, maybe."

He frowned, and disappointment crowded out all those good feelings swirling through her. He didn't want her touching his stuff. She was a fake wife, and they both knew it. All that talk about sharing responsibilities, and he didn't mean it. This wasn't truly her home. What had she been thinking?

"I don't want you to tire yourself out." He cupped her face and rubbed his thumb along her jaw. "Don't move anything too heavy. If you want to rearrange furniture, wait until I get home."

She stared at him. "You don't mind?"

"Why would I mind? This is your home, Lucinda. And you have the right to live in beauty and comfort. I'm sorry everything is a mess. I'll help you as soon as I get back, okay?"

"Okay." She turned her face and kissed his palm. Then she peeked at him. "I can really rearrange the furniture?"

"If you like."

"Oh, Gray!" She sprang out of the covers and wrapped her arms around him. "Thank you."

He hugged her, and then he pulled back just a little. "I don't know why you're so excited about cleaning up that crap. I feel rotten that you're gonna have to wade through it all. It's not fair."

"I want to contribute," said Lucinda. "I don't have much to give you."

"That's not true. You think too little of yourself, baby." He kissed her. "I have to meet Taylor. After I seal the underworld crack the gremlins escaped from, I'm going to reinforce the town's protections. It'll take about three days, though. I'll have to go around the perimeter to perform the magic."

"You're not coming home?"

"It'll be better to camp out and get it all done at once, so the spells stay strong." He kissed her forehead. "I'll call you every night. I'm not abandoning you."

Lucinda felt that inner glow again—warm, soft, safe. "No," she teased. "You've just figured out a way to not help me clean."

"You got me." He looked down at her naked flesh, and sighed. "Now get under the covers. You're distracting."

"It's too bad you're in such a hurry." She fell back against the covers and stretched, giving Gray a full view of her body. His gaze latched on to her breasts. "I guess I'll see you in . . . three days, you said?"

"Taylor can wait."

Then he dove on top of her.

Gray kissed her good-bye at the door. After she shut the door behind him, she leaned against it, and smiled. What a normal thing to do: kiss her husband as he went off to work.

She laughed, her heart full.

Safety felt wonderful.

And so did being Gray's wife.

She was determined to do him proud. She attacked the living room first. She hated that she still felt so weak. She had to take breaks far too often, but even so, she managed to get through the entire mess. By the afternoon, she had gone through every box, half of which were empty, thrown away obvious trash, and created two piles. One was for those items she thought would be good for charitable donations, and the other for items that seemed important or that she wasn't sure about. She put everything into labeled boxes, aligned them against the stairwell wall, and began cleaning in earnest.

Two hours later, the mahogany coffee table and Burmese sideboard were polished to a high shine, the two red silk camelback settees were vacuumed—as was the Persian rug—and she'd uncovered the fireplace. Oh, that was a travesty. The mantel was the same mahogany as the table, and littered with framed photos, dragon statues, and melted candles. Ash overflowed onto the brick hearth, and soot stained the edges.

She'd found two Victorian spoon-back chairs in decent shape, and she thought they'd look nice facing the fireplace with the Chinese cloisonné pedestal table between them.

Still, she'd promised Gray to wait on furniture rearrangement, even though she very much wanted to surprise him with at least one finished room.

She missed him.

Lucinda dropped onto one of the settees, and sighed. It was stupid to feel the way that she did. She needed to remember that gratitude was not the same thing as romantic love. Gray was being dutiful, and nothing more.

Her gaze traveled over the room. She still had so much more to do. The windows needed cleaning, the curtains needed burning, and the cobwebs dangling from the corners needed removal. The wood floor required a good refinish—not to mention the walls. The white chair rail could do with a little TLC, but the floral wallpaper had yellowed too much for saving. So, new wallpaper was needed—or better yet, a paint job. Hmm. A soft beige with small red horizontal stripes.

It's not your house.

Lucinda snapped out of her daydreaming. Cleaning as a contribution to their mutual living space was one thing—trying to make her mark on Gray's family home was another. There would be no repainting, or updating, or anything. She couldn't fall into the trap of caring about Gray, about his home. Not when they would be hers for only a little while. She couldn't begin to hope that he would want to keep her around after she got free of Bernard.

Knock, knock, knock.

Lucinda's gaze snapped to the front door and she jolted to her feet, heart hammering. She checked the mantel clock—it seemed to be keeping appropriate time despite its long-term abandonment. It was just past four o'clock.

She was a mess. Her hair was pulled into a ponytail and her clothes were stained with dirt and cleaning solutions. She wasn't even wearing shoes.

Knock, knock, knock.

Just because she didn't look like a hostess didn't mean she couldn't act like one. She ran her hands over her T-shirt and jeans, squared her shoulders, and answered the door.

The woman standing on the porch looked vaguely familiar. Lucinda realized she'd seen her at the wake, but she didn't remember her name.

"Hello," said Lucinda.

"Glad it's you," said the woman. "I'm Maureen Archer." She handed Lucinda a plastic-wrapped pie. "Welcome to Nevermore, Mrs. Calhoun."

Lucinda took the pie, and stared at it. Emotions crowded out her ability to speak. The silence dragged on so long, Maureen cleared her throat.

"Oh, I'm sorry. I didn't expect . . ." Lucinda smiled at her, touched by the woman's sincere gesture of welcome. "It's such a kind thing to do. Thank you."

Maureen nodded, and then looked away. Lucinda noticed the sheen of tears in her eyes, and realized the woman had come to the Guardian's home for more than welcoming his new bride.

"Please come in," said Lucinda as she stepped back from the doorway. "I apologize for the mess. I'm afraid I couldn't wait to start removing the stamp of bachelor living."

Lucinda led her to the living room and watched as Maureen took in the boxes, cobwebs, and crowded mantel. "Haven't been in here in years. Grit and Dove used to have such wonderful parties."

"Dove?"

"His wife. She passed away when Gray was, oh, about five years old. Grit never remarried."

"I'm afraid I don't know that much about the family. Please excuse me for just a moment." Lucinda put the pie in the kitchen, and realized she didn't know where the tea or coffee was kept—or even if Gray had any. Ember's tea was still on the stove, and there were clean mugs from her first attempt at washing dishes. She poured tea into the mugs and nuked them in the microwave, and then brought them to the living room.

Maureen was standing near the fireplace studying the pictures. She turned as Lucinda entered the room, her expression a mixture of confusion and pain.

"Nevermore used to be a happier place," said Maureen. She pointed to a framed photo. "That was taken more than twenty years ago at the winter festival. Back then, we'd dress up the town square, and after services, we'd eat and dance until the wee hours."

"It sounds wonderful."

"Oh, it was. Me and Henry are in this photo. And there's Gray's mama. And Sarah and Edward Mooreland, before he left town with . . . well, with another woman." She smiled softly. "Lara and Harley. A May-December romance. When she committed suicide, it broke him. Only thing he had to live for was his son. Ren," she clarified. She waved her hand around. "It's a small place. Won't take you too long at all to get to know everyone."

They settled on one of the couches and Lucinda pressed a mug of tea into Maureen's hands. She sipped on it, and nodded. "Ember's, right? She makes the best cuppa."

"I like her," said Lucinda.

"I do, too," said Maureen. "She's good people." She looked around some more, clutching the mug, and Lucinda figured that she was trying to work up the courage to spill whatever she'd come to say.

Finally, she put the mug onto the coffee table, obviously too unsettled to enjoy it. She met Lucinda's gaze. "Is it true you're a thaumaturge?"

"Yes. And no," said Lucinda. "I am. Untrained. But . . . I'm unable to use that ability." She hated the idea of ruining the beginnings of a potential friendship, but she refused to live in lies. "I was cursed. And there's no way out of it."

"You tried anyway, though."

"With Marcy," admitted Lucinda. "But I was too late."

"Doing something is better than doing nothing. Marcy was a troubled soul. My Lennie was troubled, too. And so selfish. Him and that car of his." She dashed away tears, then clasped her hands together. "But he was my son. I loved him."

Lucinda put down her mug and reached over to take Maureen's hands. "I'm so sorry for your loss."

"I loved him," she repeated, "but there's this . . . Oh, Goddess, this *relief* that he's gone." Her gaze was haunted. "It's horrible for a mother to feel that way, isn't it?"

"No. You feel what you feel. Relationships are complicated, especially those between mothers and their children."

Maureen nodded, but Lucinda knew the woman was devastated by feeling any sort of relief, no matter how minuscule, at the death of her son. Lucinda couldn't help but wonder what kind of child Lennie was that his own mother would feel that way for even a second.

"We raised five children. Four went out into the world and created good lives. And Lennie . . . he could just never get the hang of it. He wore me and Henry down. He drank and did drugs and got into fights. He stopped respecting everyone, even himself." Maureen gripped Lucinda's hands. "I think everyone's worth saving, don't you?"

Lucinda's throat clogged. She nodded because she couldn't get the words over that damned knot.

"Everyone's worth saving," said Maureen again fiercely, "but not everyone can be saved." She sucked in a breath, her eyes filling with tears. "I couldn't save my son. And I knew you'd understand. 'Cause of Marcy."

"I do," she offered softly. She had understood that kind of anguish even before Marcy. "I understand."

Maureen's lips trembled, and then she fell into Lucinda's arms and wept.

Gray collapsed into the leather wingback across from Taylor's desk. "I hate gremlins."

"We're lucky you sealed the crack before any more of 'em escaped." Taylor leaned back in his chair and tipped up his hat. "How'd the portal open?"

Gray frowned. "I don't know. The town's off magical kilter. My fault. I haven't been paying attention."

Taylor said nothing, and Gray was grateful his friend passed on the I-told-you-so moment. He deserved the lecture and more, but he was determined to honor his

Guardian role now. Nevermore would get its sparkle back—he'd make sure of it.

"I'm going to do a cleansing ritual," said Gray. "The whole town and then the farms. But first, I'm going to reinforce the magical protections around the perimeter."

"You afraid Bernard Franco will come after Lucinda?"

"She seems to think so."

"I hate gremlins." Ren strode into the office and dropped into the other leather wingback. "Little bastards. You think we got 'em all?"

"I hope so," said Gray. "After I regenerate the town's protection spells, and do a cleansing, it should keep them out. We really have to shift the alignment, get everything back into balance, or we're gonna have more problems."

"Sounds good," said Ren. "When are you starting?"

"Well, I planned to head out right after we dealt with the gremlins, but hell, it's after eight already. I'm tired, and I really just want to—" He broke off, stunned. He wanted to go home to Lucy. He felt like a part of him was missing because she wasn't around. It wasn't just the sex, either. Although he had to admit, the sex was spectacular. It was more . . . her smile, her voice, how she touched his hair or snuggled into his arms. He liked the way she made him feel. And he liked the way he could make her feel.

"You want to what?" asked Taylor.

Gray stood up. "I want to go home to my wife." He grinned sheepishly. "I'll start the spellwork tomorrow."

Taylor shook his head. "Already whipped. It's such a shame. You should probably turn in your man-club card."

"Jealous bastards like you aren't on the man-club committee."

Ren chuckled. "Gray, you going alone tomorrow?"

"Yeah. Why?"

Ren shrugged. "I think one of us should go with you, is all."

"He's right," said Taylor. "We know Marcy's killer probably wanted the eye, but we don't know why, and we don't know what else he or she wants. I'm coming with you. Ren can hold the fort for three days."

"Yep," said Ren. "Dad doesn't need me at the farm much anyway. He's hired a couple of local kids to help with chores. It would suit me to stay in town."

"All right," said Gray. He looked at Taylor and grinned. "I'll see you at five a.m. We should start the first spell at dawn—I'm thinking the lake area first."

"Fine. See you at five a.m. Your place," said Taylor. "But you have to make the coffee."

"Deal."

Gray said his good-nights and headed outside. He'd taken the truck into town, so it took him only a couple of minutes to get home. Right away he figured out something was different.

For one thing, several vehicles were parked on the street in front of his house. For another, the porch light was on, blazing like a welcome sign. Not only had the porch been swept, but two whitewashed rocking chairs occupied the space near the picture window. The living room lights were on, too, shining merrily through lacy white curtains.

As he reached for the front door, he heard female laughter.

A lot of it.

He entered the house, and stopped.

Everything sparkled, and it smelled like lemons and lavender. The wood floors shone, as did the railing and the stairs. He looked to his left and found himself staring at a hall tree. He didn't even know he had one of those.

Jackets were lined up on the pegs, too, and purses had been piled on the top of the storage bench.

He couldn't begin to fathom the amount of estrogen currently flitting around his house—and Goddess help him, they were *cleaning*.

Panic began to well.

More laughter and noise—happy, cooking-type noise—filtered from the kitchen, which was straight ahead. He veered left into the living room.

Just as he thought—the curtains were new, and the walls scrubbed, the mantel polished, the fireplace transformed. The furniture had been moved: Two couches faced the coffee table, which had a stack of marble coasters and a couple of oversized hardcovers angled at one end. Near the hearth, a small, colorful table stood between two fancy chairs. The bookshelves on either side of the fireplace gleamed, their books straightened, and the knickknacks posed. Huh. He had a lot of dragons.

"Gray!"

He turned around and saw Lucy standing in the entryway staring at him. Her gaze lit up and she ran to him, leaping into his arms. Gray caught her and swung her around. Her happiness zinged through him like a lightning bolt.

He laughed, holding her tight as she tried to squeeze the life out of him.

"You're home!" She kissed him. "I didn't think you were coming back tonight."

Gray's heart clutched. All that happiness glowing from her was for him. "I missed you."

Her eyes went wide. "You did?"

"Can't a man miss his wife?"

"Yes," she said. "I'm pretty sure it's a rule."

"If it's not, I'll make it one." He kissed her again. He loved the feel of her lips caressing his, and the way she felt wrapped around him. How had that kind of joy managed to infiltrate his rusty, cobwebbed heart again? No, not again. These feelings were different from those he'd once had for Kerren. He'd felt prideful about his new wife, as though her beauty and charm somehow amplified his own importance. "You've been busy."

"Isn't it wonderful?" she asked. "I promise I didn't move the furniture."

"Good. And yes, it's amazing." Dirt smudged her face and she smelled like pine, but she was the most beautiful creature. He felt like he'd captured a fairy, and if he wasn't careful, she'd fly away.

"Maureen dropped by," she said, "and then she activated a calling tree—I'm still not sure what that means. But then all these women showed up!" She laughed, and her joy wound through Gray. "Those two rooms are still a mess upstairs, but the library . . . oh, Gray, why didn't you tell me you had soul books?"

"You met Grit and Dutch?"

"Yes. They're adorable."

"Not the adjective I would use," muttered Gray.

"Oh, stop." She playfully slapped his shoulder. "They were very happy when we cleaned the library. I found book stands for them both." She paused. "They said you had a lab out in the backyard—in that big shed?"

"Yes," he said. "You didn't—"

"No way. A wizard's spell-working sanctuary is his alone."

"Yep. And it sure doesn't need all those girl cooties."

"Why, you—"

He swung her around again. She clung to him tightly, her laughter twining with his.

Ember stepped back from the doorway. Love had found a way between those two broken souls, and that was a joyful thing. She only hoped that they both got strength from their new bond to face what was coming—and though she didn't know what the challenge was, she did know it would arrive soon.

Show me the path, Creator Mother, she prayed, *and give me the strength to walk it.*

He hadn't meant to kill her.

Shit.

He dragged the body into the kitchen and positioned it near the stoves. Think. He had to think. He moved to the other side of the preparation station and paced.

If only she hadn't attacked him . . .

It was Cathleen's fault he'd squeezed the life from her blubbery neck. She'd wanted revenge on the Calhouns in the worst way, a hatred seeded by her mother, who blamed Grit for the death of her husband.

He'd been curious enough to cull through the public records at the library. He found the report easily enough. Jed Little liked his whiskey more than his self-respect. He had a long arrest record filled with public drunkenness and domestic violence, and he'd been cited numerous times for harassing Dove Calhoun. These days, it was called stalking.

The night before Jed got snockered and walked his fool self into the lake, he'd tried to kidnap Dove, and gotten walloped by Grit. Then the Guardian had banned him—and given him twenty-four hours to leave town. Cora filed a report claiming that the Guardian had be-spelled her husband into killing himself. On paper, Jed didn't seem the type of person willing to give up his own life so that his wife and daughter could have theirs. It could well be that Grit had gotten rid of his wife's attacker.

He stared down at Cathleen's porcine body, and felt

his gorge rise. He turned away, leaning against the stove, and sucked in a breath. It wasn't like he hated the Calhouns. He'd grown up with Grit as the Guardian and he'd done a better job than his grandson ever could. Gray didn't deserve his position—it wasn't fair he had a birthright, one he could claim proudly, without fear of reprisals. *I was a secret.* Fury burned through him. It was fitting that Gray would pay the blood price so he could have his, out in the open, right and proper.

"She wanted them to suffer, the way Daddy suffered. I promised her. Right before she died, that I'd see our justice done." She'd gotten so agitated that he'd poured her some more whiskey. She downed three shots in quick succession.

Cathleen giggled. "You think the Dark One's satisfied with ruling over death? He's been trying since the beginning of time to get hisself a piece of this world."

A being as powerful as the Dark One wasn't remotely interested in a place like Nevermore. That was when he realized Cathleen had gone all the way crazy. Her mother had spent a lifetime filling her head with lies, and she couldn't figure out the truth from her ass. All those years of living in a place that had destroyed her family, being the kind of person no one liked, giving in to greed and desperation every single day—it had all finally unraveled her.

He wanted magic and Nevermore, but maybe his dreams were too small. Living in this place had made him feel that way his whole life. Five years ago, when he learned the truth about his heritage, he'd felt minuscule. Like nothing.

He sure as hell didn't want to end up like Cathleen Munch.

"They ain't getting a happy ending. No, no, no! You kill him, y'hear? We're owed! My family is owed!" She'd thrown the whiskey bottle. It crashed against the wall and broke, the amber liquid dripping down the wall and puddling on the floor.

"It's not time to kill Gray," he'd said.

That was when she lost it completely, screeching while she tried to gouge out his eyes. She kicked at him and spit on him, all the while ranting incoherently. Damn it! He'd just wanted her to shut up. She'd rattled him with that nonsense about the Dark One. Everyone knew that the Creator Mother and the Destroyer Father could only influence their children. Not rule them. Basic magical law: *Every living thing is created out of the same fabric woven by dark and by light, and are one with the All in All.* The Dark One invading the mortal realm would be like a human trying to switch around his arms and legs—pointless.

"Stupid bitch." He returned to the body, anger coiling in his guts. Cathleen was just as ugly in death as she had been in life. Her chubby body stuffed into those pink sweats—ugh. She looked liked a badly made sausage.

Nausea rose again, and he turned, walking out of the kitchen. He leaned against the Formica counter, his head in his hands.

Eleven days until the new moon.

Gray planned to start the protections tomorrow. With the borders reinforced, it would be a lot harder, if not impossible, to open the portal for Kahl.

He just had to figure out a way to delay the Guardian.

The acrid smell of the whiskey made his barely contained nausea swish around his stomach. Then an idea began to form. He straightened and turned toward the mess of glass and liquid.

Perfect.

Chapter 11

It was just past midnight when the ladies gathered their supplies and readied to leave.

Lucy stood next to Gray in the foyer wishing everyone farewell. She was exhausted and happy, and so grateful to all the kindhearted women who'd come to help her.

Maureen explained that it was the way of Nevermore to reach out to someone in need—didn't matter how small or large the cause. Lucy was humbled by their willingness to offer assistance, especially when they received nothing in return. Her name had been added to the calling tree. The next time the women of Nevermore needed one another, she would be there, too, giving what she could.

She hugged Maureen, and doing so started a whole hugging fest. Ember was next, then Josie Gomez, Arlene, and Ronna Thomson, who was the wife of the town mechanic, Joseph Thomson, and her daughter, Alice, and then there the Wilson twins, whose organizational skills were almost supernatural. They'd berated Gray about the state of his books, especially those in the library, and he'd taken the scolding good-naturedly.

She hoped Gray, who seemed so apart from the rest of the town, didn't resent the intrusion into his home.

After the last person said good-bye, Gray shut the

door. Lucy slid into his arms and rested her head against his chest. "They are so nice. I wish—"

Gray's hands stroked her back. She wondered if he was aware of how often he did those kinds of comforting gestures. She bet it was an automatic response—trying to soothe perceived distress. Or maybe he liked affection as much as she did.

"What do you wish, baby?"

She very much wanted to host a party—like the ones Dove and Grit used to have. It would be a thank-you to the women and to the community—maybe it would repair relations between the Guardian and the townspeople. Gray had been alone, his choice, yes, but there seemed to be so many who wanted to reach out to him. They could be a genuine part of the town, and not just the wizard and witch who lived above it.

"Lucy?"

"A party," she blurted. She pulled back a little so she could look into his eyes. "We could have food—and maybe some dancing. Oh, and the kids could come. And we could do games! Maybe give out silly prizes, or ..." She licked her lips. "It's too much, isn't it? I should've called and asked if they could come over. Are you upset?"

He frowned, and her heart skipped a beat. He *was* angry. "Why would I be upset? You don't have to second-guess yourself, Lucy."

Guilt wiggled through her. *He's not Bernard,* she scolded herself, *so quit acting as if he is.*

"I'm sorry." She sighed. "I still feel like I'm walking on shaky ground."

"Is that how he made you feel? Like the earth might give way any second?"

"Yes. That's exactly it."

"You're safe," said Gray, hugging her tightly. "I promise I won't let anything happen to you."

Lucinda wasn't sure he could keep that promise, but she knew he would try, and for now, that was enough. "And the party?"

"It's a great idea."

She looked up at him and grinned; he swooped down for another kiss. Instantly tenderness turned into seduction. She melted against him, her body electric with anticipation.

Someone pounded on the door.

They broke apart. Gray grimaced. "Damn it." Then he turned and opened the door.

Maureen stood on the other side, her face pale, her eyes wide. "There's a fire in town!"

The blaze was easily seen from their vantage point. And so were the people scrambling toward the burning building.

"It's the café," said Lucinda, horrified. "The gremlins?"

"We got them all, but fire isn't their style. They like picking things apart piece by piece." Gray turned to her and in his eyes she saw both guilt and determination. How could he blame himself for the blaze?

"Arlene already called Taylor," said Maureen, her voice shaking.

"Good," said Gray. He turned to Lucy. "Stay here, baby. I'll—"

"You'll what? Find someone else with aquamancy?"

He blinked down at her, as if he'd forgotten she could magic water. "We have Bran."

"Except he's not answering his phone," said Maureen. "Arlene's already on her way to Dragon's Keep to track him down."

"All right. Get your shoes," said Gray.

Lucinda took precious seconds to pull on her worn sneakers; then they bolted out the door and followed Maureen to her still-running car. Gray and Lucinda slid in the backseat, and Maureen threw the car into drive and slammed on the gas. She made downtown in two minutes flat, and parked by Ember's. They piled out, racing across the street.

The intense heat rolled over them. Smoke clogged Lucinda's lungs, and she coughed, backing away.

"Can't get the water main open," huffed Ren. He held a huge pipe wrench. His face and clothes were stained with soot. He'd obviously been roused from bed, given the state of his hair and the fact he was in a white T-shirt, pajama bottoms, and no shoes. He noticed her perusal of his clothing. "I was crashing at Trent's. He's the one who noticed the fire first."

"You get hold of Taylor?" asked Gray.

"He's on the way."

"I can open it," said Lucinda.

Ren's eyebrows winged upward. "No offense, Lucinda, but . . . you're a girl."

"I don't need muscles." She hurried to the plug. Fire hoses lay like dead snakes around it. The bolts were rusted shut, but the deep scratches on the faded paint showed Ren's valiant effort.

Lucinda touched the plug and opened herself to the magic that pulsed all around. She used it to reach for the water . . . through the pipes . . . into the ground . . . *there*! She grabbed the water and pulled it up with a quick, hard jerk.

The top exploded upward, spinning into the air before slamming into the sidewalk. Water blasted—a fierce, huge geyser. Lucinda aimed her hands at it, called upon the sacred energies, and commanded, "Douse."

The water rose up, higher and higher. It fanned out, so powerful, so majestic, the blood of the earth, and then *boom*! It slammed down onto the café like an angry god's fist.

The fire vanished.

The spray got everyone, and the street flooded, but folks didn't care. Cheers went up, and Lucinda found herself surrounded—and nearly hugged to death.

It was wonderful.

Just past midnight, Happy trudged down the muddied shoulder of Cedar Road. Lucy wasn't gonna be . . . well, happy to see her. She was breaking her promise, but it soooo wasn't her fault. Okay, running away from the nuns was her fault, but not the reason.

The vision had compelled her to leave safety and seek out Lucy. If she didn't reach her friend in time, both she and that hot guy with the scar would die. The weird thing? Happy wasn't a magical. But she knew the vision was real 'cause the Goddess told her so. She hadn't been much of a believer before. Still. When the Goddess appeared with a vision of the future and asked for a message to be delivered, you did it.

Happy felt guilty about ditching Sister Mary Frances. She was sure they were all frantic, but since they didn't know where Lucy was, something she'd insisted on so Bernard couldn't torture them into giving information, they wouldn't be able to get a message to Lucy.

Happy wanted so much to be with Lucy. She was the only person Happy trusted. The nuns were all right, even if they were weird, and wow, did they like rules. If Lucy wanted to send her back, she'd go, but not until she was sure Lucy was a hundred percent safe. She was on a mission sanctioned by the Goddess. Surely Lucy wouldn't be too mad about her showing up.

But then . . . she might.

She gnawed on her lower lip and thought about how Lucy might react. She hoped hugs were involved—at least before the shouting. She knew sometimes people who were afraid acted angry. Her mother had told her that, and so she'd said that Bernard must've been scared all the time.

Mama had laughed, and told her she was smart.

Happy passed a sign that said, NEVERMORE, 10 MILES, and sighed. Lucy was gonna kill her for hitching, and she'd done okay until that last trucker. *Nobody rides for free,* he'd said, grinning at her. He was fat and smelly and had hairy hands. Plus, hel-*lo*, his teeth needed an introduction to a toothbrush. Ew.

He didn't figure he'd find a switchblade against his nuts, though. Yeah, that surprised him all right. Luckily, he'd parked the eighteen-wheeler right near the Cedar Road exit when he'd decided to ask for his "payment." Jerk.

Ten miles wasn't so bad. She could make it.

She wasn't scared of the dark, but she would've welcomed the occasional streetlight. Her vision had adjusted, and she was sorta getting used to all the sounds of wind-rustled grass, cricket songs, and the occasional mooing.

She'd never seen a real cow before.

Her backpack felt heavier and heavier with every step. Finally, she decided to take a break. She plunked down on the side of the road and opened the side pocket. She pulled out the crystal. It pulsed with magic, which was activated only by Happy's touch. Anyone else who picked up the gem would have only something to pretty to look at, not a homing beacon. A green arrow pointed in the direction of Nevermore. Lucy had given her the gem so that Happy would know where she was. She'd promised that one day they could be together. Yeah. As soon as it was safe, which Happy figured would be about the same time Bernard died.

She returned the gem to its pocket and then she dug

through her pack for a bottle of water and the last box of raisins.

As she munched her snack, she saw the twin beams of headlights. The truck had obviously just come from the highway exit, and as it passed by, she saw that the bed was filled with trees and big bags of soil. Then she saw the brake lights. The truck made a slow U-turn, and then pulled up close to where she was sitting.

A young guy leaned over and looked at her from underneath a ragged cowboy hat. His eyes were as dark as chocolate and twinkled the way her mom's used to before she ... Happy swallowed the sudden, awful knot in her throat.

Her stomach started to hurt, and she closed up the box and tossed it back into her pack.

"Need a ride?"

"Sure." Happy stood up and hitched the backpack over her shoulder. "But I can't give you any money. And I won't give you any pussy."

His eyes went wide, and his mouth formed a shocked O. "Your mama know you talk like that?"

"My mama's dead." She squinted at him. "You giving me a ride, or what?"

"I ought to give you a spanking," he said. "C'mon, Sassy Mouth."

She opened the door and jumped inside the cab. He wheeled the truck around and headed toward Nevermore.

"Everyone calls me Ant," he said.

"Why?"

"'Cause I use to be short and scrawny."

Happy glanced at him. He wasn't either of those things anymore. He was probably six feet tall, if not taller, and he was buff. His jeans and T-shirt were worn and she could see the dirt under his fingernails. He smelled like earth and freshly cut grass. It was nice.

"My name's Happy," she said.

"Seriously?"

"If I was gonna give you a fake name, would I choose that one?"

"Good point. How old are you?"

"How old are you?"

"Nineteen."

"I'm twenty."

Ant snorted. "Try again, Sassy Mouth. I have four sisters. I can spot a female lie at fifteen paces." He looked her over for a sec. "You're sixteen."

"I'll be seventeen in a couple months." She flinched because she sounded whiny. "If I was a magical like you, I'd be legal." She smirked at him. "We could date and everything."

"I'm not a magical," he said. "And I don't date girls with potty mouths."

"Why? You expect girls to do something else with their mouths?"

"You're not legal enough to find out."

That pissed her off. And shut her up. She wasn't too young to do anything. If she'd been born a real magical like her douche bag father, she'd be considered an adult. Sixteen was the age of majority, not eighteen like for the mundanes, 'cause they *matured* faster, and P.S. lived longer, too. Whatevs. She didn't know why Ant was being so stupid about his powers. She had no power of her own, but she could sense the powers of others. And *he* had powers.

Annoyed, she stared at the pastureland. The wind whipped into the cab through the rolled-down windows. It smelled like earth out there, too. She wrinkled her nose as the scent of manure wafted in. She saw the source—cattle near the fence line. Their soft brown gazes lifted toward the truck as it shot by.

It was so quiet out here. So peaceful. Maybe she and Lucy could stay in Nevermore together. Maybe it was safe, even without Bernard dead.

He'll never give up, Happy. Never. We have to separate. If I can come for you, I will.

If.

Lucy left her with the nuns because as long as Happy was with her, they could be tracked. But the convent had been built on neutral ground, and neither witch nor wizard could set foot on the property without the permission of the nuns. She'd known then that Lucy would probably never come back for her. Not because she didn't want to, but because Bernard wouldn't let her.

She stayed with the nuns but only because she was afraid that Lucy might be so worried about her, she would make mistakes and Bernard would find her. He'd been really mad at Lucy, and at Happy. He wouldn't hurt Happy. . . . Well, not much, anyway. But he would've hurt Lucy a lot. He was the meanest person she'd ever known.

Her stomach squeezed, and she felt like she was gonna hurl.

If she'd pressed Lucy really hard, she would've caved and not left her. Lucy didn't have anyone, either. And Happy loved her. It had to be hard to give up someone who loved you. Lucy had made a hard choice for them both.

And now Happy had to do the same.

"Who are you visiting?"

For a moment, Happy had the crazy urge to give in to tears and tell him everything. She wanted to tell someone the truth about herself, about her life. But she didn't know him, and who could trust a guy named Ant, anyway?

"None of your business," she finally said.

"Well, I'm not gonna just drop you off on a corner."

"Why not? I'm not your responsibility."

"It's the hitchhiking rule," said Ant amiably. "The pickupper—that's me—must ensure the safe delivery of the pickuppee—that's you—or he risks the wrath of the Nevermore mamas."

"You're making that up."

"Obviously, you've never met a Nevermore mama. They're scary. And they're hell with a rolling pin."

"I bet you got smacked with one a lot."

"I sure did," he admitted with a grin. "But not because I stranded a pickuppee on the side of the road."

"How many have you delivered?"

"None," he said. "You're my first hitchhiker. So you see the importance of me making sure you arrive to your destination safely."

"You mean the part where you avoid getting smacked by rolling pins?"

He laughed. "Damn straight."

Happy's entire body went tingly and hot. The sudden, fierce sensations overwhelmed her. She stiffened, sucking in deep breaths. What was happening?

"Shit." Ant pulled over to the shoulder and flipped on the overhead lights. He studied her, concern lighting his gaze. "What's wrong?"

"Magic," she whispered. "Lots and lots of it."

"You said you weren't a magical."

"I can sense it. Not use it."

"You gonna be okay?"

"This has never happened before. It's like . . . when your leg goes to sleep and you try to walk on it too soon. Only a hundred times worse."

"What can I do?"

"You're too nice," she said as her teeth started to chatter. "It kinda freaks me out."

"Tell me where to take you. Tell me who your people are."

"My p-people?"

"Your kin, Happy. Who are you coming to see?"

"I want to t-trust you," she said. She broke out in a cold sweat, and her stomach twisted. "I k-kinda hurt."

Then the world caved in, and she fell into sudden, icy blackness.

Happy floated in the twilight between awake and asleep. She felt warm and safe, but she didn't know why. She heard two men talking, their voices fading in and out. She grabbed only snatches of their conversation.

"Didn't know what to do. She passed out . . . probably just needs rest."

Happy realized they were talking about her. She felt fine now. No more tingles. She just wanted to sleep. To keep feeling that wonderful warmth. Safe. Oh, she felt so safe. Like no one could ever hurt her again.

"Someone set the fire at the café on purpose. Damn, you should've seen Lucy. If her aquamancy is a minor power, I can't imagine what her thaumaturgy must be like."

Lucy! Her friend was okay. Happy heard the admiration in the older man's voice. He liked her. And he should. Everyone should love Lucy as much as Happy did.

"Cathleen must've done it out of spite. . . . Found her body . . . least we think it's her."

She didn't like these words, so she blocked them out. People dying made her sad, and she was really tired of feeling sad. Happy drifted back into the soft dark, welcoming the oblivion of sleep.

"What do *you* want?" Bernard Franco looked into the oversized bowl of scented water at the face of Kerren Rackmore.

"Aw. You sound like you're unhappy to hear from me, and after all I've done for you."

"You mean *to* me."

"Same difference." She smiled, and the calculation behind it made him pause. What was she up to now? Gods-be-damned. She looked exactly the same as she had ten years ago at the age of twenty-two, when she'd traded her soul, and her wizard husband's, to be the immortal consort of a demon lord.

She was beautiful, the way a glacier was beautiful. Cold. Sharp-edged. Dangerous. It was too bad her eyes were not the same forest green as her sister's. Instead, she'd inherited the muddy brown gaze of their father, a color unsuited to ice. Her hair made up for it, though, glossy strands of white blond hair that snaked down her slim back. He'd had her once—when he'd made the deal to seduce and imprison Lucinda.

Kerren had damned near kill him, but it was the best sex he'd ever had.

If only her eyes could be fixed ...

"Well? Don't you want to hear my news?"

Before he could respond, a cough racked him and he fell back against the chair, shoulders heaving as the fit seized him. Rusty liquid filled his mouth, and he pressed the cloth against his quivering lips, wiping away the blood. He was getting worse. He'd been to countless medical doctors and mage healers, but none could help him. They all said the same thing: He was reaping what he'd sown, and there was nothing they could do.

He leaned over the bowl again and saw Kerren peering at him. She sought amusements wherever she could find them, and no doubt his misery gave her pleasure. She'd certainly delighted in how he'd tormented Lucinda. Sometimes, she'd watched—she'd even given him spells or techniques to help him. In fact, she'd given him the cursing magic to bind Lucinda's thaumaturgy. She'd failed to mention the repercussions it would have for him.

"You did this to me," he spit.

Her peals of laughter felt like acid splattering him. "You did it to yourself. No one forced you to use the curse. It's that lousy temper of yours, Bernard. It's finally killed you."

"You gave me the magic," he said. "You told me—"

"There was a price to be paid for everything," she interrupted. "You should've asked me what it would cost."

"How do I fix it?"

She tilted her head coquettishly. "I suppose you could kill Lucy," she said. "That might do it."

Something had changed. When Kerren had first contacted him about "securing" her sister, she'd made it clear Lucinda could not be killed. Tortured, mind-fucked, and emotionally traumatized had been fine, though. Lucinda had been a very good puppet. One of his favorite toys. Until she'd betrayed him. Until she tapped into that damned power of hers and blatantly ignored his express wishes. Lucinda had been a trial at the end. And when she escaped—and had stolen from him—he wanted nothing more than to kill her very, very slowly.

Kerren, on the other hand, was a completely different creature. She wasn't driven by a conscience and didn't worry about the morality of her own actions. Whatever she wanted, she went out and got. He had no doubt Kerren wanted him to dance to whatever new tune she was playing, but he wouldn't be her fool again.

"What happens if I die?" he asked Kerren.

"Lucinda can't remove the curse without you. Take heart, Bernard. If you croak before you find her, at least you'll have the consolation of knowing she can never use her thaumaturgy." She studied him, her ugly eyes as empty as her soul. "Ironic, isn't it, that she's the one person who might be able to cure you . . . if you hadn't bound up that very power."

"You wanted me to." He felt so weary. The only thing that kept him going these days was the bright, steady flame of his fury. Lucinda would pay for what she'd done to him—and if he could manage it, so would Kerren. "No thaumaturge will see me, and there are only a few who exist. You and your games! If her gift was such a threat, then why didn't you just kill her?"

"Kill my own sister?" she asked in mock horror. "Sure, I could rip out her heart, but after doing that a dozen or so times, the act really loses its charm."

"Instead, you gave her to me."

"Really, Bernard! Melodramatic much?"

"Will ending her life save mine?" he asked through gritted teeth.

"Where do you think the energy comes from to sustain the magic? It's being drained from you."

"But you said if I died, she would still suffer."

"It's a curse, you moron. If you die, the magic will find your closest blood relative to feed itself. So long as Lucy lives, you and your heirs will ensure her curse does, too."

Cold horror swept through Bernard. Kerren had known that the curse would drain his life force, and those of his family, when she'd given him the magic and the instructions for using it. It had been only three months since the cursing, and he was already dying. At this rate the entire Franco line could be wiped out in less than five years. Gods-be-damned, Kerren! He wanted to reach through the water and choke the life from her.

Kerren was very good at making men, human or not, want her. He had no doubt she'd been searching for ways to rid herself of the bond with Kahl, but Bernard knew from experience it was impossible to sever ties with hell's minions.

He wiped the corners of his mouth. He was tiring quickly, and needed to rest. "Why can I kill her now?"

"She's boring."

"Ah. Whatever threat she posed is gone, and so is whatever protection she had. Whose promise bound you from slitting her throat?"

"Aren't you cute? You think you know all the angles when you're really just a pawn on a much bigger chessboard." She chuckled.

It rankled that she believed she was better than him. More important than him. Before he'd enacted that damnable curse, he'd been one of the most powerful Ravens in the world. He'd sacrificed so much for his House, and they had rewarded him with power and money. It didn't matter that he could no longer have a seat on the Inner Court, or attend official functions. He'd known his worth.

And the Rackmore sisters had stolen it from him. Kerren had contacted him for her own reasons. She helped no one but herself. And she was a liar. Who knew if what she said about ending the curse was even true? He could kill Lucinda and still die in writhing agony.

"You still haven't asked about my news."

"I don't care. Go find some new toys to play with," he said.

"So petulant." She *tsk-tsk*ed. "Don't you know that Gray Calhoun is playing with one of your old toys?"

Bernard felt a hard, cold lump form in his chest. "What does that mean?"

"Little Lucy went to Nevermore," she said, "to enlist the help of my ex-husband."

"You lie."

"She married him." She laughed again. "Lucy and Gray sitting in a tree k-i-s-s-i-n-g! First comes love—"

"Shut up! Just shut up!" He coughed and wheezed, and all the while Kerren peered at him, amusement dancing in her mud brown gaze, her lips curled into a cruel smile. He hated her so much. "You betrayed him and stuck a dagger in his heart. He must be insane to marry your sister."

"Gray always loved a damsel in distress."

Something in her voice caught his attention. Bernard tamped down his own swirling emotions so that he could detect hers. Yes. Behind Kerren's amusement and her blatant manipulation of him, he sensed that she was unsettled. He'd never seen her the tiniest bit flustered. But her nervousness was there, hiding in the shadows of those awful eyes and that pristine beauty. He'd been useful to the House of Ravens for a myriad of reasons, not the least of which was his ability to ferret out secrets. "I've always been puzzled by how quickly you enacted the bargain with your new hubby. All that magic and ritual ready in so short a time?" He paused, and offered his own thin smirk. "You knew about the curse, didn't you?" he asked softly. "Before it happened."

Shock flashed in Kerren's eyes for a microsecond. Then she shrugged. "Who do you think made the bargain with my ancestors?"

"Kahl." Bernard couldn't help but admire such beautifully orchestrated treachery. "Why Gray? Did you toss some names into a hat and draw his? Or did you choose him for a particular reason?" He tapped his lips with his forefinger. "Maybe it was to keep him away from your sister."

"What the hell for?"

"Give the heart to the dragon, so he can protect all that is all, in this world and the next, nevermore."

"You're quoting me tripe from the Goddess Scrolls?"

"What's so important in Nevermore?"

"Ugh. This isn't an episode of *Torchwood*."

"Why can I kill your sister now, Kerren?"

"Oh, for the love of Kahl! You are so whiny. Okay, already. She had a protection spell on her," she admitted. "My mother wasn't a fool. But her lover kept the purse strings tight. She couldn't afford more than a few years' worth. When Lucinda turned twenty-five, the spell ended."

"That's when she completely broke free of my compelling spells, too. Then you gave me the cursing magic." Bernard considered how freely Kerren was sharing information. "Where are you on the bigger chessboard? I wonder."

"Watch yourself, Bernard."

"What do I have to lose?" he asked. "I'm already a dead man."

"You still have a soul, a soul that belongs to the underworld. If you think you're suffering now, just wait until you enter the Dark One's domain. I'll give you a personal introduction to my husband."

It was a weak threat. No doubt she had the power to draw his soul into the lair of her husband, but he suspected she didn't have the kind of power she wanted him to believe. She was dangerous, yes, but controlled by Kahl. Why would the demon lord bother tormenting an old enemy of his wife's?

"Tell me the truth about Nevermore."

For a moment, he didn't think she would answer. Then she sighed. "In the world there are several magical hot spots—believers call them 'Goddess fountains.' Nevermore is one of them."

Bernard huffed with impatience. "I've never heard of these hot spots."

"Why would you? They're secret for a reason. Magic is amplified, no matter how minute. Why do you think the Goddess figured out where these hot spots were and put in protectors?" She considered him, like a scientist might examine a plague germ under a microscope. Then she rolled her eyes. "Oh, all right. The curse can be redirected. If we transferred it to one of your kids, I could make it so that the curse followed the bloodline of the mother."

"You want me to sacrifice one of my children?"

"Don't play the father card with me," said Kerren. "There's no love in that shriveled little heart of yours. Besides, once my sister is dead, the curse will be, too. Your sacrificial lamb will live."

"And what about Nevermore?"

"If you manage to kill Lucinda and Gray, you can have it."

"Become the new protector?" He glared at her suspiciously. "Just like that?"

"Sure. Every now and then Kahl might ask a favor of you. No big deal, right?"

The shoe had finally dropped. For some reason neither Kerren nor Kahl was eager to get near Nevermore. He couldn't trust that once he'd killed off her sister and ex-husband, Kerren wouldn't show up and try to yank the rug out from under him. But if she was right about how to nullify the curse, and serious about the amplification of magic within Nevermore, then he would be strong enough to fend her off. At least until he could figure out how to permanently nullify her as a threat.

It was worth the risk.

"I'll do it," he said.

"Good luck. And hey, give me a ring-a-ling . . . if you live."

She cut off the connection. Bernard resisted the urge

to punch at the water, mostly because he had no desire to get his Armani suit wet. One day, he'd make sure Kerren got all she deserved and more. He'd watch her suffer, maybe even watch her die—damn her immortality—and laugh in her face as she met her very bloody, *painful* end.

He needed to rest. Then he would make plans. He had a new life to begin, a second chance to take.

As he moved to stand, leaning heavily on the silver cane he'd had commissioned, the bowl of water issued red sparkles. Someone else was calling?

Bernard nearly walked away, but he couldn't leave business unattended. He might feel weak, but he'd be damned if he showed it.

"What?" he snapped at the unfamiliar man peering up at him. "Who the hell are you?"

"Your new best friend."

"My last best friend tried to take off my head with a sword," he said. "So I'm sure you understand that I have trust issues."

"A gift, then, to show my trustworthiness."

"Do tell."

"Lucinda Rackmore."

Shock made Bernard reel internally. He immediately thought about Kerren and her knack for treachery, her need for games. "That gift has already been given, I'm afraid."

The man didn't quite manage to hide his surprise and his disappointment. But he wasn't deterred. "If you're coming to get her, you'll need me. I've managed to delay him somewhat, but in the next couple of days, the Guardian will start reinforcing the protections on our borders—specifically to prevent you from getting within a mile of his new wife."

He could tell that the man had hoped the news of the marriage would rattle him. No such luck, not since

Kerren had already taken all her potshots. "You can get me in?"

"Yes. And I can hide you until we're ready to act."

The idiot had no idea "we" did not exist. Bernard didn't share anything, or anyone, certainly not with a mundane. He had no doubts the man staring up at him was not a magical, though how he'd managed to enact a communication spell was mildly impressive. "What do you want in return for my friendship?"

"Gray Calhoun. And your help to summon Kahl."

If the fool wanted to kill Gray, that was one less thing for Bernard's to-do list. As for calling forth the demon lord—no fucking way. Eh. He could say anything. Promises were made to be broken. "Why do you want an introduction to Kahl?"

"It's a personal matter."

"I see. I have my own private concerns dealing with Lucinda."

"We understand each other, then."

"Yes," said Bernard pleasantly. "It looks like we can be friends after all."

Chapter 12

At breakfast, Lucinda found herself at the kitchen table, watching Gray scrape the black crust off their toast. He looked up at her, and grinned sheepishly. He was a worse cook than she was. Given the contents of the freezer, she'd guessed he usually nuked most of his meals. However, thanks to the efficient ladies of Nevermore, they had enough casseroles and pies to last the next two weeks.

Besides, Gray had other admirable qualities. He was noble and kind and affectionate. He hummed when he brushed his teeth, which she thought was adorable, and he remembered that she liked three teaspoons of honey in her tea. He gave her foot massages. He made her laugh. And the man liked to snuggle.

Who could resist a snuggler?

Last night, after the fire was out and the body, which everyone believed to be Cathleen's, had been recovered, Maureen gave them a lift home.

"Another wake," she'd said. "Another funeral. Goddess help us. I don't want to bury anyone else, Gray. You have to figure out what's going on and fix it."

"I will," he'd promised.

After they'd gotten upstairs and discarded their smoke-stained clothes, Gray had taken her into the bathroom and turned on the shower. He made love to her right there—and she hadn't even minded that the water was too tepid and the tiles were cold against her backside. Then he dried her off and lobbed her onto the bed, and ravished her again.

She'd woken up late, and found him attempting to make scrambled eggs and bacon in the newly restored and terrifyingly organized kitchen. While he tried not to set the stove on fire, they talked about restoring the garden out back, and he discussed his ideas for updating his wizard lab. It was nice to think about such normal activities.

Gray had washed their clothes while she was still sleeping, and since the sheriff had yet to release her duffel bag, she had only one outfit to wear—unless she wanted to wander around in her mother-in-law's too-big clothes. The soot smell wasn't quite out of the material, but it seemed to mix nicely with the lavender washing detergent. Okay, not really. It was sorta like throwing bouquets onto brimstone.

"You look glowy," said Gray as he crossed from the stove to the table carrying two plates.

"I do?" She touched her face. "I don't know why."

He leaned down, putting the plate in front of her, and kissed her. "It's an inner glow, baby. It's nice to see you happy."

"Because of you."

He smiled, but she saw the way his gaze flickered. No doubt he was worried she wasn't keeping their bargain. No love between them—just pleasurable business. That concept didn't particularly appeal to her now. But she wouldn't ask for more from Gray, not when he'd already given her so much.

"Thank you." She grabbed her fork and let it hover over the mess. The eggs were too wet, and the bacon was unrecognizable char, but she ate it anyway. "When will you leave to do the border protections?"

"Not for a few days," he said. "I have to cleanse the café's site. Ember's going to help me, but there's a lot of negative vibes to dissipate. We might as well continue the cleansing for the whole town. And the farms, of course."

"That makes sense. It seems like the magic here is on a teeter-totter."

"You feel it, too?"

"Yes."

They ate in comfortable silence, and then Lucy put down her fork. She'd been thinking about Maureen, and the town, and ways to help everyone. "Gray, is Nevermore poor?"

"Not everyone is on the same financial footing," said Gray. "But it does seem like more folks are struggling."

"I meant the town itself."

"No, it's not poor. Not at all." He frowned. "I handle the banking. Honestly? Taylor told me what the town needed, and I wrote a check. He took care of it. Everything. I've been a terrible Guardian. I let everyone down because I couldn't let go of my pain. . . . No, it's more than that. I've been ashamed."

"There is no shame in loving the wrong person. At least you had that."

"It was an illusion."

"Your love wasn't. Hers was. I gave myself to Bernard without any love at all. I traded my body and my dignity for room and board. That's shameful."

"You were doing what you had to for survival."

"Actually, I was doing what I had to for Dolce and Gabbana."

"So if I offered to buy you Dolce and Gabbana everything, you'd want it?"

Lucinda shook her head. "No. I'd want you to spend it on the general store." Gray was staring at her in a sorta what-crazy-pill-did-you-swallow kind of way. She licked her lips, and gathered her courage. "I talked to Maureen for a long time last night. You should've heard her talk about the general store. It was her husband's legacy, and after his great-grandfather gambled it all away, no one could ever afford to buy it back." Her words were tumbling out faster now, and she was practically tripping over her own tongue. "She said there was no place to shop here, that people had to order online or drive for hours to get to Dallas. The store is right there. It's got all that space, shelves, registers. . . . Who knows what else? Maureen and Henry want to do more than just exist here. They want to contribute."

Gray didn't say anything for a long time. Lucinda got so nervous that she thought her eggs might make a return trip.

"I own it," Gray said hoarsely.

"The store?"

He nodded. "When Nevermore was founded, the Guardian granted deeds to the families who were running the businesses. Everyone owned their land and their building, but they had to pay a percentage of their profits into the town coffers. It's kinda like taxes, I guess. That's the money Nevermore uses to pay its bills, take care of street work, and so on. If a family defaults on their payments, their deed reverts back to the Guardian."

"That's how Ember got her tea shop—the place that's the neutral ground."

"Yeah. I sold it to her, or rather Taylor did. He probably didn't realize she was going to paint it purple. That building she bought was empty for so long that no one remembers what it used to be. I didn't realize it was neutral ground until I pulled the deed."

"Do you pay the town for the general store? The taxes, I mean?"

"No. It's a little hard to explain. I am the town, and the town is me—that's what Grit used to say all the time. I oversee the town's money."

"You're the bank."

"For the town, not for its citizens." He pushed his plate away. "If a property is no longer contributing, it's not used. There's no reason to have utilities turned on or have garbage service."

"Are you poor?"

He blinked at her. "Um, no."

"Because the Archers are. I don't know if they could afford the taxes, or whatever you want to call 'em, much less the utility bills. Not right away."

"You want me to give the Archers a personal loan?"

Lucinda lifted her hands palms out. "I would, but you know . . . I literally don't have any money. But I could work there for free—until they get everything settled and can afford to hire some help." She couldn't figure out what Gray thought about her idea. He wasn't exactly leaping for joy over it. "The Archers wouldn't take charity. They'd want to pay their bills same as everyone else in Nevermore. They just need a little assistance."

He cleared his throat. "Just so I have this straight . . . you want me, as the Guardian, to hand over the deed to the general store gratis to the Archers. Then, you want me, as Gray Calhoun, to loan them the money for start-up costs, and then you, my wife, will work there for free until they can afford to hire clerks."

"Please, Gray. Just think about it. Having that store back would make them so happy. And give them a purpose. Everyone needs a purpose. And Nevermore needs that store."

"You're begging, aren't you?"

"I can get on my knees, if it'll help."

"I can hear it in your voice." He stood up, rounded

the table, and then knelt before her. "You're brilliant. I should've thought of it myself." He shook his head. "Damn it all! I was so selfish. I could only see my own pain. Five years sitting in this house thinking only about myself. I was such a fool."

"You built walls to protect yourself," she said, her heart growing fuller by the second. "I understand, Gray. You have to stop beating yourself up over past mistakes. You're doing the right things now. That's what people will remember."

"You would've begged me for their sake, wouldn't you?"

"Yes. If it meant they'd get their family legacy back, then yes, I would beg."

He sighed. "I'm not even gonna think about how insulting it is for my own wife to think she has to plead with me—on behalf of people I've known my whole life." He picked up her hands and kissed her knuckles. "The world is yours, baby. I'll give you anything."

Lucinda knew that wasn't true. He couldn't give her love. Or a baby. Or a real marriage. For all the healing his heart was doing now, there was no room in it for her dreams. Gray had his own path, and it was directly connected to Nevermore. He needed this town, and everyone in it needed him.

One day, she would be gone from here, and she hoped to do some good before it was time to seek out her own new path.

"I have some other ideas," she said.

"Okay. Let's go in the library and talk."

"You want Grit's advice?"

"No, I want to annoy him." He stood up and pulled Lucinda to her feet. "C'mon. Let's go figure out how to change our little corner of the world."

*   *   *

Anthony rolled over in bed, and groaned. His eyes felt gritty and he was damned groggy from a bad night's sleep, not least of which was caused by his inappropriate thoughts about Happy. She was sixteen, for Goddess' sake! She was pretty—all that blond hair and those blue eyes framed by a heart-shaped face, not to mention she had a woman's fulsome body. And when she smiled, she had dimples. Dimples! But her heart and her mind were still those of a girl. He felt like a lecherous old man just thinking about her in a sexual way.

He needed coffee.

And a cold shower.

He'd gone to bed in his pajama bottoms, which was a concession to their female guest. Usually he wandered around in his underwear. He pulled on a T-shirt and went downstairs, heading into the living room to check on Happy. The couch was empty. He stared at the folded blanket carefully centered on the pillow. Her backpack was gone. And so was she.

Shit.

"She went outside."

Ant whirled around. Taylor stood in the foyer, a mug of coffee in his hand, dressed in full uniform.

"Her stuff's gone."

"She left it in the kitchen. I made extra pancakes, if you want any."

Ant's mouth dropped open. "You stayed in the kitchen long enough to cook? And you made her breakfast?" He narrowed his gaze. "Who are you and what did you do with my big brother?"

"Ha-*ha*. The kid was hungry. I fed her. End of story."

"You could've poured her a bowl of Lucky Charms."

"Mama would roll over in her grave," said Taylor. "Happy's polite, but closemouthed. Wouldn't tell me why she came to town or who she's looking for." He sighed. "Maybe a good sit-down in the office will scare her into talking."

"I doubt it," said Ant. He could see that Happy wore stubborn like other people wore coats.

"Me, too. But I have a secret weapon."

"Arlene."

"Yep."

"I'll take her in," said Ant.

"Okay. Then I can meet Ren at the café. He thinks he found the point of ignition."

"What? He's an arson investigator now?"

Taylor laughed. "He's serious about law enforcement, is all. And there's not a lot of opportunities to investigate real crimes."

"I wish y'all didn't have so many to investigate now."

"I don't much like it, either." He drained the mug, and handed it to Ant. "I cooked. You clean."

"Gee, thanks."

Ant headed to the kitchen, putting the mug in the sink. He heard the ancient SUV rumble away, and he turned away from the dishes.

Happy's pink backpack lay in one of the chairs tucked underneath the table. He warred with his own conscience. The girl was entitled to her privacy, but she also needed help, which she was refusing to ask for. Maybe a clue about her identity or purpose was inside that bag.

So. What to do?

Ant walked to the table and reached down, only to stop before his fingers brushed the zipper. Damnation. He was already having lascivious thoughts about the girl. Violating her trust seemed an even worse infraction.

He'd never been so out of sorts over a girl in his life. He had four sisters. He understood the female mind well enough—at least as far as a man could. He sensed that if Happy found out he'd gone through her things, she'd never talk to him again.

He couldn't get the girl out of his thoughts, but he could get her out of his home. She was wrecking his libido and his concentration. He was grown, and she wasn't. End of freaking story.

He headed outside. She wasn't on the porch or in the front yard. He went through the house and out the back door. Over the rolling acres were his creations—gardens that came from his imagination. Every time he touched a plant, dug his fingers into the earth, inhaled the essences of flowers and grass, he felt as though he'd found his place in the world.

He stepped onto the brick path, cupped his hands around his mouth, and yelled, "Happy!"

"Back here," she answered. "I'm in the heart."

Ant felt his pulse stutter, but he didn't know why he'd had such an odd reaction. In the heart of what? Oh. He realized she was talking about the red and white rosebushes he'd used to create a huge valentine. In the middle of it he'd placed a stone bench. It was his mother's memorial garden. Sometimes, he went there to talk to Mama. He knew she wasn't around anymore, but he still felt like she heard him. *Love never dies,* she'd told him, and he believed her.

Ant found Happy sitting on the bench. He paused at the entrance to his sanctuary, feeling as though someone had struck him in the chest with a hammer. She wore a pink summer dress, which showed off the very shapely legs stretched out and crossed at the ankles. She was barefoot, and he noticed her toenails were painted purple. She wore a toe ring on her left foot.

Her long blond hair hung down in ringlets that cascaded over her shoulders. Her face was turned up toward the sun. In that moment, she looked like a flower blooming. And he knew that he could coax Happy into a beautiful blossom, fragrant and perfect, just like all his other plants.

He was having too visceral a reaction to the girl. He tried to think about jumping into the icy waters of Lake Huginn during winter, but envisioning that scenario wasn't helping much.

"You're beautiful."

The words just popped out of his mouth. Good Goddess! What was wrong with him?

She looked at him, and smiled. "You didn't want to say that, did you?"

"Not really."

"It's okay. I won't hold it against you."

"I appreciate it."

Happy patted the spot next to her. "Sit down."

"I don't particularly trust myself right now."

She laughed. "I should torture you by flirting outrageously, but I feel too wonderful. This is such a lovely garden, Ant. It's magical."

"I'm not, though."

"Yes, you are." She tilted her head. "How could you not know?"

"Both of my parents were mundanes."

"So?"

"No one in my family got powers."

"Your brother's a magical, too, but just a little. Not like you." She gestured at the rosebushes that ringed them. "The magic is here. These flowers feel like you. It's the same sorta energy. They love you, you know."

"The plants love me?" Ant chuckled. "C'mon, now."

"It's true, and you know it. You really think a regular gardener can create wonders like this? You talk to them, don't you? Coax them into beauty and light. And yes, you love them."

Ant wanted her to stop talking. He felt uneasy about her assertions. If he was a magical, he would've known by now. His family had been one of the original mundanes to found Nevermore. As far as he knew, no Mooreland born here had ever been a magical. Happy's insistence that he was, that she could sense his power, made him feel off-kilter. His world had been just fine until she'd wandered into it.

"We gotta get going," said Ant.

"Where?"

"Into town. Unless you wanna tell me where I can drop you off?"

Something akin to panic crossed her features, and then he was left only with her disappointed expression. "Town's fine."

Ant nodded. "I'll see you back at the house."

He left before he did something stupid.

Like kiss her.

Lucinda hadn't expected a cemetery to look so inviting. The huge wrought iron gates, a shiny, pristine black, were open to allow the passage of cars. On the left was a darling whitewashed cottage. She pulled into the driveway and got out of the truck. The porch and shutters had been painted a sky blue, and wind chimes shaped like stars dangled from the entryway. They made a soft, pleasant jangling. The postage-stamp-sized front yard was trimmed, and a concrete path led from the drive to the porch steps. On the far side of the yard was a gazebo with a big white swing. All kinds of plants and trees thrived. Lucinda had noticed how spring had hit Nevermore early. Nearly everything here was green and growing.

Even at the graveyard.

"Good morning!" A woman pushed open the screen

door and stepped onto the porch. She was tall and willowy, and wore a white dress that flared at her knees. Her feet were bare, her toenails painted a pale pink. Her auburn hair was drawn into a French braid, a big white blossom tucked just so on the left side. Her gray eyes were kind, and her smile was genuine. She seemed to emit peace and calm, no doubt because she'd spent her whole life dealing with the bereaved.

Lucinda shut the truck door, and walked to the porch. "You're Mordi?"

"Yes. And you're Lucy."

Lucinda nodded. "It seems odd to say this, but you have a lovely cemetery."

Mordi's smile widened, obviously in pleasure at the compliment. "Why, thank you. Did you come to visit Marcy?"

"Yes." Lucinda hesitated. Then she pulled a piece of paper out of her front jean pocket. "And to pay for Cathleen's headstone."

Mordi's eyes widened. "Whatever for?"

"Gray said the same thing," said Lucinda. "Cathleen wasn't a very nice person, but . . . some people have a hard time accepting kindness. If you've been sleeping in nettles your whole life and someone gives you a soft blanket, it hurts too much. You're used to the stinging, you see."

"Well, you certainly do."

"I know what it's like to want to be a better person." Lucinda shrugged. "Maybe I'm doing this to help me more than her."

"Either way, it's a nice gesture."

Lucinda stepped onto the porch and handed Mordi the paper. "It's a voucher. Gray said it would work just the same." She looked away. "I'm a Rackmore, so I couldn't bring the money myself."

Mordi accepted the paper. "This is fine. Come in. I'll make tea and you can look at the catalog with the headstone choices." She paused. "I thought you married Gray."

"Yes."

"Well, that makes you a Calhoun, doesn't it?" Mordi led the way into the kitchen, where a small table and two chairs occupied a nook. She gestured for Lucinda to take a seat. Then she grabbed a mason jar filled with coins from the top of the fridge. "Have you ever heard of Charon's obol?"

"Is that a band?"

Mordi paused in her efforts to dig through the change. She stared at Lucinda for a long moment, and then chuckled. "Oh. That was a joke."

"A bad one, I'm afraid. You were saying?"

"Aha!" Mordi plucked out a silver coin, and returned the jar to its place. Then she sat across from Lucinda, pushing the coin across the table to her. "In Greek mythology, Charon was the ferryman who took souls across the river that separates the living from the dead. The obol was used as a payment . . . eh, more like a bribe."

Lucinda picked up the silver disk. It looked ancient. On one side was the fearsome head of Medusa, and on the other, an anchor. "I studied religious mythologies in school. The Greeks knew about magic, but I still don't see how they came up with all those stories about gods and goddesses. The Goddess Scrolls are older than all of the known religions."

"But most were undiscovered back then," said Mordi. "It was the Romans who found the first ones—later, which is why they started the Houses. They called Charon's obol *viaticum*, which roughly means 'sustenance, or provision, for a journey.' The obol was worth one-sixth of a drachma. Either it or a danake was used, sometimes put on the eyes, or most often in the mouth."

"It's an interesting piece of history to have for your own."

"My family collects all things dead." Mordi grinned. "That sounded weird even to me. I mean, we collect stories, items, pictures. . . . Not everyone understands the fascination. It's not only my job—it's my passion."

"It shows." Lucinda offered Mordi the coin. "In a good way."

"Keep it."

"I couldn't. It's obviously valuable, and it's still money. I lose money."

"If you do, then someone else will find it, no doubt the person who needs it more than I do."

"And if I don't?" asked Lucinda as she once again picked up the coin and studied it.

"It means the curse no longer considers you a Rackmore."

Lucinda couldn't stop hope from swimming through her doubts. She wanted very much to believe that taking Gray's family name had nullified her family's curse. She was sure plenty of Rackmores had been married in the ten years since the curse initiated, and she'd never heard a word about it making a difference. As far as anyone knew, only Kerren had escaped with her wealth—but she'd paid a huge price to keep her money, and her power.

"Thank you," said Lucinda. She tucked the obol into the back pocket of her jeans.

"You are most welcome. Now, I'll brew the tea," said Mordi as she rose from the table. "And you can look at headstones."

Arlene straightened her desk for the umpteenth time. She'd done all the filing, dusted the window ledges, and swept the floor. Oh, she was *dying* to know what the sheriff had discovered at the café. She wouldn't have doubted for a minute that Cathleen would torch the place outta spite. But she couldn't imagine the woman would kill herself. Leastways not on purpose. She'd peeked out the window enough to know that Gray and Ember had started the cleansing. Purple and red magic sparkled left and right as they worked together to create balance. Humph. As off-kilter as that place was, it would probably take all day to work the kinks out.

Keeping busy was the only way to control her over-whelming curiosity (she was, as her husband so often teased her, a Nosy Posy), but there wasn't much left to do. Just when she was contemplating cleaning out the break room fridge, Ren came through the door.

"Well?" she demanded.

He halted in the middle of the checkered linoleum and stared at her, brows raised. "Well, what?"

"Did Cathleen burn down the café and her fool self?"

"Looks like." He took off his hat and slapped it against his thigh. "We found shards of broken whiskey bottle. And the basement door had been left open—even down there, it's a shambles."

"It's a wonder she didn't burn down the whole block," said Arlene. "Did the Sew 'n' Sew get damaged?"

"Doesn't look like it. It's just the café. I wouldn't be surprised if Gray tore the whole thing down and started over."

"We sure need some kind of eating place around here."

"Josie's starting up a lunch wagon," said Ren. "Her dad's fixing up an old truck with the equipment. She says she'll park in the town square and feed folks. At least for lunchtime."

"Well, now. That's some good news right there." Curiosity somewhat satisfied, Arlene sank into the chair behind her desk. "You staying?"

"With Taylor shadowing Gray and Ember while they do the cleansings, I'm the man on call." Ren sighed. "Speaking of which, I gotta head to the library. My aunts think the ghost has stolen their grandfather's ink-and-quill set again."

"They misplaced it, no doubt," said Arlene. "Poor darlings. They're getting too old to run the library."

"I imagine that's what they hoped my mama would do," he said. "Then me, at least until I asked for the deputy job."

"Now, now. They're real proud of you, Ren." Arlene sent him a sympathetic look. She'd always felt sorry for the boy. Harley hadn't been much of a father, spending too much time alone drinking away his sorrows. "I'm sorry, honey. It's such a shame what happened to your mama. You know the Wilson twins just call you so they can get some company."

Ren rolled his eyes. "I visit 'em every week. There's only so much pink and doilies a man can take."

The door to the lobby burst open, letting in the big ol' lazy carcass of Atwood. Arlene *tsk*ed. The man looked a sight. His face shone with sweat. He was panting, as if breathing was too much of an effort. He wore a gray shirt opened enough to reveal the sweat-stained undershirt, as well as gray pants, and black cowboy boots. With his lumbering gait, not to mention his balding head, small eyes, squished-in nose, and sagging cheeks, he always reminded of her of an exhausted rhinoceros.

"Y'all seen Trent?" he asked.

"Not today, Atwood," said Arlene.

"He missing?" asked Ren.

"Haven't seen him since last night." Atwood took a handkerchief out of his front shirt pocket and wiped his face. "You see him before you went to bed?"

"No," said Ren. "He woke me up, said there was a

fire. I just assumed he went down to the café like the rest of us."

Atwood shook his head. "It ain't like him. You'd think that kid would have all kinds of baggage with what happened to his folks, but he's got his head on straight. Never misses a day of work, or school. He's respectful, too. Sandra and Tommy raised him right."

"You don't think he ran away?" asked Arlene.

"Not a chance. I've done some lookin', but I cain't get far with this ol' ticker of mine." He mopped his face again, and then squinted at Arlene. "What's this I hear about Ant picking up a hitchhiker?"

"Hitchhiker?" Ren frowned. "Taylor didn't say anything to me."

Arlene waved off Atwood's question. "Her name is Happy, and Taylor thinks she's a runaway. She won't tell anyone why she was hitching to Nevermore, but don't you worry about it. She's just a scared girl who needs a hug and some chocolate cake."

"Happy?" asked Atwood. "Who names a kid Happy?"

"I think it's the perfect name for a child," said Arlene, sniffing disapproval. Sometimes, Atwood got on her raw nerve. He didn't have any kids of his own, which made him less tolerant of others'. No one had been more surprised than Arlene when he took in Trent. "Ant's dropping her by in a little bit. So I'll take care of her. You take care of your own business."

"Go on back home and wait there in case Trent returns," said Ren. "Arlene, start the call tree and round up some volunteers for a search party. Way things have been around here lately, it's better to be safe than sorry."

Atwood nodded, and he turned, wheezing as he walked out. The door slammed shut behind him.

"Man's heart is gonna explode if he doesn't start takin' care of himself," muttered Arlene. She started flipping through the Rolodex. "Where do you want folks to meet?"

"Town square, by the dragon statue. I'll meet everyone there soon as I see to my aunts."

"All right," said Arlene. Then she started to dial.

Ant hadn't said much to her since their conversation in the garden. Happy wondered what she'd said or done to piss him off so much. Then she decided his bad mood was his problem, not hers.

Anyway, Happy hoped that she could come back and visit Ant's gardens again. There was so much beauty to explore—Ant's imagination rendered in plants. How the heck he could believe he was just a mundane was beyond her. Not that mundanes couldn't be talented geniuses—they could. . . . They were. But she knew magic.

And the garden buzzed with it.

While Ant took a shower and got dressed, Happy occupied herself by doing the dishes and straightening up the kitchen. Just as she finished lining the chairs against the table, Ant strolled in looking all yummy in a tight T-shirt, faded jeans, and worn cowboy boots. He wore the same cowboy hat as yesterday. Maybe he only had one—or that one was his favorite.

"Whoa." He paused and looked around. "You cleaned."

"Your brother cooked. It seemed a fair exchange."

"That's what he said when he asked me to do it." Ant grinned, and that quirky smile drilled holes right through her. "Much obliged."

"Much a-what?"

"Obliged. It means 'thanks.' "

"Oh. You're welcome." Happy sighed. "Guess we better go."

"Guess so."

"Well, c'mon on, then," she snapped, pushing past him. "I know you want to be rid of me."

She stomped through the foyer, knowing she was acting immature, but she didn't care. He'd hurt her feelings. He could . . . could . . . kiss her backside, that was what.

"You know, not everyone appreciates a sassy mouth like I do."

Happy spun around and planted her hands on her hips. She opened her mouth to tell him to *piss off already*, but the look in his eyes stalled the words.

His gaze slid across her lips in such a way that her stomach dipped and her nipples went hard. She felt kinda breathless all of a sudden, and she stared at him, wide-eyed. His neck mottled with red. He closed his eyes, turned, and lightly banged his forehead on the wall a couple of times.

"What are you doing?"

"Knocking some sense into myself."

"You liiiiiike me," she teased. "I'm not that much younger than you."

"Enough to make you jailbait."

"I'll be legal soon enough."

"I live for the day." He sounded more sarcastic than yearning. "Quit looking at me like that. Go on with yourself."

Happy put her fingers to her lips and blew him a kiss.

"Girl, you are some kind of trouble."

"Didn't I tell you?" she asked, batting her lashes. "Trouble is my last name." Then she spun around and walked away, putting a little sway in her hips. She smiled when she heard his tortured groan.

She cleared the porch and was halfway across the gravel driveway to Ant's truck when she heard the front door squeal open, then bang shut.

"Hey," he said.

She was startled at how close he was, and she whirled, glaring at him. He stood about a foot behind her, looking like the cat who ate the cream.

"Forget something?" He held up her backpack.

How had she forgotten her bag? Argh! She swiped for it, but he just yanked it out of her reach. He grinned at her, challenge sparkling in his eyes. How could she have been such a moron? He'd gotten all mushy with her and she stopped thinking right. The crystal was in there, and she couldn't find Lucy without it. Asking around about a Rackmore witch would attract more notice than she wanted. This place was so small that there couldn't be too many places for Lucy to hang out . . . unless she was on a farm somewhere.

She wanted to tell him to stuff it, but he was trying to rile her. Besides, she needed the crystal. Her gaze narrowed, and she wondered how hard she could kick him in the balls without endangering his ability to have kids.

He shook his head. "You even think about it, and I'll get in my truck and run you over."

"Harsh," she muttered. Then she took option B: She tackled him.

He hadn't expected a full linebackeresque assault, so he went down hard, the backpack flying out of his hand. Happy landed on top of him, all wiggling knees and elbows until he wrapped his arms around her and squeezed.

She stopped moving.

"You're crazy," he wheezed out. "Damnation. You almost killed me."

"You're just mad because a girl whooped you."

"I'm not mad," he said. "That's the problem." He brushed her hair back, his knuckles skimming her cheek. "I want to be your friend."

"That's a lie." Her heart knocked so badly against her chest, she just knew he could feel it against his own.

"You're right. It is a lie. But I have to be the kind of man my mama raised."

"I understand." And she did. He was nice, even when he didn't want to be. It was sorta like Lucy's decision— doing the thing that hurt them both, separating, so that Happy would be protected. And now Ant was making the same kind of choice.

She couldn't give voice to her thoughts, or to her woes, so she scrambled off him, retrieved her backpack, and headed to Ant's truck.

In no time at all, they were headed back to town. Nerves plucked at Happy's stomach. She chewed her bottom lip as she wondered what to do next. She couldn't begin to hope that Ant would just drop her off on a corner and wish her luck. He wasn't that kind of guy.

Could she trust him?

She wanted to. She was so tired of looking over her shoulder, of worrying about what would happen the day Bernard found her again. No one should live a life in fear—Lucy said that. All Happy had known since the day her mother died was fear. Hers, Lucy's, everyone's. Scared all the time because of Bernard.

It felt like giving him power, to be so terrified. She knew he thrived on creating that emotion in others. It made him strong. It gave him the kind of pleasure other people got from eating chocolate or kissing.

"You all right?"

"Yeah." She clutched the backpack. "So, where are you taking me?"

"To the sheriff's office." He glanced at her. "My big brother will help you. There's no one in town more reliable than Taylor, I promise."

"What's your promise worth?" she asked wearily.

"Happy, I . . ." He trailed off, staring straight ahead, his knuckles white from gripping the steering wheel too hard.

She heard the anguish in his voice. She hadn't meant to hurt him, not really. She supposed that was an indication that he really did like her. But what did it matter?

Happy focused on the scenery. It was so pretty here. So quiet. Nevermore soothed her troubles in a way no other place had. It was too bad she wouldn't be able to stay here. The only thing she could hope for was that Lucy would go with her when she left.

The two-lane road was edged in tall grass, and scrubby bushes. Up ahead, she saw a huge oak tree, its canopy so huge, it blocked out the sun.

Her admiration turned to ashes. *Oh, no!* The tingling of this magic was far too familiar. "Ant, turn around," she cried. She felt as though she were starting to burn from the inside. Flames licked her bones. Heat snaked over her skin. "You have to turn around!"

"Whoa, Happy. What's wrong?"

"Please," she said as the tears started to flow. Pain and fear wound together like a dagger, stabbing her chest. *"Please."*

"All right, sweetheart." He hit the brakes. The truck didn't slow down. He pumped them hard, but the truck lurched ahead. "What the hell?"

The vehicle picked up speed.

"It's too late," she whispered. She looked at him, at the handsome, sweet man too nice to woo her. "I'm sorry."

"What are you—"

The truck veered, bouncing over the uneven ground, crashing through the bramble, and then it slammed into the trunk of the oak tree.

Happy jerked forward. The seat belt snapped into place seconds too late to prevent her head from smacking the dash. Stars exploded before her eyes, and then she fell into the darkness, into the cold terror of her worst nightmare.

Chapter 13

Gray sat at the bar, leaning over the mug of tea. He had to admit that Ember's place created a deep sense of tranquillity—even with all the purple. He inhaled the spicy smell of the liquid, feeling rejuvenated already. "What is it?"

"Good for you, dat's what," said Ember. She sat on the barstool next to him. They had finished the cleansing of the café a few minutes earlier, and Gray felt wiped. He wouldn't have been able to do the work alone—there had been too much negativity. The magical alignment had shifted even worse than he thought. Cathleen had managed to turn the whole place into a swirling vortex of awfulness.

When Ember had suggested they take a break at the tea shop, he agreed. Taylor had gone off to check on the progress of the search for Trent. Gray hoped the kid was just sleeping off a hangover or off with a girl. Anything a typical teenager might be doing, because that kind of trouble was far better than the kind that had been stalking the residents of Nevermore.

"Where do you think we should go next?" asked Gray.

Ember sipped her own concoction. "I think it bein' decided for us."

"You like talking in riddles, don't you?" The tea was

spicy, but there was also an underlying sweetness to it. Cinnamon, definitely. Maybe . . . Huh. Chili powder? No matter what the ingredients, the tea was doing the trick.

"You been hidin' from yourself so long," said Ember. "You tink everyone hidin' someting, too."

"You're talking about that so-called gift, aren't you?" He put down the mug and swiveled to face her. "It's not what you think. I spent five years finding ways to control it. I wouldn't have returned to Nevermore at all if my family didn't need me." He smiled bitterly. "Lucy doesn't know. She . . . no. It would scare her."

"If you tink she can't love you just da way you are, den you don't deserve her."

"Love me?" Panic shot through Gray like a poisoned arrow. "Our relationship is . . . um, well-defined. I care about her. And she cares about me. But it's not a love match."

Ember stared at him for a long moment. Then she laughed. "Oh, Goddess. You really tink dat, don't you?"

Gray was nettled by her reaction. Was it wrong to enjoy being with his own wife? Just because they'd married as a business arrangement, that didn't mean they couldn't get along. "My relationship with Lucy isn't your concern."

"Humph. How long she gonna be your wife, den?"

"Until she's free of the curse. And Bernard is no longer a threat."

"I see." Ember nodded. "If I told you dat today she'd be free of both curse and enemy, you'd let her go?"

"Yes," said Gray, although his heart sank to his stomach. He didn't like the idea of Lucy leaving him today, or any other day. "But that's not gonna happen."

Ember looked down at her mug, and sighed. "Everyting dat must unfold is already in motion. You need everyting inside you to win, Gray. *Everyting.*"

Gray felt his stomach pitch. He had never told anyone his secret, although he'd wanted to tell Lucy. He
found that he wanted to tell her everything. He didn't
want to keep a wall between them, one built by lies and
doubts. He hated to admit it, but he was afraid. Would
knowing what had happened to him that night scare
her? Would she turn away? Goddess help him, he didn't
want to see a look of disgust or pity in her eyes when he
told her the truth.

Could Lucy accept a man who had a demon dormant
within him?

Lucy spun the dial on the radio, looking for a station
that didn't play country music. No such luck, though.
Well, what did she expect from Texas? It was cowboy
country, and, apparently, the country of lamenting about
losing stuff—hearts, trucks, dogs, ranches, guitars.

Sighing, she turned off the radio.

She'd had a pleasant chat with Mordi. The girl was
odd, but in a completely charming way. After she'd chosen the headstone for Cathleen's grave, Lucy had gone
off and visited Marcy. Mordi said that talking to dead
people could be cathartic. Lucy had sat next to the fresh
pile of earth and tried saying something meaningful, but
whispering to the ground where Marcy had been in-
terred didn't make her feel better. There they were, she
and Marcy, surrounded by silence and regret.

She wondered if Gray had finished the café's cleansing, and where he'd gone off to next. She missed him.
She couldn't believe how quickly he'd turned into her
safety net. She felt like nothing bad would happen to her
as long as he was within arm's reach. It seemed selfish to
want to feel that way all the time, but she did. And she
wanted him to feel safe, too.

She knew he wanted to tell her something. He'd been

unnerved when she told him she'd seen his scar glowing while he wrestled with his nightmare. She thought maybe he would confide in her, but he'd changed the subject.

It was getting difficult to remember that she was in a temporary relationship. Worse, though, was the ache that gathered in her chest every time she saw him, or thought about him. It was echoes of the desperation she felt before Bernard found her.

Nevermore was becoming her home, but it belonged to Gray. *I am the town, the town is me.* Yes. He was beginning to live that truth now. Even if he offered her continued sanctuary, she couldn't reside in Nevermore and not be with him.

As the truck crested the hill, she saw a young man walking on the side of the road. He stumbled along, weaving, and it seemed he was muttering to himself. He was dressed head to toe in black. She recognized him from Marcy's wake.

She stopped the truck. Earlier, she'd rolled down both windows to let in the fresh spring air. "Trent!"

He paused, turning toward the car. His skin looked pale and waxy, and his eyes were red and puffy. He stared at her for a long moment, and her skin prickled with unease.

"Are you all right?" she asked.

"Don't know. Woke up in a ditch." He blinked at her. "You're Gray's wife. The Rackmore witch."

"I'm Lucinda Calhoun now," she said. "Would you like a ride back to town?"

"Yeah. Thanks." He opened the door and crawled inside. "I dunno what happened to me."

"What's the last thing you remember?"

"Going to sleep in my own bed."

"You don't remember telling Ren about the fire?"

Trent blinked at her owlishly. "What fire?"

"The café. Cathleen set it ablaze, but she didn't get out in time—unless she didn't want to get out."

"She's dead?" Trent rubbed his face. "I don't remember the fire. I don't remember anything. You got any water?"

"Sorry."

"I feel like I swallowed metal shavings. My head is pounding."

"Sounds like a hangover."

He sighed. "I'm not gonna lie and say I don't have experience with hangovers, but I've never blacked out."

"Maybe we should get you to a doctor."

"Don't worry about it." He frowned as he pointed toward the windshield. "What the hell is that?"

"Oh, Goddess!" Lucinda pulled off the side of the road. She and Trent scrambled out and headed toward the accident.

The blue pickup had hit the massive trunk of the oak tree hard enough to make its hood crumple like an accordion. Both doors were open.

Lucinda heard a faint groan.

They rounded the hood and saw a young man lying on his side. He was scraped up good, his clothing ripped and stained. His eyes were closed, but from the rise and fall of his chest, he seemed to be breathing all right.

"Holy shit. It's Ant."

"You're worried about ants?"

Trent sent her an astonished look. "Anthony Mooreland. This is the sheriff's little brother." He squatted down and patted the man's face. "Ant. Dude. You all right?"

Ant coughed, then grabbed his ribs and moaned. Lucinda felt helpless. She had a gift, a gift Bernard had stolen, one that could help this young man. She knew it would do no good to try, so she knelt next to him and helped Trent lift Ant into a sitting position.

"I feel like I've been danced on by elephants wearing clodhoppers," said Ant. "Where's Happy?"

"Seriously, man. Now you wanna find your bliss?" asked Trent incredulously.

Lucinda felt chilled to her bones. He couldn't mean . . . no, no, no! Happy would never try to find her. She was safe at the convent. Bernard couldn't hurt her while she lived on neutral ground.

"That's her name, moron." He hissed in pain. "She was hitching into Nevermore and I picked her up. I was taking her into town—to Taylor."

Panic welled. "What happened? Tell me!"

"I don't know. She was scared. Told me to turn around." He stared at Lucinda, his brown eyes shadowed with pain. "Something took control of the car and we hit the gods-be-damned tree. Then it was lights out."

"Happy!" she yelled. "Happy!" Lucinda stood up and hurried around the truck. She peered into bushes, circled the huge tree, checked the ditches, and screamed for her friend over and over.

"Lucinda!" Trent grabbed her shoulders and shook her. "She's gone, all right? Maybe she went down the road to get help or something."

Hope speared her for a brief moment . . . then faded. No way would Happy abandon someone injured. Not without at least seeing to his comfort. She was smart and brave and loyal. Tears dripped down Lucinda's cheeks. Who had caused the accident? And had someone taken Happy? "I promised to take care of her. I promised her mother that no harm would come to her daughter. Oh, Goddess!"

"I know you're freaked, but you need to hold it together. Call Gray and let him know what happened. I'll stay with Ant, and you can go search for the girl."

"Okay," said Lucinda. She sucked in a calming breath, and then went in search of an aqueous surface. Trent was right. Gray would help them. She just hoped he could forgive her for keeping one last dangerous secret.

Gray and Ember stood on the sidewalk in front of the Sew 'n' Sew watching Taylor fiddle with the lock. Gray couldn't decide if he was annoyed or amused by Taylor's stubbornness.

"Damn thing is stuck," muttered the sheriff.

"Or the locks have been changed," said Gray.

"No one's been in here since the owner." Taylor kept trying to shove in the key, which fit but wouldn't turn.

"Maybe it unlocks the back door," offered Gray.

"Your puddle's ringing," said Taylor. "Why don't you answer it and leave me alone?"

Gray looked at the dip in the sidewalk that had collected murky water. Blue sparkles burst from it and then he saw the expression on Lucy's face. His smile faded instantly. "What's wrong, baby?"

He and Ember leaned over the water.

"There was an accident. The sheriff's brother hit that big oak tree, the one where Brujo Boulevard forks."

"Is he all right?" asked Taylor sharply. He pushed between Gray and Ember and damned near stuck his face in the puddle. Gray understood his friend's concern. His own worries were dropping like stones into his stomach.

"He's alive, but injured. And Happy is gone."

"Shit," said Taylor. "Shit."

Gray and Ember turned questioning looks to Taylor. He grimaced. "Ant picked up a girl hitchhiking to Nevermore last night. She passed out in the truck, so he brought her home and let her stay the night. I knew that runaway was trouble the minute I laid eyes on her."

"This isn't her fault," cried Lucy. "I'm going to look for her. Please, Gray, please come."

"I'm on my way. But wait for me."

"Ren's in that area searching for Trent," said Taylor. "He'll get to her faster than we can."

"Trent's here," said Lucy. "He was walking toward town. He says he woke up in a ditch and—" Her head jerked up. "I see Ren!" She waved at someone, purportedly Ren, and then her eyes went wide. "Oh, my Goddess! Trent! Stop, please. No!"

Gray's heart nearly stopped. "Lucy!"

The puddle went dark.

All Gray could think about was getting to his wife. Panic clawed at him. Had Trent hurt her? Goddess! Lucy had his truck. Shitshitshit. He looked at Taylor, feeling raw and helpless.

"I have a portal in my office, remember?" Taylor was already striding across the street. "And there's another one near that tree. It'll only take us a few seconds. C'mon."

Taylor insisted on going first, even though Guardian trumped sheriff. In this case, Taylor said, he was protecting the Guardian from his damn fool self, so Gray had let him go on ahead.

Gray hadn't been sure what to expect when the three of them arrived, but Trent holding a protection bubble made from sparkling black swirls around him and Ant wasn't even on the list.

Lucy and Ren were nowhere in sight.

When Trent saw Gray, Taylor, and Ember, the kid looked relieved. He dropped his palms, muttered his thanks and a prayer, and the magic dissipated. Ant was propped against the tree, his eyes closed, one hand closed over a knobby root. Taylor squatted near his brother and put his hand on his shoulder.

"Not yet," muttered Ant. "Almost there."

"He's been communing with that tree for the last couple of minutes," said Trent.

"Communing?" Taylor's gaze jerked to his brother's placid expression. "You're not a magical."

"Ah yes," said Ember. "Earth magic. I see it now."

Gray hadn't. He'd never sensed that Ant was a magical, and certainly not Trent. All he really cared about was Lucy. He wanted badly to charge into a battle, any battle, to save his woman, but he knew doing so could endanger her further.

"I'm a necro," admitted Trent. "With some earth magic thrown in. It's not something I advertise."

"I didn't sense you at all," said Gray. He looked at Ember, and she shook her head. She hadn't known, either.

"Mom and Dad taught me how to hide it. I don't want my life defined by other people's idea of what I am, okay?"

"I don't care if you're magical or mundane," said Gray impatiently. "Where's Lucy?"

"Ren took her."

Everyone stared at him, and Trent took a step back and lifted his hands in a don't-kill-the-messenger gesture.

"Why the hell would he take off with her and not take Ant with 'em?" asked Taylor.

"Dude. You're not listening. He *took* her. He whacked her across the temple with his gun and then tossed her into an SUV. He was gonna shoot us."

That was why Trent had enacted a protection spell for him and Ant. Even so, Gray couldn't wrap his brain around what Trent was saying. Ren had kidnapped Lucy, and tried to kill two of his own friends?

"He didn't know you were magical, did he?"

"No. He kinda freaked out. He dumped Lucinda in his truck then took off up Old Creek." Trent sent an apologetic look to Gray. "I'm sorry. I couldn't get to her."

"You did what you could. I appreciate it."

Trent nodded, but he still looked miserable. Gray felt the same, except a hundred times worse. Why had Ren taken Lucinda? And where?

"Son of a bitch," said Taylor. "He's been under our noses the whole time."

Ant's eyes popped open. "Ren killed Lennie. That's what Tree says. He was waiting here, waiting for Lennie to come charging down the road. He'd been drinking, as usual, but it was Ren who made the car swerve into Tree. It hurt her." He sighed, rubbing the trunk. "And so did my truck."

"You're creeping me out." Taylor stood up and backed away, eyeing the tree as if it might suddenly start talking. "Why would Ren kill Lennie?"

Gray understood all too well. "He was the link to Marcy. She asked me how she could love someone who did awful things. She must've been talking about Ren. She wanted to protect the town, but she couldn't bring herself to betray him. So she stole the demon's eye and left town."

"Lennie was dumb as a rock and as big as a black bear," added Trent. "He would've done anything Ren told him. They were tight."

"Lennie killed Marcy," said Taylor. "I can't believe it." He kicked the tire of the wrecked truck. "What the hell does Ren need magical objects for?"

"He has magic," said Ant. "But it's very weak. He

uses objects to magnify his power. Tree says if he didn't live in Nevermore, he wouldn't have even discovered what little power he has."

"What does that mean?" asked Taylor.

"Nevermore was built to protect a Goddess fountain," said Ember softly. "Magic is amplified here."

"I thought Goddess fountains were a myth," said Gray.

"Better that they are thought of as myths than proven to be real," said Ember. "Very few know the real locations. The Dragons who founded Nevermore knew the truth—they were sent by the Goddess to protect this place."

"The Goddess told you all that, did she?"

"Yes, Gray. The Creator Mother told me. And She also say no more secrets! Not for dis town or for you."

"Message received." Gray turned away and walked to the edge of the road. He couldn't imagine what Lucy was feeling now. Scared. Alone. In fear for her life. As far as he was concerned, Ren's life was forfeit. He'd hurt Lucy, and that was an unforgivable offense. He sucked in a steadying breath and then returned to his friends. All they could do was puzzle everything out and make a plan. He was filled with a razor-sharp sense of urgency. *I'm coming, baby. Just hold on.*

"This doesn't make sense," said Taylor. "Why would Ren take Happy, and leave Ant alive . . . only to return to take Lucy and try to shoot Trent and Ant? He could've killed Ant easily after the accident."

"Tree says Ren didn't cause my wreck. She says it was a man whose magic felt . . ." He frowned. "I think she means sickness. The guy's ill."

"Ren has a partner, then." Taylor eyed the tree with something akin to respect. "Someone we may not know."

What Gray couldn't figure out was how Lucy, and this

girl Happy, fit in with Ren's plans. Then an idea occurred that chilled his blood. "He wants to be a full magical."

"That's impossible," said Taylor. "You can't just turn yourself into one."

"But you can bargain for such power," said Ember, horror coating her words. "And you can sacrifice for it."

"Enough dillydallying," barked Taylor. "Ember? Can you take Ant back to the tea shop and fix him up?"

"Of course."

"Take Trent with you." Taylor looked at Gray. "We'll port to Ren's farm and see if Harley knows where his son is." He swore. "That's how Ren got around so fast. He knows where all the portals are . . . and he's got a key to 'em."

"I'm coming with you," said Trent.

"Kid, go home and let your uncle know you're not dead."

"You don't get it, do you? Ren was setting me up to take the fall for the café fire. He knocked me out somehow and tossed me in a ditch. He knew I'd wake up without a memory, and I wouldn't have an alibi."

"Why would he—" Taylor's eyes went wide. "He wasn't sure if we'd buy the story that Cathleen torched it."

Gray nodded. "It makes sense. He told us that Trent woke him up to report the fire. He made sure Trent disappeared long enough to look suspicious."

"Bastard had a plan B ready." Fury etched Taylor's expression.

"So I can go?"

"Not a chance."

Trent opened his mouth—probably to argue—but Ember reached out and patted the boy's arm. "This is not your journey to take, but you'll be needed soon. Help me take Ant back to the shop."

Trent sighed, his shoulders sagging. "All right."

Ember took Gray aside, laid her hands on his shoulders, and looked him deeply in the eyes. "You must close the circle Ren opened with his avarice. Bring peace to Nevermore, and to yourself."

"I will."

"Good luck, Guardian."

Ember and Trent helped Ant to his feet. Then Ember opened the portal with a wave of her hand, and they all disappeared.

"C'mon," said Taylor. "Let's go find us a traitor."

Chapter 14

Lucinda woke up to the sounds of two men arguing. She immediately recognized one voice—she knew too well the cadence of Bernard's fury. As her eyesight adjusted to the dim lighting, she realized she was in a barn—tied up and placed upright against a rough wood wall. The scent of manure was thick enough to stick in her lungs. She tried to breathe through her mouth to dampen the awful stench.

A few feet away, she spotted Happy lying on a decrepit door that had been propped on two sawhorses. The girl was sweating, her body quivering. She wasn't tied up, but Lucinda sensed the magic keeping her flat against the surface. Bernard was powerful—and he'd done something awful to her friend. She couldn't let Bernard hurt Happy. She'd failed the girl's mother, but she wouldn't fail her. *Think, Lucinda. Think!*

But her mind felt too foggy, and pain throbbed in her temple. Her head ached where the gun had impacted. She couldn't believe Ren had hurt her. He'd seemed so nice. Everyone liked him, trusted him. And if betraying his friends and his hometown weren't enough, he'd been in league with Bernard.

"Gray will come for her. We have to summon Kahl." He pointed to a rickety table where various items gleamed. "I have the eye, and the spell."

"But not the magic." Bernard laughed, and a chill went through her. He got that kind of amused only right before he did something nasty.

Apprehension flashed through Lucinda. Ren had made a deal with Kahl to take Gray? She had to stop them before they called the demon lord. She'd fight to her dying breath to protect her husband from suffering through all that again.

"You shouldn't have taken the girl." Ren's anger was tainted with alarm. Lucinda guessed that he'd figured out how dangerous Bernard was—but the realization was surely too late.

"Can't a father reunite with his daughter?" Bernard reached down and stroked Happy's hair. "Now my daughter sustains Lucy's curse, and I'm free to become Guardian of Nevermore."

Ren screamed, cocking his fist and aiming toward Bernard's sneering visage. Bernard aimed his hand at Ren, palm out, and said, "Electrify."

The air went thick and hot. Goose bumps broke out on Lucinda's flesh and she bit her lower lip to keep from crying out. Her heart pounded fiercely as the familiar beat of fear pulsed within her.

Blue magic sizzled out from Bernard's palm and hit Ren full in the chest. The man lifted off the ground and flew across the barn. It was too dark to see where he landed, but she heard the crash.

Then nothing.

Bernard turned toward her, smiling.

Everything inside her went cold.

"Well, my darling. Here we are. Together, at last."

Lucinda swallowed the knot clogging her throat. She wouldn't show her terror even though it crawled inside her like a living thing. "What did you do to Happy?"

"I've told you many times that my daughter is not

your concern." He walked toward her, his gaze fastened on her mouth. "You are still quite lovely. It's too bad I have to kill you." He paused and lifted one elegant shoulder. "Maybe I'll just let my pain-in-the-ass kid die and keep you instead."

"No!" She wouldn't let Happy die. "Tell me what you did!"

"I can't resist you," mused Bernard. "It's that delicious Rackmore charisma, I suppose. All right, then. I'll indulge my little ice queen. Your curse requires feeding. Think of it like a vicious pet. Happy's life force is its food. The thing is, it feeds on a bloodline—in this case, her mother's. I was trying to figure out which of my children should help out Daddy when who do I discover? My missing daughter. And here you are, too, my missing lover. It's been a very good day."

Lucinda sifted through the information. She'd never learned much about curses beyond the idea of "Curses are bad; don't use them." Then she understood. She felt sickened by Bernard's selfishness. The man had no conscience. "It was feeding on your bloodline. Oh, Goddess. You transferred to Talia's?"

"Well, Talia was the only child of two only children, whose parents and grandparents are all dead. If Happy dies . . . so does your curse."

"And if I die?"

"She lives." He squatted next to her. "I'm surprised that I'm suffering from indecision. I've dreamed of killing you for so long. Slowly, of course. Just imagining your screams . . . mmm . . . delicious." In his gaze swirled fury and lust and all those terrible emotions that made Bernard so powerful and so terrifying. He was going to hurt her, just like he'd hurt her all those times before. "You know, I didn't think I would enjoy the countryside that much, but Nevermore has a certain ... magic to it. Don't you think?"

"Gray will kill you."

"Doubtful." Fury flashed in his gaze. "You ungrateful bitch. You married him—knowing that you belong to me."

He raised his hand and slapped her hard. Her head snapped back and she tasted blood. Anger spiked through the icy ghosts of her old fears. Lucinda thought of Gray, of how he made her feel, and she latched on to those emotions. Duty. Trust. Loyalty.

She glared at Bernard. "I belong to him," she said. "I belong to Gray."

He leaned back on his heels and studied her. "You've gotten some of your old spirit back." His eyes went dark, and he licked his lips. "That was my favorite part, you know. Breaking you. At the end, when you used your power to save Talia, I was ... enthralled by your rebellion. And rather looking forward to the challenge of breaking you all over again. Then you disappeared. And you kidnapped my own flesh and blood. It was arrogant and foolish." He threaded his fingers through her hair, and she flinched. He grinned as he leaned forward, his lips angling toward hers. "You need to be punished."

"So do you." Lucinda reared back and slammed her forehead into his. Stars burst behind her eyes, and her aching head imploded with agony. She sagged against the wall, trying to push down the nausea. Damn it. That hurt a helluva lot more than she thought it would.

Bernard was knocked on his ass. Even though Lucinda's vision was wonky from her head-butt, she snapped out her bound legs and managed to nail him in the crotch. With her ankles duct-taped together, the kick wasn't hard enough to cause real damage, but the connection still hurt him. He rolled onto his side, roaring in pain. "Bitch," he wheezed. "I'll kill you."

Good. She wanted him to. Because then Happy would live. And Gray would conquer Bernard. She knew he would. Bernard didn't know true power, didn't understand it. She wished she'd be around to see Gray kick his ass. Soon, the Raven bastard wouldn't hurt anyone else ever again.

Taylor barely restrained Gray from blowing up the barn. When they saw the department's decrepit SUV parked in front, they knew Ren had taken Lucy inside. The house was nearly a mile away, with a separate driveway accessed from the main road.

Harley had been passed out drunk on the couch. They'd wasted precious time getting the old man upright and pouring coffee into him. Harley wouldn't say anything against his son, but mentioned that Ren had been spending a lot of time at the abandoned barn at the edge of the property. They'd left Harley in the kitchen with orders to finish the whole pot.

The doors were closed, but even so, there was a sliver of space between them. They paused there and heard voices—a man's and a woman's. They were too muffled for Taylor to understand the words, much less whom the voices belonged to.

"Lucy," whispered Gray fiercely. He lurched forward, his hands splaying out as magical fire licked his fingertips.

"Hold it." Taylor grabbed his friend by the shoulder and then yelped. "Shit. Why are you so hot?"

"It's my magic," said Gray, but he frowned, and Taylor realized that Gray wasn't sure why his skin was overheating. "I want my wife."

"If we burst in there without knowing what's going on, we could get her killed. C'mon, man. Think."

Gray nodded. "You're right." He studied the building. "Look."

Taylor followed Gray's line of sight. On the barn's left corner, several boards had rotted away, leaving a huge gap. It was big enough for them to squeeze through. Hopefully there was a place to hide while they checked out the situation.

Taylor was trying really hard not to think about Ren's betrayal, or what might've already happened to Lucinda and Happy. And he couldn't begin to figure out the identity of Ren's partner—whoever it was, he owed him payback for what he'd done to Ant. Fury boiled inside him. He might be acting coolheaded, but it was an effort. Like Gray, he had the impulse to rush in and shoot someone.

They picked their way through high grass and uneven ground. Taylor stepped through the jagged opening, trying to be as quiet as possible. Gray followed him. Luckily, a rusted tractor and moldering haystacks blocked the makeshift entrance. The dirt-packed floor concealed the sounds of their footsteps. They stayed close to the wall. The conversation between the man and the woman continued. The man's tone was smarmy, and Lucy's was constrained.

They heard a low moan, then a ragged, pain-filled cough. They paused, staring at each other.

This part of the barn was filled with shadows. Taylor's eyes adjusted to the lack of light. He and Gray searched the hay-littered ground for the source of the noise.

"Taylor." Gray jerked his head to the right.

Ren lay in a tangled heap of barn debris. He'd landed on a spike of wood that pierced his chest. Taylor's stomach roiled. The metallic stench of blood was overwhelming, especially mixed in with all the smells of mold and manure.

Taylor knelt next to Ren. The boy's gaze tracked him. Even though Ren had betrayed him, had betrayed all of them, he couldn't stop the waves of horror. "He's alive."

Gray's expression was ice-cold. "Not for long."

"Brother," Ren whispered. Blood bubbled from his lips. Then his eyes glazed over, and what little light was in them faded.

Taylor wished he had Gray's ability to cut out those pesky interfering emotions. He wanted to hate Ren, but he didn't. Not even knowing that Ren tried to put a bullet in Ant and Trent, he couldn't work up anything but fury and shame. Gods-be-damned. He couldn't forget his friend's finer moments, even though his kindness had hidden such an evil soul.

"Why the hell did he call me brother?" asked Taylor. He stood up and joined Gray at the edge of the darkness that hid them.

"Does it matter?"

"Yeah," said Taylor, annoyed with Gray's dismissive tone. "It does."

"Ponder it later. We have a bigger problem." Gray pointed to the man squatting next to Lucy. "That's Bernard Franco."

"Shit. He was Ren's partner?" Taylor's gaze caught on the girl flattened on a weathered door propped on sawhorses. "That's Happy. He's got her laid out like a solstice feast."

"He's keeping her pinned with magic. I'll free her and you grab her. Take her to Ember's. I'll get Lucy."

"And Franco?"

Gray's ice-blue eyes met his, and Taylor knew then that Franco wouldn't live to see the sunset. He might've had a regret or two about Ren, but he had no qualms about Franco breathing his last. Taylor was a lawman, sworn to protect the laws of Nevermore and the state of Texas. But he had another oath, one more binding than any other: Protect the Guardian and the citizens of Nevermore.

No one around these parts would be safe so long as Franco lived.

And that was that.

"I'll create a distraction," said Gray. "Then I'll free Happy. Get her and run. Franco will be too busy to follow."

Taylor heard a thwack. He watched as Lucinda head-butted Franco and then kicked him in the balls. "Wow. She's got some moves."

Franco writhed on the ground, and then he screamed, "I'll kill you!"

Taylor felt the change in the atmosphere as Gray gathered magic. A huge red fireball appeared between his outstretched hands. Then he lobbed it—right at Franco. The blackhearted wizard was too good at protecting his own hide to get bombarded that easily. Franco rolled away from the flames and popped to his feet. Gray made some other gestures aimed toward Happy, then yelled, "Go!"

Taylor took off toward the girl.

Gray fully engaged Franco in a war of magic. Fire and lightning roared between them. Taylor scooped the unconscious Happy into his arms. He caught Lucinda's gaze, and saw the relief and gratitude in her eyes.

Taylor wished he could save her, too. He took a step toward her, even though it meant getting between two battling wizards. The air smelled like ozone, and the ground trembled. But Lucinda shook her head fiercely, then jerked it toward the doors. "Go," she mouthed. "Please."

He had to trust that Gray would save his wife.

Taylor took off at a full run. He turned so that his shoulder hit the door hard. Pain exploded down his arm, but he ignored the agony. The doors burst open, and he kept going.

All he had to do now was get to the portal.

Gray's fury fueled his magic. He threw everything he could at Franco. The wizard retaliated quickly, but he was still forced to move back, away from Lucy.

Sweat poured off Gray. He'd expended a lot of energy on the café's cleansing. He wasn't as strong as he needed to be, but his worry for Lucy kept him from giving in. Franco was too good, though. Every time Gray struck at him with fire or electricity or wind, the bastard gave it back twofold.

"This is pointless!" screamed Franco. "She's not worth it."

Gray didn't respond. He wasn't going to waste his breath talking to Franco. Lucy was worth everything. He wouldn't let Franco hurt her, not ever again.

"Enough!" roared Franco. He created a huge ball of black-edged flames. Gray prepared his own magic to dissipate it, but he shouldn't have bothered. Obviously, Franco was getting as tired as Gray, because his aim was way off.

Behind him, he heard Lucy scream.

And realized Franco's aim had been perfect.

Gray turned around and ran toward her, but he was too late. His wife was consumed by the dark magic. Franco's laughter echoed in the barn, wrapping around the sounds of Lucy's screams, and the horrific crackle of the magical fire.

"Lucinda!" Gray tried to grab her, but it was like trying to scoop up shadows. He called forth the sacred energies, but neither wind nor water responded. She was dying, and without her, he was nothing. She gave his life meaning, she made him whole.

He wouldn't let her die alone.

He jumped into the flames, felt the heat, the power, and nearly collapsed from the darkness of it all. Now that he was within Bernard's heinous spell, he could see Lucy was intact, but suffering. *I'm here, baby, I'm here.* She was sobbing, and so terrified, and he couldn't bear it. He wrapped his arms around her and held tight.

Together, they burned.

Are you not the master of fire, Chosen?

The world froze. The flames surrounding them, binding them, stopped flickering. Lucy lay statuelike in his arms, tears glittering on her pale face. She lay against him, eyes squeezed shut, her bound hands trying to hold on to his shirt.

Even the world beyond the spell held still, crystalline and immovable.

"What's going on?" he asked.

He swore he could smell . . . spring. Wet earth, cut grass, sweet flowers. Warm wind wrapped around him, as soft and comforting as a mother's arms, and he realized he was feeling Her presence.

"Goddess?"

The night Kerren killed you, your spirit called out for help and your ancestor Jaed answered. The essence of your family's symbol fused with you.

"I don't understand."

You are not demon. You are dragon.

He was infused with the truth of Her statement, and he knew that the creature he'd so feared, the one he'd fought off for the last ten years, was not evil. It was an innate part of him, spirit dwelling within spirit.

More of my Chosen will be drawn to Nevermore. You

must welcome them. You must prepare for what is to come.

"What's coming?"

Do not worry. You will be prepared. Take your second form, Gray. Claim your power.

The world unfroze.

The flames returned, but now Gray understood. He commanded the flames, no matter real or magic. *Go away,* he told them, and they instantly turned to smoke. He heard Bernard's cry of disbelief, but it sounded like the mewl of a scared kitten. Yes, Gray was the master of fire, and he, too, was the master of the beast within him. *Come forth, dragon,* he demanded. *Save our lady.*

Lucy had passed out, and he gently laid her on her side.

Then he stood.

The magic of Gray's second form unfolded within him.

He watched Bernard stomp toward him, and then he hesitated, eyes going wide. "Impossible!" he screamed.

Gray's scar pulsed with light, with purpose. His skin flaked away to reveal the shiny red of his scales. Then the magic burst forth, red fire and gold sparks, and the human receded, giving way to the dragon.

The creature expanded, growing wider and taller, filling up the space in the barn. Dragon's massive head brushed the wooden ceiling beams. *How annoying.* He lifted a wing to cover his mate, then aimed his snout at the ceiling and issued a fireball. The roof became instant ash, its crumbling edges falling to the ground below.

The human screamed. He scrambled backward, and stalled, cowering in the darkness beyond. His face was bloated with shock, his eyes bulging and his lips flopping open like the mouth of a freshly caught fish.

Disgusting.

"You tried to kill Lucinda," accused Dragon, his voice booming.

"No," the man protested hoarsely. "No."

"You dare lie?"

He turned and ran, but he tripped over debris and sprawled on the floor. He was wailing and crying. Dragon sniffed the air, and snorted. The ugly little thing had soiled himself, as well. He was crawling through the dirt and hay scattered on the floor, sobbing like an orphaned hatchling.

Dragon spit fire. Just a little. Flames licked across the man's feet, melting his shoes and toasting his pants.

He shouted in agony and rolled over and over. Dragon watched the human's actions with bored interest. Hmm. Fry him? Not worth his precious fire. Eat him? Someone with so foul a stench would surely give him indigestion. Ah. That left one option.

"Do you not know what Lucinda is?" asked Dragon. He leaned down, though it took some maneuvering. With one claw, he rolled the man onto his back and peered into his tiny face. "She is the heart of the dragon."

Then Dragon rose to his full height, his magnificent head poking out of the ceiling's hole, and he stepped on the awful human. The crunch of bones and the squish of flesh were most satisfying. Dragon shook his foot to get off the bits, and then wiped his claws on a pile of hay. Humph. Messy.

Dragon looked at the sky, feeling the siren call of the wind. His nature was entwined with his human, and he understood that playing in the clouds and kissing the sky with his fire must wait. They had work to do yet.

So Dragon closed his eyes, and slipped back into the ancient magic that bound him with Gray, and set his master free.

*   *   *

Gray woke up in his own bed. At least he thought he was in his own bed. The covers had been changed and the room itself was clean. It smelled like vanilla and lemon oil. He stared at the empty space next to him, and panic welled. He shot up and whipped off the covers. "Lucinda!"

The door to the master bathroom burst open and Lucy stood there in one of his old T-shirts, her toothbrush brandished like a sword. "What?" She looked around. "What is it?"

Gray was so relieved to see her that he scrambled outta bed and swept her into his arms. He rained kisses on her face. "I thought you were gone. I thought I lost you."

"You saved me," she said softly.

"You saved me first." He sucked in a breath. "What happened?"

"You've been asleep for almost a day. I woke up a few hours ago and got all the skinny. Ren's dead."

"I remember that part. I'm fuzzy on everything that happened next."

"Bernard got squished."

A memory flickered. *You are not demon. You are dragon.* "Define squished."

"Like something the size of the Chrysler Building stepped on him."

"Lucy." He swallowed the sudden knot in his throat. "I talked to the Goddess. She told me I was . . . a dragon."

She stared at him. "Okay."

"Okay?" He blinked. "It's that easy?"

"I saw you. I came to for a few seconds just before you shifted back. You were magnificent."

The tightness in his chest unfurled. "When I was trapped in hell, I called for help, and Jaed answered. The dragon saved me. All this time I thought I had somehow brought a demon with me. I was so ashamed."

"I wouldn't care if you brought a demon with you," she said fiercely. "You survived. And however you managed it, I'm glad." She kissed his chin. "You did. Taylor said when he returned with the cavalry, we were lying together, unconscious. You were naked. Kinda like you are now."

Gray was immediately distracted. "You could be naked with me."

"We have guests. And Happy still hasn't recovered." She looked at him, devastation in her eyes. "The curse will kill her, Gray. Unless I"—she gulped—"die first."

"No. We'll find a way, Lucy. I'll save you both."

"Ember's working on potions and spells and who knows what." She pulled him over to the bed, considered him in such a way that his cock perked up, and then went to the dresser. She pulled out a pair of sweats and tossed them to him. "I can't tell you how much I regret covering up even an inch of that spectacular body."

"If you want me to be serious, you might not want to give me compliments like that. It makes the blood rush out of my brainpan and into other areas."

Lucy cocked an eyebrow at him. Gray sighed and pulled on the pants. Then he sat on the bed. "All right. Let's chat."

Lucy joined him on the bed, pulling her knees up to her chest and wrapping her arms around her legs. "About six months ago, I turned twenty-five. I started to question what I was doing with Bernard. That was my first clue he'd been using compulsion magic—just to ensure I'd stay with him. I don't know why, Gray, but he wanted to make sure I didn't use my thaumaturgy. After I became less malleable, he took me to a guarded penthouse, and that's the first time I learned he had a harem of mistresses. That's where I met Talia Ness and her daughter, Happy."

Gray looked at her incredulously.

"Yep. Talia named her daughter Happy Ness. Because her little girl was all the happiness she had. Talia was very sweet. She was smart in her own way, but . . ." Lucinda sighed. "Bernard liked her because she never said a word to him, no matter how nasty he got. She did anything he asked, no question. Talia didn't see the point in fighting Bernard, or trying to escape. Not even after she got pregnant with his child. She was seventeen when Happy was born."

Gray sensed her sadness and rubbed her back. "You okay?"

"Not really." She smiled at him, but he could see she was trying to hold back tears. "I stayed there three months. Talia, Happy, and I became friends. A family. Then one night, Bernard visited the penthouse and he was upset. Furious. Of course, he took Talia, because he could be as mean as he wanted. He beat her to death."

"I'm so sorry."

"That's not the worst part. I saved her. I don't know how I got my power to work. I haven't been trained that well, and I just . . . oh, Goddess. I just wanted so badly to save her. And I did.

"Bernard was enraged that I'd undone her death. I'd usurped his power with my own, and he couldn't tolerate that. Two of his goons held me and he made me watch while he slit her throat. She bled out in minutes, and I couldn't save her again. He made sure of it."

Gray wrapped his arms around her and kissed her hair. If he could find a way to flatten Bernard again, he would. He felt approval from the dragon, too. It was an odd feeling to embrace the creature he'd spent so much time trying to ignore. "That's when he cursed you, isn't it?"

She nodded. "Only he didn't know that I'd already

set a plan into motion to escape. I was wearing pajamas and cashmere socks, but I managed to get us both out of there. I found her a place to stay—a nunnery built on neutral ground. Then I tracked down everyone I ever knew to ask for help."

He squeezed her tighter, feeling the renewal of his own guilt. How could he have turned her away? He didn't think he'd ever forgive himself for ignoring her pleas of help.

"You helped me," she said softly, as though she could read his thoughts. "You came back for me. You're an honorable man, Gray. And even honorable men can lose their way." She lifted her head and stared at him. "The important thing is that you find your way back."

"You gave me that," he said. He kissed her, his heart full, and even his dragon snorted with approval. "You know, maybe we should keep the whole dragon thing quiet for a while. Until I figure out how it all works."

"Your secret is safe with me."

Gray looked down into his wife's face, to the acceptance and tenderness she so easily showed him. "And everything you are, Lucy, is safe with me."

"You look like shit."

Ant jerked up and met the pain-filled gaze of Happy. "You should talk, Sassy Mouth. Seen a mirror lately?"

She grinned, and his heart skipped a beat.

He leaned forward and pulled up the covers, tucking her in more securely.

"Where am I?"

"Guest room at the Guardian's house. You ask that every time you wake up."

"Oh." She blinked. "You're here every time I wake up?"

"Yep. There's nothing good on TV."

She snorted. "So you'd rather watch me?"

"Best show there is," he said easily. "You've got that drooling-in-your-sleep thing down pat."

Horror entered her eyes and her little pink tongue flicked out. Then she realized he was teasing. "So not cool."

The rocking chair he sat on had ceased being comfortable, but he wouldn't leave her side. So many people had abandoned her, and she needed to know that she was worth sticking around for. She looked too pale. Her life was literally draining away, and there was nothing he could do. Every day the shadows deepened under her eyes. She couldn't eat, and the only fluids that stayed down were Ember's crazy tea concoctions.

Happy was dying.

And his heart was breaking.

"It's okay to let me go," said Happy. "I'm all right with taking a dirt nap."

"That makes one of us." He leaned forward and brushed her hair back. "You're not gonna die."

"I have to. If I don't, Lucy will stay cursed. And the world needs her."

"The world needs you, too."

"Uh-huh." She rolled her eyes. Then she grinned at him again. "I was right about you bein' a magical, huh?"

"Yep. I put a gold star on your chart an' everything."

"Yeah? How many stars I got on that chart of yours?"

"Just the one."

She laughed, but the joyful noise turned into a vicious cough. Blood dribbled from her mouth, and Ant grabbed a towel from the nightstand and pressed it to her lips. After a moment, she ceased trying to hack up a lung, and fell back against the pillow. "Hard to breathe. My lungs feel squishy."

He couldn't bear that she was in so much pain. But he hid his worries behind a smile, digging into the pocket of his jeans. "Hey, Sassy Mouth. I got something for you."

"Is it shiny and expensive?"

"Nope."

"Well, give it to me anyway."

He pulled the bracelet out. He'd been playing around with his new power and he'd created the jewelry from strands of grass and flower petals, binding it with the gossamer of a spider's web. Green was the main color, and glittering between the thin strands were dots of pink, purple, white, and blue. He slipped it on Happy's thin wrist. "This here's a promise band."

"You made that up." She studied it. "It's beautiful, Ant."

"Just like you are."

"I think you get a gold star deducted from your chart for being a liar, liar, pants on fire."

"You are beautiful, Happy. Not just on the outside, but the inside. Your heart is the most beautiful thing about you." He cleared his throat. "So. I promise to always be your friend. To be there when you need me. To give you a free hug any time you need it, and to always give you a shoulder to cry on."

She stared at him, her eyes filled with longing. "All that for me?"

"All that and more." He got on his knees next to the bed and gathered her frail, cold hands in his. "If you're still interested, later, as in three, maybe four years, there's a romance upgrade that's part of the package."

"You won't wait for me," said Happy. "It's, like, *eons* away. And let's not forget that I'm kinda probably not gonna be alive." Her eyes narrowed. "Are you just doin' this because I'm biting the big one?"

He groaned and pressed his face into the covers. Then he raised his head. "I wouldn't lie to you, not even on your deathbed. Which you're not. Have some faith."

She looked at him, and he saw in that gaze the wisdom of a woman who understood things about life he never would. It rocked him, that look. She smiled so sadly, and said, "I believe that you believe."

"I'll take it." He kissed her knuckles. "Now rest."

Her eyes fluttered closed, and when he was sure she was asleep, he got to his feet and left the room.

Trent waited in the hallway for him.

"I think I know how to save her," he said. "And if it works, Lucy's curse will be gone, too."

Hope leaped inside him. He grabbed Trent by the shoulder. "How?"

"Well, you're probably not gonna like the first part," said Trent warily.

"Which is . . ."

"You know," he said, wrenching free of Ant's grasp and backing up a step. "The part where she has to die."

Chapter 15

Harley Banton sat in his living room and cried. On the coffee table was an almost empty bottle of Jack Daniel's, photo albums filled with pictures of his family before Lara died, and a loaded Colt .45.

What he'd done twenty years ago haunted his every waking moment. Not even the whiskey helped no more. 'Cause of his sins, he'd lost Lara. And now his boy was gone, too.

Weren't nothing left living for.

Guess he could give the Moorelands some kind of peace. He supposed folks should know the truth of it all.

He took the pen and the notebook paper he'd scrounged from a kitchen drawer.

Dear Taylor,

Twenty years ago, I killed your daddy. Him and Lara took up, you see. After Ren was born, she tol' me what she done. She wanted a baby, and I couldn't give her one. Your daddy liked her a lot. 'Bout the time he made Ant with your mama, he made Ren with my wife.

Harley's hand trembled, and he stopped writing long enough to take a pull from the whiskey bottle. The burn took some of his edge off, and he started writing again.

> *I didn't want your mama to suffer none, so I wrote the letter sayin' he'd left with a Rackmore witch. Seemed like the thing to do. I can see now it was worse for y'all, and I'm real sorry.*
>
> *Lara found out what I done. All the light went out of her. She wouldn't hold Ren no more, she stopped eatin', and she cried all the time. She couldn't live with my sin, so she took all them pills. I guess I killed her, too.*
>
> *'Bout five years ago, Ren found Lara's suicide letter. I kept it from the sheriff 'cause she confessed my shame an' her own. Then he kept goin' on about bein' a magical. I didn't know Edward had Wolf blood, but somehow Ren found out about it. He turned into a man I didn't know. Collecting magic objects, sneaking around, lying. He wanted more than the world could give him, than I could give him, just like his mama.*
>
> *It don't matter to me that Ren came from your daddy's seed. He was my boy, and I loved him best I could.*
>
> *Sincerely,*
> *Harley Seymour Banton*

Harley reread the letter, and figured it told the tale just fine. He picked up the pen, and added one last line:

> *P.S. I buried your daddy in my basement.*

Harley finished off the Jack. Then he picked up the Colt and put the barrel to his temple. For the first time in his miserable life, he felt like he was finally doin' something right. He cocked the hammer.

"Lara," he whispered.

Then he pulled the trigger.

Chapter 16

Lucinda sat on the bed next to Happy and held her hand. Ringing the bedside were Gray, Ember, Ant, Taylor, and Trent. Rilton was downstairs with other folks, handling all the questions and worries and giving away a lot of tea and scones. "You sure about doing this, Happy?"

"I'm gonna die either way," she said. "So, it'd be way cool if I died for a few minutes instead of forever."

"Yeah," said Lucinda. "I like that better, too."

Happy glanced at Ant. "I . . . want Ant to hold my hand when I . . . go." She looked at Lucinda anxiously. "Is that okay? What if I . . . don't return? Will you be mad?"

"No," said Lucinda. "I love you."

"Love you back."

Lucinda's worry filled her up like cement, hardening with every damned breath. The idea was for Happy to drink poison. When she died, Trent would use his necromancy magic to grab hold of her soul and keep her long enough for Lucinda's curse to break. Then Lucinda would use her thaumaturgy to heal Happy.

The risk, of course, was that Happy had to die long enough for the curse to break. Too short, and it could renew itself, too long and Happy couldn't be brought back. And it all depended on whether Lucinda could use her power the right way.

"Oh, I almost forgot. I didn't mean to break my promise—you know, about leaving the nuns. But the Goddess asked me to. She said you would understand. She said you would need me, and when I got here, I should tell you"—Happy frowned, obviously trying to remember the exact words—*"Give the heart to the dragon, so he can protect all that is all, in this world and the next, nevermore."* She nodded. "You're the heart, and he's the dragon," she added. "That was the important part."

Lucinda glanced at Gray. He looked slightly dazed, as though Happy's revelation had unlocked another secret inside him. "Thank you, Happy. You're a brave girl."

"Actually, I'm terrified."

"That's my cue," said Ant. He turned to Trent. "You don't bring her back, and you're headed to the underworld next."

"Dude. I got this." Trent sounded confident without any swagger. He looked at Lucinda. "Just because I kept it secret doesn't mean I don't take my gift seriously. I can do it."

"Okay," said Lucinda. She slid off the bed and joined Gray, who put his arm around her. She grasped his waist and held on tightly. *Please let this work,* she prayed. *Please.*

Ant took her place on the bed. He didn't content himself with just holding Happy's hand, though. He put his arm around her and tucked her in close.

"It works quickly, chil'," said Ember as she handed Happy the teacup. "Drink it all. You'll go right to sleep."

Happy nodded. The cup trembled in her hand, but she managed to down the liquid in three big gulps. Ember took the cup and put it on the nightstand.

"How long do you think . . ." Happy's words slurred and faded. Her eyes drifted closed and she fell against Ant's chest.

He held her close, his gaze latched on her face.

Her breathing slowed. . . . Then Happy gave one long hush of sound . . . and died.

Trent stepped forward, his eyes focused on the space above Happy. Ant gripped the girl tightly, and Lucinda saw the tears in his eyes. Her own grief hovered inside like a trapped bird.

Trent lifted his hands and sparkling gray magic emitted from his palms like glittery smoke. It swirled and twisted together, creating a bubble. When the large globe was finished forming, Lucinda could see the pure white light contained within.

Happy's soul.

"I have her," said Trent.

"How long?" asked Ant, his voice hoarse.

"Five minutes should be enough," said Ember. "I'll keep the time."

Each minute seemed to last a century. As soon as Ember intoned, "One minute left," Lucinda felt her whole body go white-hot.

She cried out, her knees buckling. Gray caught her and scooped her into his arms.

Snap. Snick. The sounds started at her feet and kept issuing over and over, faster and faster. Up her legs, torso, arms, neck, head. *Snap. Snick.* It was painful, this release. The magic clung to her, reluctant to leave its host, not wanting death any more than Happy. *Snap. Snick.*

She felt herself go stiff, and then her eyes rolled back in her head. The light burst inside her, gold and black, light and dark. Then she heard a female voice echo inside her mind, *You are my Chosen. You and your mate shall protect the All in All, in the soul, in the heart, nevermore.*

"Lucinda!"

The pain left her in a rush, and when it was all gone, she was left with the sure knowledge of what to do next.

She looked at Gray, who held her so tightly, his gaze worried, and she smiled. "Put me down. I know what to do now."

He did as she asked, and once Lucinda was on her feet, she walked to the bed where Ant cradled Happy's lifeless form. It was so simple. She plucked Trent's glittery gray bubble from the air, and his magic hissed away. "Go home," she whispered to the soul. "You still have work to do."

Then she placed her hand briefly on Happy's still chest. Where her palm had lain, light glowed. The soul sank down into the light, and as soon as it disappeared into Happy's body, the glow faded.

Lucinda leaned down and kissed Happy's forehead. Then she whispered into her ear, "Awake."

Happy sucked in a huge gulp of air, and her eyes flew open. "Holy shit!" she cried. "I can't believe that worked."

Gray couldn't believe everything had turned out all right.

Lucinda was free of her curse.

And if she wanted, free of him, as well.

He was glad Happy had survived the experience. She'd been too excited to stay in bed, so Ant carried her downstairs so the rest of Nevermore could fuss over her. They were all still here, bringing her tea and scones, fluffing her pillow, and with Ant there, by her side.

Gray wondered if Ant knew what a goner he was. Sure, the kid was nineteen and Happy sixteen, but he knew love-struck when he saw it. For instance, his own expression in the mirror.

Lucinda played the hostess, filling teacups and plates until Ember and Rilton shooed her away. She stood in the living room leaning against the doorjamb and watching everyone chat. It was sort of the party she'd wanted, but he hoped ... he hoped she would stay. He'd help her host a party every night if that was what brought her joy. He wanted to see her smile, hear her laugh, feel her hand in his. He wanted to wake up next to her and lose himself in her every night. He wanted to argue with her, and then have hot, stupid makeup sex. Goddess help him, he wanted to do the dishes with her, and sit in the library, even with Grit and Dutch carrying on, and read to her. They'd sit by the fire, her head on his shoulder, while he regaled her with Poe. He'd read "The Raven" to her first because that poem seemed the most appropriate.

Did she want him? Now that she was free of her curse and could do anything, have anyone ... would she stay with him still?

He watched her intently, his heart trapped in his throat, his hands shoved into his pockets. He was riddled with doubts, but so in love with her that every centimeter of him ached with it. She seemed so serene now, as though she'd figured out her place in the world.

He wanted to feel that way, too.

But with her by his side.

"Let's go upstairs," he whispered.

She smiled. "We don't have time for that."

"Just for future reference, there's *always* time for *that*," he said, "but I just wanted to talk to you."

"Okay."

He took her hand and led her upstairs to their bedroom. The whole way there, he rehearsed in his head what he planned to say. Yet, when they arrived in the room, and he'd shut the door to ensure their privacy, he blurted out, "Don't leave me. Please."

"I won't leave you in the lurch," she said carefully. Her gaze searched his face. Could she not see his desperation? His love? He wasn't trying to hide from her anymore.

Gray's throat knotted. If she wanted to go, he'd let her go. He wanted nothing more than her happiness, even if that meant a life without him in it. But he wasn't going to pretend he didn't love her, or that he didn't want to spend the rest of his life with her.

"I love you, Lucinda."

Her eyes widened.

"I'm not pressuring you. If you don't feel the same way, it's okay. I don't want any lies or secrets between us. And I won't make you stay if you want to go. Just . . . please think about it, would you? About being my wife . . . forever."

"You love me."

Tears fell down her cheeks, and Gray felt like an asshole. He'd made her cry. What kind of an idiot made the woman he loved *cry*? He took her into his arms and wiped away her tears. "I'm doing this all wrong! Damn it. Baby, I'm—"

Lucy pressed her fingers against his lips. "Shush. I don't think I can take much more. I love you, too, Gray. When you're not around, I feel like half a person. I'll stay here, by your side, for as long as you want me."

"Until the end of the time?"

"Hmm." She tilted her head. "I may have to check my calendar. . . ."

"Why, you—" He scooped her up and tossed her onto the bed.

"Gray, our guests . . ."

He kissed her until she went pliant beneath him. Then he grinned. "Our guests are fine. They won't miss us."

"You really don't understand the concept of a calendar, do you? I can probably pencil you in on Tuesdays."

"Every day," he muttered, yanking up her shirt and

planting kisses on every inch of smooth flesh. "For the rest of our lives. No. For the rest of *eternity*."

She threaded her fingers through his hair, and he looked up. In her eyes shone her love for him, and finally, oh, finally, he felt as though he'd found his place. In the world.

And in the heart.

Read on for a sneak peek at the next book
in the Wizards of Nevermore series,

NOW OR NEVER

by Michele Bardsley

Coming soon from Signet Eclipse.

Thirty years ago ...

Millicent Dover loved children.

She would never, ever be able to have any of her own. So, she funneled all that unrequited tender regard to her charges at the Raven's Heart orphanage.

Raven's Heart was a repository for those darlings who were too different to succeed in their mundane families. Should an infant begin to show signs of magical heritage or be born with hex marks or, in some sad cases, otherworldly extremities—tails being the most common—the parents could drop off their newborns, or any child up to the age of four, at Raven's Heart.

No questions asked.

A death certificate would be issued and if necessary, a coroner's report.

And the poor, sweet dears would be left in Millicent's care.

Since the House of Ravens funded the orphanage, their members received priority access to the young magicals. Even so, she worked very hard to place the children in good homes, and she worked even harder to make sure the children were well mannered, strong in mind and in body, and above all, obedient.

Millicent didn't tolerate sass.

If by the age of five, the children at Raven's Heart had not been adopted, some were sent to the workhouses in Mexico, and others were gifted to European businesses that catered to a . . . well, *particular* and wealthy clientele.

And then there were Millicent's angels.

Like the adorable cherub who now held her hand so tightly.

She was such a good girl. Smart, pretty, duteous. Millicent loved her angels the best—she really did—but it seemed as though Lenore had more to offer this world.

There was just something about the girl. She had a . . . sparkle.

Well, thought Millicent, *perhaps that shine would serve her well on the other side.* Yes. Sweet little Lenore would be the brightest of all the angels.

Millicent opened the door to the special room. Only her angels were allowed to see it. It was all pink and ruffles and lace. Cheerful. Like walking into a pile of cotton candy.

In the corner sat a white chaise longue, the perfect spot for an angel's repose. They always looked peaceful as they lay down to rest. It was a point of pride for her that they never suffered. She photographed their final moments and put those pictures into the scrapbooks she kept. Sometimes, she would take her dinner breaks in this room, and remember all the children she had loved, and who had loved her.

"It's very pretty in here, Miss Millicent."

"Thank you, dear." She patted the girl's bouncy black curls. "Go sit in the chair. We'll have cookies and tea. And while you enjoy your treats, I'll read you a story."

The tea service was already set up, and so was the plate arrangement of paper-thin cookies.

Lenore took her seat and waited for Millicent to take hers.

"One lump of sugar, or two?" asked Millicent as she picked up the teapot.

"Two, please."

Oh, she was so polite. Such a treasure. Millicent smiled as she poured the fragrant liquid into the delicate china cups. "You must drink all of your tea before taking a cookie."

"Yes, ma'am."

The girl placed the edge of the cup to her lips, and for the tiniest moment, Millicent had the urge to knock it out of her hand.

No. She'd been given her directive. The girl's father himself had insisted his five-year-old daughter be put into Millicent's care, and more specifically, that Lenore be given angelic treatment. Even though it was rare for magicals to give up their own children—especially a powerful Raven like Lenore's father—it wasn't exactly unheard of, either. She'd seen the disappointment in the father's eyes as he looked at his daughter.

Mundanes gave up their children for being too magical.

Lenore's father had given her up because she was not magical enough.

Such a shame, too, because the girl was otherwise perfect. Ah, it was sad, yes. But Millicent had long ago learned that she should not question her betters. Her life was devoted to the children at Raven's Heart. And though she was experiencing unusual qualms about seeing Lenore to the other side, she would do her duty.

The girl took the barest of sips before grimacing. "Miss Millicent, this tastes funny."

Startled, Millicent stared at Lenore's light blue eyes.

She'd seen a crystal like that once, so light blue it was nearly white. Like ice.

Like judgment.

A chill stole through Millicent, but she would not be cowed by the girl. She frowned. "It's very rude to make disparaging comments about what your hostess is serving. You are a guest, Lenore."

"I apologize," she said in a soft, penitent voice. "But isn't it rude of the hostess to put death into the tea?"

Millicent blinked. The brew was her own special blend of herbs and alprazolam. She used just the right amount of jasmine and magic to disguise the taste.

"I would like to go home," said Lenore. She put the full cup into its saucer then folded her hands onto her lap. She stared unblinkingly at Millicent. Those glacier eyes seemed more tinted now, more blue, more . . . magical.

The back of Millicent's neck prickled, and sweat beaded her brow. Lenore really was the most amazing child. None of her angels had ever suspected the tea had been doctored. None had ever uttered a complaint.

"I'm afraid you can't go home," said Millicent.

She nodded, and sighed. "Father does not want me."

"You really should drink the tea, dear. It's for the best."

Lenore glanced at the cup. "No, thank you. May I go now?"

"Where would you go?"

Lenore considered this question, one finger perched on her chin. "Away," she said. "Far, far away."

"That's not a destination," said Millicent. She rose, smoothed out her dress, and smiled at the girl. "While you decide where you would like to go, I will get the book. Do you like the story of Cinderella?"

"Yes," said Lenore.

Millicent turned toward the bookshelf. Not only did the tall, pink case house a well-stocked array of children's titles, but the bejeweled box on the upper shelf held a syringe. It was her plan B. Thirty-four angels she'd sent to the other side, and she'd never had to use it.

Lenore was an amazing child, indeed.

She opened the box and withdrew the syringe, cupping it in her hand to hide it, and then she pulled the oversized pop-up book from its place on a lower shelf.

"Now," she said brightly as she turned, "let's—"

Lenore stood by the table, looking at Millicent with such a sad gaze. "You really aren't very nice," she said. She looked around the room. "They're all here. And they're mad."

Millicent swallowed the sudden tight knot in her throat. She brought the book up to her chest, almost as though it might serve as a shield. "Who's here, Lenore?"

"The children you murdered. They told me about the tea. They told me what you did."

"I would never, ever hurt my angels," she said sharply.

Pity entered Lenore's gaze. She had such an adult look about her. And she was so eerily calm.

"Good-bye, Miss Millicent."

She turned to go. She was even so bold as to take steps toward the door. Millicent was stunned by the chit's gall. Lenore actually believed she could walk out of here. Leave the only person who would ever, *ever* love her.

Rage thrummed through Millicent. She uttered a cry, dropped the book, and raised the syringe. She'd been wrong about Lenore. She wasn't special. She wasn't amazing. She was a horrid, horrid child. She didn't deserve to be an angel. Not ever.

"Evil girl," she hissed as her arm came down. "You will burn in hell."

Lenore stopped, and turned. "Not me," she said, her voice filled with such sorrow. "You."

The syringe never made contact.

Lenore's odd blue eyes blazed as hard and cold as crystal, as ice . . . as death.

Violent wind came out of nowhere. It shattered the china, knocked books off the shelves, ripped the lace curtains. Lenore stood in the middle of the chaos, watching with distant eyes as Millicent was flung backward, the syringe falling uselessly to the pink shag carpet.

She landed on the white chaise, her eyes wide, her mouth opened in a silent scream. Pressure from little hands crushed her chest, and tiny fingers scratched at her windpipe.

Her lungs flattened.

Her heart slowed.

Her vision grayed.

She saw her angels then, all around her, pushing and shoving and clawing.

And as she struggled for her life, to escape from the vengeance of those she had loved so very much, she saw Lenore Thelma White give her one last pitying look, and walk out of the room.

The quiet *snick* of the door closing was the last sound Millicent heard.

Present day . . .

Sheriff Taylor Mooreland glanced at his ever-efficient assistant's desk, just as big and old as his own. It gave him a sense of satisfaction to see everything in its place. The office had been changed here and there over the years, but, like most things in Nevermore, it had mostly stayed the same. He liked the continuity of it all, the way this building and all that it housed had been used by those who'd stood vigil over the town before him.

Arlene kept everything spotless and orderly, just the way he liked it. The black-and-white checkered linoleum floor gleamed despite its age. He suspected Arlene bŏught maĝic-enhanced cleaners, which was fine by him. He didn't want to dip into the coffers to replace anything, for one thing, and for another, he wasn't a big fan of new and different.

New and different meant trouble.

He thought about Lucinda Rackmore—well, Lucinda Calhoun now. She was all kinds of new and different. She turned Gray's world upside down, not to mention the whole town, and it seemed like—though he didn't much like admitting it—everything was somehow better.

Taylor clasped his hands behind his back and looked around. Off to the left of Arlene's desk was a locked door that led to the archives. Only Arlene ventured inside there, and not even he risked invading that domain. To the right of the foyer was the entrance to his own office, which faced Main Street. The picture window allowed him a proper view of downtown, not that there was much to watch.

He did a quick check around, a habit motivated by Ren's betrayal. The deputy had used his access to the office to cull through files, break into Taylor's safe, and paw through Arlene's precious archives.

A narrow hallway led to the former deputy's office, a supply closet, the bathrooms, and the break room, and the back door that opened onto the alley. Beyond the break room was the secured door that led down to the basement, and to the rarely used jail cells. One had been built especially to dampen the powers of magicals, but he'd never had cause to use it.

Satisfied with his inspection, Taylor returned the foyer, and breathed deeply. Yep. Life was all right so long as it had order.

He checked his watch, and frowned. Arlene had been gone for more than half an hour. A couple times a day she'd go across the street and check on Atwood Stephens; the man, who looked like an exhausted rhinoceros, owned both the town garbage service and the weekly paper, *Nevermore News*. His health had been deteriorating rapidly, and not even Lucinda's gift of healing had been able to do much more than slow the decline. Atwood's nephew, Trent Whitefeather, had been taking over more and more of his uncle's responsibilities, and he'd still managed to get straight As in all his classes. School had let out a week ago, so at least the kid didn't have to worry about studying *and* working over the summer.

Taylor turned to go into his office, but he heard the rattle of the entrance door open, so he turned back. He expected to see Arlene chug inside, already complaining about Atwood's stubborn hide, but to his surprise, he saw Gray Calhoun.

"Gray," he said, offering a congenial nod.

"Hey, Taylor," said Gray, smiling.

He did that a lot these days. He was the happiest son of a bitch in town, and a sliver of Taylor felt, well, jealous of his friend's connubial bliss. It made him feel petty, so he heartily shook Gray's hand, and said, "C'mon. I've got fresh coffee."

"You might want something stronger," said Gray as he followed Taylor down the hall and into the break room. "I just got word that my mother will be here on Friday. With all twelve of her *lictors*."

"A dozen bodyguards?" Taylor gestured for his friend

to sit at the table, and Gray grabbed a chair and slid into it. "I thought she only traveled with three."

"Things are tense in the Grand Court," said Gray. "Especially after Leopold White's arrest. Every Consul has been encouraged to keep all their *lictors* close, at least until the fallout can be assessed."

"You got enough room in that house?"

"Not for twelve giants and certainly not for my mother's angst. When I told her about marrying Lucinda, I think her head exploded."

"Well, you did marry the sister of your ex-wife, the one who sold your soul to Kahl to keep her wealth."

"I'm aware," said Gray drily.

Taylor handed the Guardian a mug and then took the spot across from him. "I'm surprised Leticia didn't come down long before now."

"No doubt she stayed away so she could plot in private." He shook his head. "That's not fair. She's upset, I know, but once she meets Lucy, she'll be fine with it." He gave Taylor a sly grin. "And I have an ace in the hole."

"Oh?"

"I get to play the 'mother of your only grandchild' card," said Gray, "because Lucy's pregnant."

Taylor almost dropped his mug. Instead, he put it on the table, and reached over to smack Gray's shoulder. "Congratulations!"

"Thanks."

For a moment, Gray looked dazed, and then he offered such a goofy grin, Taylor couldn't help but laugh.

"How long is your mother staying?" he asked.

Gray blinked. "Ah. Well, through the Summer Solstice festival."

"So, she'll be here for . . ." Taylor narrowed his gaze. "Oh, crap. You haven't told her?"

"No. Other than you and Ember, we haven't told anyone."

"Well, you don't have to," said Taylor, rolling his eyes. "Not with all the reports I've been getting."

"Sorry. We try to be discreet, but it's not easy."

Taylor smiled. "Shifting into a dragon is no small feat." He sent Gray a level gaze. "And neither is flying around with Lucy on your back."

Even vampires can be afraid of ghosts...

After the death of her husband—and the end of her dreams of motherhood—Elizabeth Bretton returned to the family estate in Broken Heart, Oklahoma. Little did she know she would also give up her life as the Silverstone heiress.

But escaping the past isn't that easy—especially with a vengeful ghost trying to kill her, a 150-year-old mystery to solve, and an outrageously hot were-jaguar named "Tez" trying to get into her boudoir...

Available wherever books are sold or at penguin.com

Everybody makes mistakes—and my first one was named Connor, a heart-stealing Scottish hottie. I thought our night together was the beginning of a love story, which turned out to be my second mistake. I, Phoebe Allen, lifelong Broken Heart resident and vampire, am now mated to a half-demon.

Thankfully Phoebe's four-year-old son Danny is safely away at Disneyworld with his human father. Because Phoebe is right in the middle of major paranormal drama, helping Connor and his rag-tag group of friends retrieve part of an ancient talisman in order to ward off Connor's vicious stepmother, an über-demon named Lilith. Phoebe swears she isn't falling for any of Connor's demon charm. But still, he's willing to do anything to protect her and prevent demons from storming into Broken Heart. And her undead heart can't resist a bad boy with identity issues...

Available wherever books are sold or at penguin.com

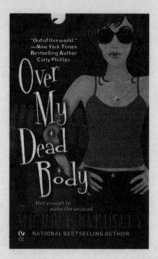

Hot enough to wake the undead...

Moving into Broken Heart seemed like the perfect
transition for Simone Sweet and her young daughter, Glory.
With her ex-husband gone after attempting to murder
Simone, and Glory being mute since the incident, it is one
place where Simone can feel safe and almost forget she's a
ravenous vampire.

No one is without secrets, but Simone's are big. She'd hate to
have them interfere with what's developing with local hunk
Braddock Hayes. When not turning her legs to jelly, he's
building an Invisi-shield around Broken Heart and helping
Glory speak again. But when Simone's past resurfaces, it
threatens to ruin her second chance...

"Michele Bardsley's vampire stories rock!"
—*New York Times* bestselling author Carly Phillips

Available wherever books are sold or at
penguin.com

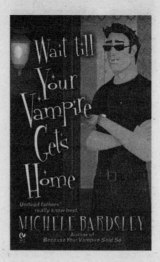

Undead fathers really do know best...

To prove her journalistic chops, Libby Monroe ends up in
Broken Heart, Oklahoma, chasing down bizarre rumors of
strange goings-on—and finding vampires, lycanthropes, and
zombies. She never expects to fall in lust with one of them,
but vampire/single dad Ralph Genessa is too irresistible. Only
the town is being torn in two by a war between the undead—
and Libby may be the only thing that can hold
Broken Heart together.

**"Has action aplenty and a free-spirited, wittily sarcastic
heroine who will delight [Michele Bardsley's] fans."**
—*Booklist*

Available wherever books are sold or at
penguin.com

When you're immortal, being a mom won't kill you—it will only make you stronger.

Not just anyone can visit Broken Heart, Oklahoma, especially since all the single moms—like me, Patsy Donahue—have been turned into vampires. I'm forever forty, but looking younger than my years, thanks to my new (un)lifestyle. And even though most of my customers have skipped town, I still manage to keep my hair salon up and running because of the lycanthropes prowling around. They know how important good grooming is—especially a certain rogue shape-shifter who is as sexy as he is deadly. Now, if only I could put a leash on my wild teenage son. He's up to his neck in danger. And my maternal instincts are still alive and kicking, so no one better mess with my flesh and blood.

"Lively, sexy, out of this world—as well as in it—fun!"
—*New York Times* bestselling author Carly Phillips